WINTER AT MISTLETOE GATE FARM

HELEN ROLFE

Boldwood

First published in 2021. This edition first published in Great Britain in 2022 by Boldwood Books Ltd.

Cover Design by CC Book Design

Cover Photography: Shutterstock

A CIP catalogue record for this book is available from the British Library.

Paperback ISBN 978-1-80415-595-0

Large Print ISBN 978-1-80415-597-4

Hardback ISBN 978-1-80415-596-7

Ebook ISBN 978-1-80415-598-1

Kindle ISBN 978-1-80415-599-8

Audio CD ISBN 978-1-80415-590-5

MP3 CD ISBN 9978-1-80415-591-2

Digital audio download ISBN 978-1-80415-594-3

Boldwood Books Ltd
23 Bowerdean Street
London SW6 3TN

1

Tilly hummed along to a Christmas playlist as she unboxed a glass vase ready to put on display in her shop, Tilly's Bits 'n' Pieces. She was glad to be tucked up inside away from the cold and even happier that the storms of the last few days had subsided to a drizzle and a wind that was so half-hearted it was hard to believe the weather had created such chaos in Heritage Cove.

Into the vessel she placed a white pillar candle and over it looped a wire ring decorated with artificial gypsophila. The look was elegant, classic, traditional. In fact, the look was everything that Tilly was not. She'd inherited her late grandma Shirley's dress sense – not that Tilly dressed dowdily or in a style that was inappropriate for a woman of thirty, but rather she dressed in a way she'd describe as boho-chic. She favoured floaty fabrics, funky designs, and charity shops were her go-to for a clothes spree. On her latest spree she'd found the lime-green, flared-sleeve top embellished with florals in red, bottle-green, and amber – the same colour as her eyes – that she was wearing now teamed with flared jeans and brown, suede, ankle boots.

Tilly had been lucky enough to be privately educated; she'd

excelled academically but then she'd backed away from the career in law everyone had assumed she was well suited to. Ever since Tilly had turned down a place at university, her decisions had been a source of conflict in her family, particularly with her dad, and Tilly still wasn't sure he'd ever approve of her life choices even though he'd been the one to hand over the shop to her when it was passed down to him from Grandma Shirley. She liked to think it was a sign that deep down he respected her choices and was proud of her, as much as he wouldn't admit it openly. And now, rather than spending her days hunched over black-and-white law texts at a desk, revising papers and putting together depositions or interpreting rules and regulations, Tilly was following a different path altogether, which had begun by studying textiles and working in soft-furnishings retail on a casual basis. Eventually those choices had led to her being here in the Cove, in the shop she'd loved even as a little girl.

As soon as Tilly had taken on the shop it was like she'd found her calling. What had once been a place to buy only candles and candle accessories became a place to find the odd piece of antique furniture, handmade cards, fashion jewellery and accessories. And having larger items gave the added benefit of hiding the peeling wallpaper, the same wall coverings that had been in the shop ever since Tilly could remember. There were no longer many rules when it came to what went in her shop. Tilly chose beautiful things that she thought customers would like and – so far – her method always worked. She even bought some larger items: a rocking chair in Tudor oak with spindles and slats and a plank seat, an ivory-painted chest of drawers, a Welsh dresser. And while each item waited for someone to fall in love with it, in turn it served a purpose in the shop as an extra place to display other pretty pieces – the velvet cushion embroidered with designs for the twelve days of Christmas sat on the rocking chair, the silk scarves in a variety of colours and patterns were tied on the handles of the chest of drawers with others folded on top, and a whole range of candles with unique fragrances were lined up along the Welsh dresser.

Tilly sighed as she placed the new candle holder onto a flat, silver plate and positioned it on top of the cream table tucked into the bay-window area. The display here was set on a platform slightly raised from the rest of the shop and facing out onto The Street, the main road that ran through the pretty village of Heritage Cove on the east coast of England. From the local pub, the Heritage Tea Rooms, and Tilly's shop, to the recently renovated bakery, the ice-creamery, and the waffle shack, each and every business here in the Cove was cemented in village life as much as were its residents.

Tilly looked out at the four-foot snowman she put in situ every Christmas, set back enough to be under cover. Grandma Shirley had introduced him a long time ago and Tilly had carried on the tradition – although when she'd found him out from storage this year she'd needed to fix up his black felt hat, dust off his pink-dotted cheeks and sew one of the buttons back onto his body. She supposed that was what happened when he was kept in a bag for so long.

Moving gingerly to the other side of the bay window, she plucked the cloth from the back pocket of her jeans and dusted the walnut table, on top of which sat three owl ornaments that needed their heads wiping too. She picked up a glittery squirrel decoration that had fallen off the tree that stood proudly in the centre of the bay window and repositioned it on a branch thick enough to take its weight. The tree with all its twinkly lights was especially welcome on a day like today. It was cheer amongst the grey clouds and murkiness beyond.

As she backed out of the narrow space and stepped onto the shop floor, Tilly almost collided with Lois, coming into the shop.

'Sorry!' Lois pushed the door closed behind her to shut out the cold. 'I didn't see you there, Tilly.'

Tilly dismissed her concern. The shop was beginning to feel the size of a doll's house as she added more and more pieces to her collections, passion overtaking common sense some of the time, so this wasn't the first time people had collided with one another. Tilly picked up the empty cardboard box she'd unpacked. 'I'll get rid of this; feel free to browse.' Her tummy rumbled at the sight of what Lois had in one hand – a paper bag emblazoned with the name of the local bakery and surely containing something delicious judging by the smell. Owned by sisters Jade and Celeste, who lived in the cottage behind their business, The Twist and Turn Bakery never disappointed.

Lois set the paper bag and her handbag down on the stool near the counter. 'Retail therapy is always a good thing,' she grinned. 'You get on, I'm happy to look around.'

Tilly narrowly avoided tripping over a basket of fabric cases she had on sale for those who used e-readers. Honestly, this place was simply far too small now she was stocking bigger items. Customers had to stay in single file along the aisles, of which there were two, and those were narrow enough. Tilly didn't get too many breakages but that was only because she made a point of putting the more fragile items on shelves or on furniture pushed against the walls. In the centre of the shop there was a raised area but the whole place still felt cluttered no matter how often Tilly tidied or rearranged things. What she really needed was to do out the upstairs, which currently was nothing more than a few empty and neglected rooms, but that was only a dream right now, partly for financial reasons but also because she was risk-averse. She'd never wanted to prove right her dad's claim that she was throwing away her future by going off to study textile design at a college rather than pursue the degree she'd applied for. She'd thought her parents would be pleased she wasn't stopping her education just like that, that she would be studying alongside working in retail, but her dad, busy with his own work back then, had never really asked her much about it. And then Grandma Shirley had died and he'd handed the shop to Tilly and they'd never talked about that either. She knew they had a serious problem with communication, going in for pleasantries but never talking at a deeper level, but she'd long since given up trying to work out the way her parents' minds worked. She'd taken on the shop, set up her new life, and the family tensions had lessened enough that they could go through the motions when they saw one another, which she supposed was better than nothing.

Out the back, Tilly finished flattening the cardboard boxes, some of which she recycled, others she'd use as needed. Sometimes customers bought so much it was easier to assemble a box for their new belongings than pack them into a number of bags. By the time she returned to the shop front, Lois had hold of a cute cushion covered in a hedgehog design and she was checking her hair in a small ornate dressing mirror to see that it was sitting in its usual obedient bob.

'Just checking I don't have hat hair,' Lois explained. Her Irish accent hadn't softened at all since she'd been reunited with Barney, the love of her life. She set the cushion on the counter by the till and found out her purse. 'It's dangerous coming in here – you have way too many gorgeous things. I could spend a fortune.'

Tilly handed Lois her receipt. 'You're welcome anytime and I do aim to please.'

Purchase made, Lois picked up the bag from the bakery. 'Barney's helping over at the florist today while they do their repairs in time to reopen for the Christmas demand so I took over his lunch and when he saw I'd included some treats for later on, he suggested I deliver one to you. It's not too early for you, is it?' She opened the bag to reveal mince pies dusted in icing sugar – the hole in the top, the irresistible sweet scent.

'It's never too early for a mince pie.' Tilly smiled as Lois took out one for her and one for herself. And she looked at the clock for the first time in hours. 'I've been crazy busy. A coachload of tourists en route to Cambridge decided the Cove would be a lovely place to stop and explore. They're lucky the council cleared the storm debris first thing this morning or they'd never have been able to come through the village.'

The storms had shaken residents up as well as their properties. Tilly had been talking to her friend Harvey last night and he'd said he hadn't ventured down to the cove itself yet because he wasn't sure how safe it was to walk Winnie, his dog. Apparently he'd gone to the end of the track that ran parallel with the chapel and cemetery behind and had stood looking out at the sea, the waves white-crested and still rolling fiercely.

'Did they buy much?' Lois ate her mince pie over a cupped hand.

'Plenty, although I had to limit how many people came in here at once – I was terrified something might get broken.' Her casual assistant Dessie, who did hours in the shop whenever Tilly needed, was spending the entire month of December with her gran and at first Tilly had thought managing this place completely solo would be fine but if this morning was anything to go by, she may have underestimated how difficult it was not having someone she could call on when custom swelled unexpectedly. Some days she could go along with a steady trickle of customers, as though they'd all pre-agreed when to go in and were forming a very orderly queue to do so, but on other days it was the complete opposite.

'The tourists were in the tea rooms when I went past,' Lois confirmed and as she lifted her mince pie to take another bite, her diamond wedding band flashed when it caught the light. She'd only been married since the summer after rekindling her romance with Barney, local favourite and a man who'd been like family to Tilly. He'd been good friends with her grandma Shirley and ever since Tilly had come to take over the shop in the Cove he'd always been there for her without question. Barney was one of those people who immersed themselves in the community and that meant helping out whenever and wherever he was needed. And everyone loved him for it.

'Etna would've been beside herself... in a good way, with all her tables filled, plenty of people to chat with.'

'It certainly seemed that way when I went past. I waved through the window to her and the tables were chocka. I saw a group heading up to the waffle shack as well so Daniel will be just as busy.'

Talk turned to Tilly's parents and their winter cruise. Since her dad had retired they'd been all about travelling and this time they were cramming lots in – France, Spain, Italy, and Portugal.

'I'd love some winter sun,' Lois confessed. 'You'd think I'd be used to rain, having lived in Ireland for so many years, but it can get me down sometimes.'

'The storm here can't have helped.'

Lois turned and looked to the front door. 'You'd never know the glass had been smashed.'

'The glazier did a brilliant job.' A brilliant but expensive job it had been to repair the broken window after the storms. Businesses and homes in the village had hunkered down while the deluge did its best to wreak havoc, with winds well over fifty miles per hour hitting the small village and its surrounds and enough rain for a month falling in the space of forty-eight hours. Tilly's neighbour had lost an entire garden fence, and the person who lived opposite her had a tree uprooted that narrowly avoided crashing right through the sitting-room window. The village chapel, which sat over the road from Tilly's Bits 'n' Pieces, stood strong as it had for so many years but the cemetery behind it was a total mess, with branches of trees hanging across headstones, offerings left by grieving visitors nowhere to be seen. Hazel, who owned and ran the local riding stables, had told of frightened horses; she'd burst into tears with the stress of it all when she'd met with friends in the pub last night. Zara from the local ice-creamery had left her tables and umbrellas out following a very mild start to the winter, with plenty of customers happy to buy her festive flavours in December and content to linger outside bundled up against the cold. The umbrellas had been completely wrecked, one of them found way past the bus stop on the bend. The local florist had had a smashed window at the back of the property, and although the tea rooms and bakery had stayed safe on this side of the street, Tilly's shop had been the target of an enormous tree branch that came out of nowhere and crashed through the glass in the door.

'Barney said your cottage was relatively unscathed.' Lois brushed the crumbs from the counter and dropped them into the paper bag.

'Thank goodness. I was lucky, by the sounds of it. Jade said they lost a chimney pot from the roof of their place and several slates from the roof of the bakery. My cottage fared well with only a bit of damage to the front fence.' Tilly shrugged. 'It was on its last legs anyway so it's not the end of the world.' She'd replace it with a small picket fence in the spring and paint it in a bright white. 'What about your place?'

'The house escaped damage. And the chickens are blissfully unaware anything was amiss. We locked them in the coop, made sure there was no garden debris nearby. Barney was so worried about them all, obsessed something was going to blow in from far away. Thankfully it didn't. And we're just grateful that when we agreed to take those chickens and keep them on our land we went for top-of-the-range everything.' She began to smile. 'I nicknamed their coop The Palace.'

'Good name,' Tilly grinned as Michael Bublé came on the Christmas playlist, making her really feel as though Christmas was fast approaching. She'd seen The Palace – it might house chickens but with its beautiful dark, strong timber, sections for egg collection, a run, sleeping quarters, and a sturdy roof, it was like high-end real estate but for animals. She wasn't surprised it had stood up to the storm and kept the chickens safe.

'We weren't so lucky with the barn,' Lois added.

Tilly had a bad feeling about this. Her good friends Harvey and Melissa were due to get married in the barn in only a few weeks. 'Oh no... Harvey and Melissa will be devastated.' She'd always thought of the barn as being like the chicken coop – sturdy and not going anywhere. 'What's the damage?'

'A tree smashed through the roof and the back wall, one of the main doors is badly damaged, and the inside flooded with water. It's not a pretty sight. Our first concern was the chickens but when we saw the barn after the storm had calmed down, we realised we hadn't escaped quite as well as we'd thought.'

'Why didn't you tell me earlier? I feel terrible now – Barney was over here last night fretting about the glazier finishing up, he's had the chickens to deal with, he's over at the florist now, sending over baked treats for me. That man needs to worry about himself, too.'

'He's devastated. We had someone come out this morning to assess and quote on repairs but I don't think we'll even get materials in time.'

Tilly's heart sank. 'What does this mean for the wedding?'

'Barney knows he has to tell Melissa and Harvey today that the wedding can't be held in the barn. They're going to have to find another venue. Barney is so upset he won't be able to give them the wedding they deserve – you know how he is about those two.'

Tilly did. Both of them had been in Barney's life since they were kids and they'd spent many happy days in the barn that sat adjacent to his home. They'd played there, hung out after school, and it had always seemed the natural choice for their wedding, even all those years ago when marriage had still been a long way off.

'He's waiting on one more phone call from a timber supplier as his last hope.' Lois crossed her fingers on both hands. 'For now, until he has to tell them, he's trying to keep busy.'

Tilly had known Melissa and Harvey for years. They'd split up for a long while but had been together again for around eighteen months, their engagement and upcoming nuptials no surprise to anyone. Melissa had asked Tilly to be a bridesmaid at the wedding alongside her friend Tracy, who with her husband Guy owned and ran the Heritage Inn, the guesthouse that sat on the corner as you came into the Cove from one direction. Their dresses had been chosen and as well as being key members of the wedding party, their job as bridesmaids was to keep the bride happy – Tilly just didn't know how they were going to do that in light of this terrible revelation.

'Is there really no way the repairs can be done in time?'

Lois shrugged her shoulders. 'We've made a lot of calls. The best person to do the work would've been Harvey, especially with it being so close to Christmas, but of course he has his own work – he's flat out with loft refitting for his day job before he and Melissa get married and head off on honeymoon. And it's not just the labour, it's the materials. Barney has always used the supplier Harvey uses for maintenance of the barn but he can't get a delivery date until after Christmas. Barney thinks we should offer to have the wedding at the house if they can't find anywhere else.' Lois looked at Tilly. 'You know Melissa better than I do. Would she be incredibly disappointed?' She swished her hand through the air to quash her words the moment they came out of her mouth. 'Silly question, of course she will. I loved getting married in the barn and I didn't grow up around here.'

'The house could be just as special,' Tilly assured her, this poor woman who would be feeling Barney's pain as though it were her own. 'And if Barney is there, that's what will mean the most to Melissa and Harvey. Besides, it's better than not getting married at all.'

'Barney has already walked around the house talking about how we can decorate it – fairy lights, more than one Christmas tree, we could move the table and sofas to the sides of the room to make a dancefloor.'

Tilly had a thought. 'What about the chapel?'

But Lois shook her head. 'They're hosting a visiting choir on the morning of the wedding and then the primary school is holding a nativity performance in the afternoon.'

The door swung open and in came a trio of women clucking noisily about gifts. Tilly helped one of them find a present for her granddaughter who was graduating at the end of the week. She showed her the necklaces on the jewellery tree near the till, pointing out a sterling-silver design with heart and mortarboard pendants on the same chain that the woman instantly fell in love with before moving over to peruse the hand-stitched cards as Tilly wrapped her purchase at the till.

'I don't know what else to suggest,' she told Lois as she broke off pieces of sticky tape to secure the tissue paper. 'I can't hold it here. The tea rooms are way too small. The waffle shack is beautiful but not big enough either. There's the pub? But no… couldn't do that to Terry and Nola, not at such a busy time of year, although they'd probably oblige if asked.'

'I'm wondering whether Melissa might choose Tumbleweed House.'

'That could work.' Tumbleweed House had been in Harvey's

family for years and although the rooms weren't large, getting married at the home they now shared would certainly have a special appeal.

'I think Barney will offer our place, then they'll talk about Tumbleweed House,' Lois concluded, pulling on her hat and gloves to brace herself for the cold. 'Thanks, Tilly. I suspect Barney sent me in here as much for my sanity as to give you a sweet treat. I'm worrying, about him mostly, and of course that means he's stressing about me.' She began to laugh. 'Life's never simple. See you tonight at the tree-lighting ceremony?'

Tilly nodded and waved her off, and as the Christmas playlist continued she thought of her friends. She hoped they'd find somewhere perfect for their special day because they both deserved it so much.

* * *

The storms had been nasty enough to cause a lot of trouble throughout Heritage Cove and its surrounding villages, but almost as though they'd timed it the best they could, the winds and rain had subsided enough for the village tree to be transported from Mistletoe Gate Farm, which sat out past the pub, beyond the florist.

The tree, an impressive fifty-foot Norway spruce from the Doyle family's farm, stood tall and proud now as onlookers huddled against one another or in groups clasping big cups filled with mulled wine from the cart that the pub had put out on the grass area especially for tonight. The village needed this, Tilly thought to herself as she took a sip of her wine and savoured the taste of traditional mulling spices. Everyone had been somewhat melancholy clearing up, sweeping footpaths, removing debris from gardens, booking in with tradesmen to do the jobs they couldn't manage. But now, there wasn't a downturned mouth to be seen.

When Tilly spotted Benjamin Doyle – son of Heather and Danny who owned Mistletoe Gate Farm, chef at the local pub and a friend she sometimes imagined being more than just that – her smile only widened further. Ever since the summer, she'd been convinced he was on the verge of asking her out. They'd flirted, they'd chatted long into the evenings when he came off shift at the Copper Plough, he'd walked her home more than once, but he didn't seem any closer to moving beyond their friendship.

Benjamin held his cup aloft, his gentle, soft-caramel eyes focusing solely on her. 'Great minds think alike.'

'Everyone knows your recipe is the best,' she replied. Benjamin's family recipe for mulled wine was used every year and never disappointed. Or perhaps Tilly was biased.

'I'll take that compliment.' He tilted his head in acknowledgement of the praise. 'It's freezing tonight – I'm still getting used to not having the extra hair to keep warm.' He patted a hand to the back of his neck. Benjamin's hair had been tied back in a ponytail for years but a month ago he'd had it all cut off. Tilly had been in the pub the night of the local fundraiser, which collected over a thousand pounds from friends and punters eager to support a charity that used hair donations to make wigs for children and young people who had experienced hair loss.

'Totally worth it,' she beamed at him.

'I don't know why I kept it long, to be honest. It's much easier to look after this way.'

And way sexier, she thought to herself. His hair was cut short at the back; she'd seen the clippers run gently from the nape of his neck upwards, stopping so it remained spiky at the top. And the cut suited the well-groomed designer stubble he favoured.

'I think the whole village needed this tree-lighting tonight.' The mulled wine had warmed her up already and as they gazed around at the swelling crowds Tilly could just about make out Daniel up at the Little Waffle Shack watching from the veranda, his arm around his girlfriend Lucy's shoulders. She'd already seen that Barney and Lois were closer to the tree, but Tilly was glad she and Benjamin were both standing further back, in the shadows, as it was nice for it to be just him and her.

'I almost came in to see you in the shop earlier today,' he said.

'You did?' She looked up at him. This was it. He was going to ask her out at long last. She was relieved she'd had a chance to go back to her cottage and freshen up, to put on some lip gloss and mascara, to spritz her perfume.

'I still need a gift for Mum and I've no idea what to get her this year.'

Tilly's heart sank. 'Right, well, whenever you're ready.'

He seemed oblivious he'd made her hopes soar and then been the one to cause them to drop from a great height. They both turned and watched the crowds gathering by the tree; it was almost time for the lights to be switched on.

'Your family does us proud every year,' said Tilly.

Even beneath his thick jacket she could see his chest swell with pride. He had his own career – as chef at the Copper Plough he'd transformed the menu more than once – but he still helped out a lot at the farm, the family business that held a sentimental significance for him as it likely always would. It was the same for her with the shop: there was rarely a day that went by when she didn't have a recollection of her grandma or consider what Shirley would think of any changes Tilly made, the stock she now kept on sale. It made her strive to keep improving the shop, too, as though her grandma was watching over it and all of Tilly's hard work could meet with her approval.

'Do you have a tree for your cottage yet?' he asked her.

'I need to sort that, don't I?' She'd already seen his mum, Heather, handing out business cards for Mistletoe Gate Farm to people who might not be from around here but may well be interested in picking up a real tree this season.

'We're open at nine tomorrow morning; stop by and I'll help you choose one. I'll even carry it back to your cottage for you – how does that sound?'

It sounded pretty perfect to Tilly. If only. 'I have the shop.'

'Couldn't Dessie watch it for you?'

'She's away with family.'

'I'll do it,' came a voice from beside them.

Hand clasped against her heart, Tilly smiled at Lois. 'You gave me a fright. You were down nearer the tree a minute ago – you sneaked up on me.' She gave Lois a kiss on the cheek, then leaned over to kiss Barney, who'd positioned himself the other side of Benjamin.

'Better view from right back here,' Barney concluded.

And when Barney told her about the barn and how hard it had been to tell Melissa and Harvey today, Tilly made a mental note to text Melissa later and tell her she was thinking of them both and to offer her help if it was needed. Casting her eyes around she couldn't see either of them right now as the crowds swelled.

'Choosing a tree cannot be rushed,' Lois insisted, turning the subject back to Tilly, 'and your shop is busy – I saw that today for myself. I've helped you out before, so just remind me about the till and the card machine and I'll come in for an hour or two.' Another thing Barney and Lois had in common was that despite both being in their seventies, neither of them showed the slightest sign of slowing down.

Benjamin whistled between his teeth. 'I reckon once we let her loose at the farm she'll spend way more than an hour choosing her tree.'

Tilly reddened. Good job it was dark and nobody could see. It wasn't that she was embarrassed about spending forever choosing the perfect tree from Mistletoe Gate Farm last year but she was uncomfortable that he could remember it – and by the way he was looking at her now, he wasn't thinking of her like any other customer but as someone he wanted to share more than a friendship with.

It was last winter when Tilly had started to feel attracted to Benjamin, not that she'd let on to anyone because he'd been with his girlfriend then and so Tilly had pushed her feelings aside. But in the summer, after he'd been single again for a while, she'd got the impression he liked her too.

'If you're sure, Lois, then that would be brilliant,' said Tilly. 'Once the village tree is up it always feels weird not to have one at home. I grabbed one for the shop last week but the one for home takes longer to select.'

'You want to get one before all the good ones go,' Barney advised.

'I'll have you know they're all good.' Benjamin turned to face Tilly. 'So, will I see you in the morning?'

She told him that he would just as Danny's voice boomed out from beside the tree through a microphone that he held in his hand to be heard above the crowds who gathered on the grass area beyond the village bus stop on the bend that led out of Heritage Cove. The tree lighting was about to happen and onlookers counted down from ten.

As the crowds reached zero in their countdown colour burst from the foot of the tree all the way to the top. Squeals of excitement accompanied a round of applause and seasonal cheer spread at the sight of the tree that had been quite a feat to get into position this year. The ground had had to be cleared of storm debris with everyone from Mistletoe Gate Farm mucking in, Benjamin too, and on her way to the shop this morning Tilly had seen the tree laid out along the length of the trailer, a cherry picker waiting in the wings for Benjamin's dad and anyone else he worked with who had no problem with heights to do the honours, as they did every year, and deck out the festive beauty with hundreds and hundreds of baubles, decorations and lights.

When someone walked past with waffles Barney told Lois they'd better get up there quickly before the masses had the same idea. He led the way but Lois hung back for a moment. 'He needed this tonight,' she assured Benjamin before reconfirming she'd be at the shop half an hour before it opened in the morning so Tilly could go and choose her tree.

After they'd carried on up to the shack Benjamin was confused. 'Why did Barney in particular need this tonight?' he asked Tilly. 'Has something upset him?'

'You haven't heard?' When he shook his head she elaborated, explaining the damage to the barn, the predicament about the wedding. 'I haven't seen Melissa and Harvey tonight, have you?'

'No, but if they found out this afternoon then no doubt they'll be in panic mode trying to sort out an alternative venue. The path of true love, eh...' His eyes held hers and her stomach clenched. 'I'd better get to the pub, there'll be plenty of hungry people to feed tonight. I'll see you tomorrow.'

But before she could reply, her phone rang. 'Sorry, I'd better get that – I'm expecting a call from a supplier about delivery in the morning and if they change the time, I'll have to tell Lois.' She picked up the call from the unrecognised number and soon realised it wasn't a supplier at all. 'Mum? Is that you?' She put a finger in her ear – she could barely hear – and she turned her back on the crowds and moved to the very edge of the field as though it might make some difference.

'Mum, speak up,' she urged again. 'What did you say?' But she could already tell it wasn't good news, and so could Benjamin because he was no longer looking at the tree to give her some privacy, he was watching her and her mounting distress.

'What's wrong?' he asked the minute she ended the call.

'The police contacted my parents. Their house was broken into. The neighbours called the police when they noticed a curtain billowing from a smashed window at the back of the house – which would've been the kitchen.' Her words continued to spill out. 'I need to get up to Nottingham. Mum's fretting that the house is wide open. I'll need to arrange repairs, go through their things, and attempt to itemise what's missing.' She put a hand to her forehead. 'This is the last thing I need. I'll have to go tonight, get it done as soon as possible.' But then she looked at the near-empty cup of mulled wine in her hand. 'I've been drinking. I can't go. And I have the shop – how can I leave Lois to manage it for a day or more? And I can't close, I—'

Benjamin took hold of her shoulders. 'First, breathe.'

She looked down and could barely make out the blades of grass amidst the muddy soil beneath their feet, so dark was the sky surrounding them. 'There's another coachload of tourists due through tomorrow afternoon. It would be good for business.' And it would top up the all-important cash reserves, especially since she'd had to call the emergency glazier.

'Let's go and get you some waffles,' he insisted, leading her towards the shack. 'For the shock. And why don't you ask Lois about the shop? She's offered to help in the morning; perhaps Barney could step in too and between them they could handle it for the day.'

'It's a big ask.' She was so distressed she barely registered Benjamin's arm around her shoulders, she had no chance to savour being tucked against his chest and the feel of his voice vibrating against her hair as they reached the waffle shack. 'And with everything Barney has on his plate at the moment, I don't know if I can do it to them.'

'I think it'll make Barney feel like he's helping in some way,' Benjamin assured her as they stepped onto the veranda and opened the door, the sweet aroma snaking out to grab them. 'It'll take his mind off the barn and Melissa's wedding plans.'

A thought occurred to her. 'I was going to choose my tree in the morning.'

'Plenty of trees, Tilly. You stop by in a few days, any time.' He had hold of her upper shoulders again as though it was the only way to get through to her.

But now she had to stop thinking about Benjamin and the way he looked at her, the way she wanted to stay near him and move closer into his arms. She had to ask Lois and Barney for an enormous favour.

And tomorrow she had to drive up to Nottingham and assess the damage.

2

Mistletoe Gate Farm had been in the Doyle family since it was established in 1951 by Benjamin's grandparents. And every December, business boomed.

This year was no different. Benjamin woke to the sound of a chainsaw cutting down another tree beyond his bedroom window at the front of the family's stone-built house. The property was surrounded by a generous fifteen acres of land, most of which was filled with Norway spruce, Nordmann fir, and Fraser fir trees. The land was accessed via a long driveway just wide enough for cars to pass either side provided they were going slowly, or via a pedestrian path marked out by a gate surrounded by mistletoe growing in trees and bushes. Not far from the house was a hexagonal shed, each of its Georgian-styled windows outlined with twinkly lights and sprigs of mistletoe now it was into December, and from there they sold fairy lights, decorations, pre-cut mistletoe, ready-made wreaths, and rings of greenery that customers could buy and decorate themselves, as well as hot chocolates with marshmallows.

From his window Benjamin could just about see the field allocated as a parking area and cars were already arriving, people eager even at this early hour. He pulled on cargo trousers, a long-sleeved top, and a thick fleece. He'd got used to living at home again after splitting up with his girlfriend, although living with your parents when you were in your early thirties, especially having moved out once, definitely felt like a step backwards. But it had its perks – the house was big enough that he had one side of it to himself, he was saving a heap of money with his parents refusing to accept much for board and lodgings, and it was so close to the village high street and therefore the pub that it took him less than twenty minutes to walk to work.

Benjamin had a long shift at the Copper Plough today. Thankfully he was in charge of a hardworking, efficient team of staff and so they'd manage to do the prep without him, meaning that by the time he got to the pub they'd already be organised and raring to go with the lunchtime rush. This morning he'd be starting his day helping out at the farm – there'd be work out in the fields to ensure the trees were at their best, there was helping customers locate their preferred variety within the height range they required, and with some customers preferring to take their own tree home rather than have it delivered, he'd help net trees and fix them onto car roofs in the generous parking area at Mistletoe Gate Farm.

Benjamin found a pair of thick socks and ran a hand through his hair – so much easier now it was short and without tangles. He'd begun to get the odd grey already but he'd always known it inevitable since his dad, Danny, was fully grey by the time he turned forty. He put the pillows on his bed back in position and tugged the end of the duvet so it was straight. He'd dreamt of Tilly last night, of her amber eyes as she smiled or laughed, the way her hair curled up at the ends as though she'd purposely made it go that way, although he suspected she hadn't. He couldn't imagine her spending much time in front of a mirror, not that she didn't look good. Quite the opposite – she was pretty, and the warmth she had around people drew him to her as much as anything else. They'd been getting closer for a while but he hadn't wanted to rush into anything new when he and Zoe had gone through an unpleasant breakup less than a year ago. And now, he and Tilly seemed to be solid friends and he'd hate to mess that up by moving too fast.

Benjamin headed downstairs. As tradition dictated, garlands already wound their way along banisters and newel posts on the staircase, there was already a sprig of mistletoe above the doorway going into the sitting room, one above the dining-room entrance, one as he went into the kitchen that was so big it actually served as kitchen, dining area and a place to relax on one of the two sofas or the leather armchair. It was an unusual set-up for a period farmhouse but this was his favourite room, a room that had always brought the family together. It held plenty of childhood memories, too – Christmases with his parents and his sister Charlotte, stockings hung above the fireplace in here rather than the one in the sitting room, their tree filling the space in the corner.

He noticed another sprig of mistletoe had been put up at the doors that led out onto the veranda. His mum had always liked to put mistletoe everywhere and when they were kids Benjamin and his sister had frequently caught their parents kissing beneath it whenever they could like a couple of newlyweds. Benjamin hadn't seen them do that in a long time, though – certainly not this year. And no such luck for him. The only girl he wanted to kiss was Tilly and she wasn't even in Heritage Cove right now.

'Good morning.' His mum, Heather, was in the kitchen at the table eating a bowl of steaming-hot porridge. She'd done the same thing for as long as he could remember, always in the azure bowl from the Denby collection kept in the sideboard that housed the overspill from the kitchen. On top of the porridge, as usual, were slices of banana and a drizzle of honey the same colour as her bobbed hair with its long fringe that she hooked behind her ears.

Her friends had often joked she couldn't possibly be a farmer's wife as she was far too glamorous despite her getting stuck in with all the jobs around the place that Danny and Benjamin did: planting seedlings and saplings and continuing their care, weeding, mowing – although she left the ride-on to Danny or Benjamin – cutting back brambles along the track, shaping trees that didn't attain the beautiful festive shape all by themselves.

Benjamin took a mug from the sideboard and set it beneath the spout on the coffee machine as his mum carried on reading the newspaper. Although it was usual for her to be quiet first thing in the morning, she seemed even more so lately. He pressed the pre-programmed button for his choice of coffee and waited for the grinding, the water, the creamy milk froth on top to finish before taking it over to the double doors that looked out over the veranda. From here he could see the fields stretching out beyond, the rows upon rows of fir trees standing to attention. In all the years he'd been alive he'd never grown tired of this view; it was spectacular.

The timber veranda that stretched along the back of the house and around the side provided shelter and character to the property and had little on it in the winter apart from a porch swing facing out to the fields and a side table. Even when it was freezing, he'd often sit out there bundled up in his jacket and let the cold blast his cheeks while he enjoyed a coffee, his fingers kept warm by holding the cup. He'd listen to the sounds of the farm going on around him – his dad calling out to someone about which trees were ready to be cut down, frustration from him when the netting machine played up again, his mum gathering up pieces of greenery, plucking berries, and bringing a filled basket back to the house, ready to seat herself at the big, oak dining table and put together the festive wreaths they sold at the farm – but today he knew that if he sat on that porch swing he wouldn't want to get up again. Christmas was a busy time here and at the pub and already he was looking forward to easing up a bit come the new year.

Once Benjamin had finished his coffee he turned to his mum. 'I'm making poached eggs. Interested?'

'Porridge will be enough for me, thank you.' She smiled at him. 'You'll find spinach in the fridge if you'd like it... in the bottom drawer.'

He found the spinach, mushrooms, and tomatoes too, and cooked himself a breakfast that would help his body prepare for the manual labour ahead.

When the family had bought the farm all those years ago it wasn't actually a farm at all; it was land with a wooden gate that had a few trees and bushes with some mistletoe already growing. Benjamin's grandparents had known all along that, once married, they wanted to raise a family right here in the Cove on this parcel of land, and that they wanted to start their own business selling Christmas trees. Benjamin's grandad had already been growing a dozen trees every year as it was, cultivating them in his very small garden near a major city in England before selling them to friends, and so the idea was born. He'd continued to work in his job as a junior accountant and at the same time, thanks to a windfall from Benjamin's grandmother's family, had got the business going. When the Doyle family first opened up to sell Christmas trees they'd made the gate itself a big feature. They'd tended the mistletoe in the bushes and trees that already grew so well and surrounded the gate that marked the pedestrian access and the way the family and plenty of customers accessed the farm. The original gate had been repaired over the years and then replaced during the last decade but mistletoe carried on growing just as well on both sides as though it knew its place.

After a hearty breakfast Benjamin shrugged on an older coat that he wouldn't mind getting dirty or damaged in amongst the trees and went out to ask his dad what was most needed this morning.

Danny trudged over from his position at the netting machine and handed Benjamin an axe. 'We need more logs chopping, I've got a few orders to deliver this afternoon.'

'Nothing like the hardest work for your son, eh?'

'You could do the netting instead if you like.'

But Benjamin laughed. 'You're sixty-seven and I've no idea how you do it but if I want to be as agile as you are when I reach your age, I'll need to take a leaf out of your book and get to work.'

Benjamin soon got into the task around the back of the largest shed that housed the tractor, lawnmowers, and all the equipment they needed throughout the year. He split logs and it wasn't long before a coat was too much despite the bracing chill and the frost that lingered on the tops of trees and the roof of the house. He stacked the logs at the side of the shed so they could be divided into batches and put a whole load in the bags already positioned on the back of his dad's truck. Danny would still have plenty of room left for the trees so he could do all the deliveries in one go.

Benjamin set aside the axe and blew out his cheeks. It wasn't as if he was a stranger to being on his feet all day but working on a farm was something else – no wonder neither of his parents showed their age when their daily routine was so physical. But, if he wasn't careful, much more of this manual labour and he wouldn't have the strength to lift a knife in the pub kitchen, let alone race around on a double shift preparing, cooking, and delivering customer orders.

He wandered over to the trees closest to where he was. These were the Nordmann firs in heights ranging from three to eleven feet. They were fatter at the bottom than some of the other varieties, with excellent needle retention. He reached out to touch the rounded needles of one and then another, and the one after that.

Any of them could have a place in Tilly's cottage – she'd be spoilt for choice. They'd all look spectacular with their dense foliage and deep, rich colour, and nothing beat that farm-fresh smell of citrusy pine that came with every tree. He wondered how she was getting on. She'd been flustered last night, unable to think straight when she'd got the call about the break-in at her parents' house. She didn't have the sturdiest of relationships with her mum and dad, by the sounds of it, and some people might have used that as a reason not to leap to attention in their hour of need, but not Tilly. She thought of others and put them first whenever she could. It was one of the things he loved and admired about her the most.

Danny had netted a tree and, with it over his shoulder, was heading towards the car park. He was fit, no doubt about that, but there wasn't the usual festive spring in his step this year and Benjamin didn't really know why. Usually, as soon as they hit December, Danny would have a different Christmas hat on each day, his smile would never slip even when he wasn't with a customer, he'd take every opportunity to talk at length with visitors, asking about their Christmas plans and listening to details Benjamin knew he couldn't possibly be that interested in just to be polite and a part of it. He hadn't been as attentive to his wife lately, either. Danny and Heather usually held hands when they were out walking, they snuggled up on the sofa even after a good thirty-five years of marriage. And those absent snatched kisses underneath the mistletoe this year kept playing on Benjamin's mind.

He lifted a hand to wave to his dad, who was walking over to him after finishing off with the buyer. Maybe his parents were just busy. It wasn't only the most wonderful time of the year – for the Doyles it was the craziest time of the year.

'Cheers, son.' Danny patted Benjamin on the shoulder. 'It's a tough job, I know.'

'You look tired, Dad.'

'It's been a hectic few days.' His breath came out cold. He took off his thermal work gloves. 'The storm made such a mess.'

Benjamin had helped clear up debris to make the farm passable for visitors coming to select their tree – the last thing you wanted was someone tripping over an errant branch, or a child falling onto a sharp stick, or, worse, one of the trees falling on someone. The rows and rows of fir and spruce trees stood strong but it was always a worry and they were regularly checked, never more so than after a big storm that had the power to uproot even the sturdiest of species.

'The logs are done. Anything else you want me to handle before I have a shower and go to work?'

'No, we're good from here and I appreciate you pitching in so much.'

'Hey, family business, right?' But he didn't get much of a response and as his dad led the way around to a new bunch of awaiting customers, Benjamin asked, 'Is there something I need to know? I mean, is there something going on?'

'No, not at all. Why do you ask?'

It suddenly dawned on Benjamin that perhaps this was financial. 'You would tell me if the business was in trouble, wouldn't you?' Maybe this was the year they'd realised they weren't making the profits they used to. With a business such as this it was always a risk and Benjamin didn't have a hand in the accounting side so he'd never know.

'Of course I would.'

'I can give you more for my board – you charge me next to nothing.'

'This is your home, son.' Danny stopped and raised his hand to indicate the scene before them, the laughter and merriment of people all around, some carrying trees, others just arriving and ready to make a selection. 'And does it really look as though the business is in trouble?'

Benjamin had to admit that no, it really didn't.

But as he set off towards the house he still had the niggling feeling his dad was keeping something from him.

* * *

At the Copper Plough, Benjamin went out to the back, hung up his coat, and took off his fleece, which definitely wouldn't be needed in the kitchens that got too hot even in the winter. It could be minus ten outside and he'd still fling open the back door to go out for a break and would stand there without a coat, in his chef whites or an apron, and cool down.

'Morning, Marnie,' he greeted the youngest and most enthusiastic member of his team. Not that anyone slacked off, just that Marnie was usually the first to volunteer for extra hours whenever there was a chance. She was the one he pegged as most likely to go and run her own business one day. 'Where are we up to?' he asked.

Familiar with the briefing that came whenever someone else arrived at work, whether it be him or Billy or Henry, Marnie gave him the low-down: the fish she'd filleted, the meat she'd prepared and already rubbed with marinade, the sirloins that were ready for the steak Diane special today. She'd even ducked out to the convenience store to pick up a couple of extra cartons of double cream with the delivery coming late today. Steak Diane had been popular for the last week; it seemed word had got around, and it had certainly been the item of choice with the out-of-towners yesterday and the day before.

Benjamin had studied hospitality at college and enjoyed the entire course, but once he got to the food-service management and catering parts of the syllabus, including some work experience at a gastro pub for eight weeks, he knew he'd found what he wanted to do. He arranged some casual work at the Copper Plough as a glass collector, table clearer, general dogsbody, and then as a kitchen hand until finally when the chef there approached retirement – which some said was a little overdue – he'd been waiting in the wings. Luckily for him the owners, Terry and Nola, had been thrilled someone local was interested. And since taking over the role as chef, Benjamin had transformed the basic menu from its run-of-the-mill chips with burgers, chips with chicken, fish and chips, and the fish curry that Melissa – but nobody else – had loved. Plenty of those choices were still there – they were pub favourites, after all – but with tweaks to lift them to another level. But the fish curry had had to go, and now Benjamin provided the pub's clientele with good all-round choices, honouring the seasons as they fell and turned to the next.

Benjamin had grown up always knowing that there was a job for him at Mistletoe Gate Farm but for a long time he'd doubted he would ever want to take it on full time, with sole responsibility. His sister, Charlotte, had been thrilled – because she did want the farm. She currently lived in Dorset, where she was a business development manager, and ever since Benjamin's admission one year that actually he wanted to pursue a career in food, Charlotte had been more than happy to step up, telling their parents she was very interested indeed. She'd seen her future at the farm, had always had a good eye for business and an ability to make solid decisions. And whenever she was home she asked all the questions – about the crops, about the financials, consumer behaviour – she joined in with the manual labour and was always on about what could be improved or altered to maximise the farm's effectiveness as a business. It hadn't taken long for their parents to realise Charlotte had inherited Danny's sheer devotion to Mistletoe Gate Farm, whereas Benjamin's strengths and passions lay firmly in the kitchen.

Benjamin had Marnie prepare the Diane sauce, starting with the chopping of mushrooms and garlic, while he set to making the beef-and-ale pies that were always popular in the pub. They took forty minutes to cook, another ten to cool, so he'd make eight now and have mixture and pastry on standby if any more orders came in. He prepared the pastry, careful not to overwork the dough, and rolled part of it out into thickish rounds. He lined eight individual pie tins, each with an overhang, and using the filling he'd made yesterday with beef, dark ale, onions, mushrooms, and thyme as well as parsley, left in the fridge overnight, he used a slotted spoon to fill the pie cases. The secret of a great pie was pastry that could stand up to fillings and wouldn't get soggy from the mixture yet would remain light enough to flake. He rolled out more of the pastry dough and assembled the tops, finishing with a brush of egg, before putting them into the oven. With twelve o'clock fast approaching, Terry had already come in and pinned the first order on its piece of notepaper to the service area where assembled dishes would be taken from kitchen to table.

At one time Benjamin had dreamt of opening up a restaurant at the farm and he still wouldn't rule it out – something Charlotte would likely encourage and plan for if he so much as hinted at it – but for now the kitchens at the Copper Plough were his domain.

* * *

'It's nice to be on this side of the kitchen,' Benjamin told Daniel after he'd placed an order for waffles just before nine o'clock. Daniel, Harvey's younger brother by just a couple of years, owned and ran the Little Waffle Shack and with the village tree an even bigger draw card for the eatery, it was busy in here.

Melissa and Harvey had commandeered the biggest table in the joint and it looked as though they were consoling themselves about the alteration of wedding venue by demolishing two portions of waffles with chocolate sauce and cream if the remnants on their near-finished plates were anything to go by. A handsome couple – Melissa with her heart-shaped face, hazel eyes and auburn hair, Harvey at well over six foot like his brother, with dark hair and stubble on his jaw that was rarely pared back to clean-shaven – had been childhood sweethearts and it meant a lot to everyone in the Cove who knew them to see them getting married at long last.

'Mind if I join you?' Benjamin checked, but of course they didn't mind at all, or at least Harvey didn't. Melissa was making a call but ended it after Benjamin sat down.

'She's back tonight,' Melissa told Harvey, putting her cutlery together on her plate so it would be picked up and taken away.

'You talking about Tilly?' Benjamin asked before turning to thank Daniel for the ultra-speedy service when his ginger-and-cinnamon waffles topped with a scoop of vanilla-bean ice-cream appeared. Funny how working around food dulled your appetite, yet the second you were out of the kitchens it came back with a vengeance. He unwrapped his cutlery from its serviette.

Harvey and Melissa had obviously been in touch with her. 'I am, and she seems to have it all sorted,' Melissa explained. 'She called out a handyman to fix up the back door that had a bit of damage, a glazier for the glass panel and the smashed window, and a locksmith just in case the thief got hold of a spare key from anywhere.'

Benjamin finished his mouthful. 'She'll be anxious to get back to the shop – you know what she's like.'

Melissa rested her chin on her clasped hands, smile in place. 'I do know what she's like.'

Benjamin chose to ignore the look she was giving him. 'Christmas is her busiest time.' It was kind of obvious but he didn't really know what else to say when they were both looking at him registering his interest.

Melissa watched him carefully. 'It's a very busy time. I should know, I was in there all day.'

'You were?'

'Tilly asked Lois and Barney to help and they'd both leapt at the chance to do something, but it was so busy by mid-morning that Barney called me to come over. Lois was already flustered with the till and she was fretting that she wasn't able to help customers and serve others at the same time. Neither of them had had a break by the time I got there so I sent them over to the tea rooms for sustenance and between the three of us we had a much better rest of the day after that.'

'The shop was still standing when I walked past.' Benjamin collected another piece of waffle onto his fork along with ice-cream that was fast melting. 'You must've done something right.'

'Tilly would do the same for any of us.'

'You're not wrong there.' And when the focus seemed to be on him, Benjamin ventured, 'Dare I ask you two about wedding plans?'

Harvey frowned. 'You can ask but we haven't sorted anything yet. Barney has offered his home but we really couldn't expect that of him and Lois. They do well enough at their ages to hold the Wedding Dress Ball every year; a wedding is a big ask, and they'd have to shift furniture around without the barn to store it in. Neither of us would want to do that to them both. Lois has relatives from Ireland visiting over the Christmas period too, so we wouldn't want to get in the way of that.'

Benjamin and everyone else in Heritage Cove knew what Barney meant to Melissa and Harvey. They'd both spent their childhoods hanging out in the barn – Harvey because his home life was less than good with a father who showed no love and so the barn had become a hideaway for him, Melissa because she simply enjoyed herself and the freedom she had there. And when Melissa's parents died, Barney had become a father figure to her too.

'I don't want Barney to feel any pressure from us,' Melissa went on, 'so we need to stop feeling sorry for ourselves. I've made enquiries at the hall in the next village, a chapel less than ten miles away.' She held up her phone as though it might ring with news at any second. 'I'm waiting to hear.'

Benjamin hated to say it but this close to Christmas, that phone wasn't likely to ring.

'The other option is our place, Tumbleweed House,' said Harvey. 'Not ideal and neither of us wanted to get married at home, especially because there isn't a room big enough to host it. And outdoors we don't have anything under cover unless we put up a marquee.'

Melissa leaned her head briefly onto Harvey's shoulder. Then, straightening up, she met Benjamin's gaze. 'By rights we should both be panicking just about now, but we're holding it together.'

'You are, I admire that.' Waffles devoured, appetite satiated, he put his cutlery together and took Daniel up on the offer of coffee, as did Melissa and Harvey. Daniel and Etna had agreed that the waffle shack wouldn't sell coffee or hot beverages when it first opened this time last year. At Etna's tea rooms she had a fancy coffee machine and didn't want this place stealing her customers, but over time she'd soon realised she still had her locals, that there was room in the Cove for the both of them as well as the bakery and the pub. And Etna was no stranger in here, either. She'd even begun to request a pot of tea with sweet waffles for herself. Benjamin and Tilly had laughed once, saying that was probably the reason Etna had allowed the serving of hot drinks here – to satisfy her own cravings.

'Tracy even floated the idea of using the Heritage Inn,' Melissa told Benjamin, 'but, again, it's too much to ask of someone. She and Guy have a full house as it is.'

'We're pleased everyone is trying to help us,' said Harvey. 'It's a good reminder of why we live here in the Cove – it's for the people as much as the village itself.'

Benjamin felt the same way.

When Melissa's phone buzzed with an incoming message she snatched it up and he wondered whether he was about to be proved wrong, whether a venue could be scored at the very last minute.

She looked up at both of them after she'd read her message and must've realised what was going through their heads. 'Just Tilly,' she explained. 'She just got home to her cottage and had a message from Barney telling her that it had taken three of us, but that takings were up and the shop was in one piece. She wanted to pass on her thanks.'

Benjamin leapt in as Melissa began bashing out a reply. 'Could you tell her I'll be around at the farm in the morning if she wants to come and choose her tree?'

Melissa's gaze flicked up. 'She needs you to hold her hand?' No matter what she had going on, Melissa was always at the ready with a teasing quip. They'd known each other a long time and although she'd been away from the Cove for years, since she'd returned it hadn't been at all difficult to fall back into their easy way together.

'Of course not, but I said I'd help. I'm being kind.'

'You most certainly are.' She finished the text and sent it Tilly's way.

He stirred the coffee set in front of him and looked up to see Melissa still grinning. At least he'd managed to cheer her up a bit and get rid of the worried look on her face for now. 'You're watching me,' he said.

'I'm not.'

'You were,' Harvey butted in, sipping his own coffee.

'Okay, I was. But only because I'm wondering whether you're ever going to ask her out.'

Benjamin pulled a face as if to deny it, but what was the point? 'You know I want to?'

'Yes,' she said.

'Does everyone know?'

'Of course they do,' said Harvey. 'So, what's the hold-up? Tell her how you feel... life's too short to mess around.' He shared a look with his bride-to-be, an acknowledgement of the years they'd spent apart when they should've been together.

Benjamin had to wonder whether Tilly really was the only person who didn't know how he felt, because everyone else seemed to.

3

Tilly was glad to be home. It was amazing how stressful twenty-four hours could be, and how busy. She'd arrived at her parents' house to find their concerned neighbour basically camped out on their doorstep. She and the man who lived the other side of Tilly's parents had taken turns to keep a lookout and the whole neighbourhood was on high alert in case the burglar decided to target any of them.

Right now it felt a relief to head to Mistletoe Gate Farm to choose her tree and the warm smile Benjamin greeted her with when he answered the back door told her all she needed to know – she was glad to be back in the Cove.

'You're sure this is all right?' she asked him as he pushed a foot into one of his boots out on the veranda. 'I know you're busy here and you have the pub…'

He stood back up to full height. 'I offered, remember.' He pulled on his other boot. 'I'm happy to help, and besides, I need to know how it all went in Nottingham.'

'There was a bit of damage to the door, a broken window, and of course the locks needed changing, but apart from that it was just some tidying up.' She'd fallen into bed last night, exhausted from the stress, the drive, the clearing up and coordinating the repairs, not to mention worrying about the shop in her absence, although Melissa stepping in to lend a hand had been a relief because when Tilly had called Lois she'd sounded as though she and Barney didn't know whether they were coming or going. 'The hardest part was knowing what was taken. But after a few messages back and forth with Mum and Dad it seems not much is missing at all and we made a list.'

Tilly had found that apart from the mess where the intruder must have emptied drawers and shelves in search of money or anything of value, there wasn't much cleaning up to do. She'd heard some terrible stories of burglaries and, unsurprisingly, all of those had replayed on a loop as she drove up to Nottingham, but within a few hours she'd welcomed the locksmith who was already booked in, the repair man had sorted the door, and she'd tidied enough that you would never even know anything untoward had gone on.

'They took all the cash lying around,' Tilly added. 'Dad had about a hundred quid's worth of notes in the dining room in a pot that he uses when he has to pay the window cleaner. They took some of Mum's jewellery so she's upset about that. But the television was still there, as was the computer.' She began to laugh. 'The thief must've thought all his Christmases had come at once when he picked up the swear jar I bought Dad. It was totally full and coins had been replaced by notes. It's been building up for years – Dad doesn't hold back when he feels a curse coming on.'

'Did they smash the jar?'

She shook her head and smiled. 'They left it intact, and seeing as I said plenty of naughty words while I was at the house, I made a fresh start and dropped in a few coins.' She had a fluttery feeling in her stomach at the way Benjamin was looking at her and swiftly moved the conversation along. 'I hope there are some trees left here for me.'

He took the lead and stepped off the veranda. 'Come on, you've got your pick of a beautiful bunch, just you wait.'

The smell out here at the farm was heavenly – a mixture of a spicy Christmas tree scent and the earthy aroma that came as they trudged up along one row of trees, crossed to another. There was a distant sound of an electric saw, families huddled in groups chatting, another family bickered about what would make the best tree – *that one's too tall, that one is way too fat, no not the right shape* – and the sun had at last peeped out from behind a cloud enough to add some brightness to a cold December day.

'Do you have a preference as to which variety?' Benjamin wanted to know.

'Not really...' Her wellies squelched into the mud as he led her down a different row. 'But remember I live in a small cottage.' They'd passed stunning trees so far but all of those would bend over on the ceiling they were so tall. Others were so wide at the base that they'd take up the entire room.

'I remember.' But he stopped so suddenly she almost crashed into him and her feet slipped. He caught her arm.

'Thank you, I don't much fancy landing in the mud.'

'It's still slippery in parts after the big storm – mind your step.' He looked down at the bright red wellies she'd found at a charity shop last year. 'We certainly wouldn't lose you out here in those.'

'They're fur-lined,' she bumbled. 'I couldn't resist.'

'Fur-lined, you say – well, I might have to get myself a pair.' His eyes didn't leave hers as they stood surrounded by the rich green of Christmas as though they were the only couple on the farm and everyone else had faded into the distance.

'I don't think red's your colour.' They were flirting and Tilly felt as though she were floating on air; at least she did until a kid barrelled past, slipped in the mud and wailed.

Benjamin scooped him up in his arms, the boy's sky-blue coat covered in muck that was now also coating Benjamin's jacket, until the boy's dad found them. 'I think I have something that belongs to you,' Benjamin told him and the man took over consoling the boy, who looked as though he'd got overexcited in the madness of the run-up to Christmas.

'He'll be hyped up on the sugar,' Benjamin said quietly when they were left alone once more. 'I saw that kid having a hot chocolate. I'm not sure how much milk was in the drink but it was definitely piled high with marshmallows – we're a bit generous with those here.'

When she began to feel awkward standing so close, both looking at each other but neither of them able to think of what to say, Tilly declared she had to make a decision. 'I need to get a move on, I've got a shop to open.'

He led her to the right. 'These are the Nordmann fir variety. And don't worry, they're not all this big.' He cocked his head to indicate she should follow him a bit further, past a couple of dozen trees or so, and they came to a row of specimens that were all much shorter. 'These are below six foot. See how they're much fatter at the bottom than some of our other trees.' He'd crouched down and was pointing to the shape he referred to and after removing his glove put a palm beneath a branch so that the greenery sat against his skin. 'The needles are soft and the retention is good, so less sweeping up for you.'

'That's always a bonus.' She took off her glove and felt the silky leaves, leaned in to inhale the scent some more. Then she stood back to assess the height, regard the width at the bottom.

'It'll fit in your cottage,' he assured her.

'I have beams, remember.'

'How could I forget?' His smile reminded her of the one time he'd been to her home. It was a couple of months back and the local artisan blacksmith, Lucy, had made several items for Tilly to keep for herself rather than sell at the shop. Benjamin had seen Lucy struggling with the heavy box and had offered her a lift. He'd gone inside with her to help deliver the goods and had promptly bashed the top of his head on one of the beams as he headed from the front door to the kitchen when Tilly offered to put the kettle on and make them both a cup of tea.

'If you put it in the corner of your sitting room then it'll be fine,' he advised. 'It'll be far enough from the log burner that it won't dry out, close enough that you'll be able to see both when you're relaxing on the sofa.'

A family nearby were talking about tagging a tree and Benjamin stepped in to help, pulling from his pocket a couple of pink labels that explained the colourful strips on the tops of several trees Tilly had seen this morning flapping about like masts on a sailboat.

He turned back to Tilly. 'Saw.'

'Excuse me?'

'I didn't bring a saw, only tags. I'll tag this, or else you could stay here on guard and I'll run back to grab one.'

'I think tagging it'd be better anyway, then I can have it delivered later.'

'I'm happy to cut this down now and take it straight back to yours, if you like.'

'I don't want to be any trouble.'

'It's no bother at all. I just hope I can find my way back to you again,' he winked before setting off towards the equipment shed to grab what he needed.

Tilly didn't mind hanging around at the farm. As much as she loved her shop, there was just something about being out in the open air at this time of the year. And while some winter days were damp and relentless with the chill reaching your bones somehow, being out here at Mistletoe Gate Farm with Benjamin had been the perfect antidote to the last twenty-four hours and the stress over her parents' break-in.

Tilly was busy trying to decide which had been the best thing for her today – the fresh air or Benjamin's company – when the man in question reappeared. His light brown hair was highlighted beneath the sun, and the smile that came with him warmed Tilly through.

'What's the piece of cardboard for?' she asked as he laid it down on the ground.

'I don't mind the great outdoors but I'd rather not get any dirtier than I am already.' He lay down on his side, saw in hand.

'Need me to do anything?' She tried not to look at the hair snaking down a taut stomach as his layers rode up when he reached further beneath the base of the tree with the saw. At least he couldn't see her staring, his own face well hidden in amongst the branches by now.

'Hold the tree by the trunk and tilt towards you when you feel it give a little,' came his muffled voice.

She'd been expecting a *No thanks* to her offer of help but was glad she wasn't just standing around watching and so slotted her hand through the branches to the trunk as Benjamin sawed away at the bottom. When she felt the tree move she did as instructed and eventually a puffed Benjamin emerged.

Although not easy to stand on tiptoes in chunky wellies, Tilly managed to reach up and pull a couple of needles from one side of his hair when he took charge of the tree.

'Hazard of the job,' he laughed. 'Now, let's get this to the netting machine.'

'Which end do you want me to take?' At his surprise she added, 'You think I'm going to make you carry it by yourself? I'm not so girlie I can't pick up part of a tree – it's all a part of the tree-choosing process.'

'You fit in very well around here,' he complimented before lifting the top of the tree as she took the bottom and they marched over with it to join the queue of customers waiting for their trees to be netted.

While Benjamin stood in line, Tilly took her chance to pay for her tree and choose two fresh wreaths – one for the shop and the other for her cottage. She selected one with cinnamon sticks and pine cones and studded with plump, red berries, and another covered in natural green foliage with small, frosted, red apples and sprigs of holly.

'Don't forget your mistletoe,' Heather encouraged at the hatch of the shed. 'You can cut your own near the gate – there's so much, Tilly, you'd be helping us out.'

'And what am I going to do with a load of mistletoe?' Tilly laughed.

'You never know when it might be your lucky day,' Heather shrugged. Looking glamorous all wrapped up in a puffy jacket with a looped scarf around her neck, make-up in place as always, she gave Tilly a somewhat knowing glance. 'I'm sure you'd get some use out of it, a beautiful young girl like you.'

When Benjamin came over, tree hoisted onto his shoulder, Tilly waved goodbye to Heather.

'What's my mother up to?' Benjamin asked.

'No idea,' she lied, because she'd seen Heather look first at her and then at her son and back again, the sort of look a parent gives that leaves no doubt as to what they're thinking.

Tilly had her wreaths, one over each arm, but before she could offer to somehow help with the tree as well, Benjamin told her he'd take it by himself. 'Much easier to carry once it's netted,' he said, resting it on one shoulder as though it weighed nothing at all.

Back at Tilly's cottage, she set down the wreaths and helped Benjamin negotiate the doorway that was lower than most and once he was through, minding the beams in the rest of the cottage, he took the tree into the sitting room.

'I've got the stand in the kitchen, let me grab it.'

Already she knew the tree would be perfect just where he'd said, in the corner. Last year she'd had the tree the other side of the fireplace but she'd gone for a slightly taller, skinnier variety then.

'Scissors?' Benjamin asked once he had the tree in its stand.

Tilly grabbed a pair and began to cut the netting from bottom to top and as the branches splayed out, so did her smile. 'I love how fat it is at the bottom.'

'It's a great tree. Hate to say I told you so, but...'

She shoved his arm playfully. 'I'll make sure I get this variety every year from now on – it fills the part of the room that needs it.' All the rooms in the cottage could be described as compact and the sitting room, with its low beams, was no exception. It was at its cosiest in winter, with the log burner and a tiled hearth, two sofas – one along the far wall, a smaller one at an angle – and a flatweave, pale-blue rug covering a carpet that really needed replacing at some point.

'Now it feels like Christmas is coming.' She stood next to Benjamin as they admired the tree and when his fingers accidentally brushed hers, she felt her heart skip a beat.

'Did I see Mum trying to tempt you into buying some mistletoe earlier?' he asked.

'She did her best. Do you have lots in the house? Back at the farm... inside, I mean.' She tripped over her words in an eagerness to shift the focus away from herself.

'Mum puts sprigs here and there.' A frown knitted across his brow.

'What's that look for?'

'I'm not sure why she does it, really – she and Dad don't seem to make the most of it any more. Not this year, anyway.'

'I suppose they've been married a long time.' She hoped it was the right thing to say and that it didn't sound as if she was trying to trivialise his worries. Her parents were as solid as they came as a married couple but Tilly couldn't really see them pausing in their daily routine to snatch a kiss under the mistletoe. Then again, if Benjamin's parents usually did and mistletoe played such a big part in their business, maybe he was right to be concerned.

'Would you like a cup of tea to say thank you for your help with the tree?' She hoped the offer would take his frown away and give her back the relaxed Benjamin she was used to. She did need to get to work but another twenty minutes or so wouldn't matter. 'Hold that thought,' she said when a knock on the door disturbed them.

Tilly opened the door to find Jade from the Twist and Turn Bakery armed with a plastic container that had a see-through lid. 'Treats for you,' Jade announced. 'Chocolate, cranberry and orange cake for morning tea. I did come to the shop but you weren't there.' A puzzled look passed across her face. 'You're not sick, are you?'

'No, I'm not sick.'

Benjamin stepped into Jade's eyeline. 'Hey there.'

'Good morning,' Jade smiled, a knowing look on her face.

Hands pushed into his jeans pockets, he looked at Tilly. 'I'd better be going, no worries about the tea.' And with a nod to them both, off he went down the short path and away from the cottage.

Jade bustled inside, her lips sealed until she'd shut the front door to the cottage. 'Okay, give me details!'

But Tilly shook her head. 'Nothing to tell. He helped me choose a tree and bring it back here, end of story.' She pulled on her coat from the hook near the narrow staircase, looped her scarf around her neck, picked up her bag and keys, and took the plastic container from Jade. 'Thanks so much for these – we can enjoy them together, but I really do need to get to the shop, if you don't mind.' She opened the door again.

'Not at all.' Jade followed after her, down the path, still wrapped up against the cold. 'We can walk and talk.' And when Tilly said nothing, Jade prompted her. 'Come on, give me the gossip!'

But Tilly was already striding on ahead of her friend. 'Nothing to tell,' she called over her shoulder.

And there really wasn't... but did that mean that there wouldn't ever be?

4

Benjamin had his work cut out for him at the pub. Henry had been off sick with a cold, Marnie burned her thumb and forefinger on the lid of a casserole pot, which meant she slowed down so as not to do any more damage, and in the weeks leading up to Christmas it was always a busy time for the Copper Plough, this year being no exception.

When Tilly came into the pub late afternoon with Melissa and Tracy, her presence gave Benjamin the lift he needed to work through the final hour before his shift finished. He delivered the two portions of chunky chips with aioli and sweet chilli sauce in miniature bowls on the side and picked up on the theme of their meeting: weddings. Had to be, he supposed, with it getting so close to the big day. Melissa looked as though she was stressing – she gave it away because she'd looked the same way when she'd first come back to the Cove after an absence of five years, worried about what people might think of her.

Tilly came over to the bar as Benjamin was finishing his shift and, one arm cradling a plastic container filled with leftover herby lamb cobbler to take home, he lifted up the hatch to make his escape. Tilly had just waved goodbye to Tracy and to Melissa, who was meeting Harvey at the Little Waffle Shack for their supper and so they could make a start on writing out wedding invitations with the details of the now-decided change of venue. Not many couples would write their invitations in a food outlet, Benjamin thought, chuckling to himself. But if he knew Melissa and Harvey, it was all a part of their togetherness, which made it so much easier for them to manage this major change they were facing.

'How are their plans going?'

'Hectic,' Tilly replied as he lowered the hatch to the bar once more. 'But Tracy and I have had our final fittings for our bridesmaid dresses so that's one more thing crossed off Melissa's list, at least.'

'And what about the all-important venue?'

Tilly pulled on her woolly hat. 'It'll be at Tumbleweed House – not ideal, but they haven't come up with anything else. They're enquiring about marquee hire.'

'Sounds stressful.'

She looked about to agree but instead squinted at him. 'If you don't mind me saying, you look wiped out.'

'Er, thanks.'

'Sorry, that didn't sound very nice, did it?' She pulled a face. He loved it when she scrunched up her nose and cheeks realising she might have said something inappropriate.

'It's all right. If I'd felt on top of the world then what you said would've been a real insult, but as it is, I am knackered.' He was tired – tired from work, the farm, trying to work out what was going on between his mum and dad despite their protestations that nothing was up.

He tilted his head in the direction of the door and they left the warmth of the pub, emerged into the biting cold of winter, and Benjamin stood for a moment and took a breath. His jacket was still undone but man, it felt good to escape the confines of the kitchen.

He went on to tell Tilly his woes, the staff issues today, how busy it was.

'You probably could've done without bringing us chunky chips,' she said.

'Always happy to be of service.' As he adjusted the container to get a better grip he noticed Lucy coming towards them along The Street. 'What have you got there?' She had a box in her arms and by the way she was holding it, it had to be heavy.

She rested it on her drawn-up knee for a moment, using her other hand to tug a wisp of blonde hair away from her mouth and behind her ear. The box in both arms again, she told Benjamin that she was on her way over to his place with it. 'It's for Heather – well, actually, ordered by her for Jared, who works for you guys. I assume it's a Christmas gift.'

As if by mutual agreement, Tilly took the container Benjamin had hold of and Benjamin took the heavy box from Lucy.

'My knight in shining armour.' Lucy, dressed in her work dungarees with dust all down the front, had her coat open and gave her arms a good shake.

'What's inside?' Without a free hand he couldn't peek into the box.

'It's a set of two cast-iron skillets to use for cooking, keep the food sizzling at the table.'

'Ah, that makes sense. Jared was talking to me the other day at the farm about his foray into Mexican cooking – he wanted some top tips for making fajitas. I told him the first thing to do was get a skillet so you can serve them up properly. Mum overheard our conversation and told me she was going to try to get him some for his Christmas gift, she just hoped he didn't manage to get to the shops first.' Although he doubted it. Jared was a hard worker and did long hours at the farm so this should be a timely gift, ready for his long break over Christmas and New Year.

'You should've driven it up there,' said Tilly, peering over to see inside the box. She nodded her approval before looking at Lucy. 'Do your coat up, you're making me feel cold.'

'It gets really hot in the workshop,' Lucy laughed. 'I thought I'd get some fresh air – hence the walk – but I didn't realise how heavy the box would get once I'd carried it all the way along The Street.'

'I can take it from here,' said Benjamin.

And as Tilly still had hold of the container of leftovers, just like that he got to spend more time with her and sent up a silent thank you that Lucy had chosen that moment to head over to the farm.

Lucy said her goodbyes while Benjamin and Tilly set off in the direction of Mistletoe Gate Farm.

'You've gone quiet,' Tilly noticed as they passed the florist and turned down the lane. 'It must be very heavy.'

'Swap?'

'You're joking, no chance.' Her laughter echoed in the night air.

'We'll drop this off and I'll walk you back home. Stay for a mulled wine first, though.'

'I won't say no to that.' Tilly did the honours and undid the pedestrian gate surrounded by mistletoe on either side.

'I made some last night as it's always nice to have at home. I swear at this time of the year I have it flowing through my veins.'

'You and me both, I love it.'

It was so dark as they walked that he couldn't see whether she was smiling but he sensed she was as he told her to tread carefully. She didn't have her wellies on and he hoped there weren't any potholes of mud that would mess up her footwear.

When they reached the veranda he set the box down. 'Jared owes me some home-cooked fajitas for carrying these,' he said, quietly in case Jared might still be around. Customers weren't here at this time but there was still a bit of noise coming from the fields as Danny and other workers milled about finishing up jobs for the day, chopping down any trees that had been tagged and needed delivery, putting away the equipment, and closing up the sheds.

'You'll have to write out a recipe for him and pop it in with your mum's gift.'

'That's a great idea.'

'Happy to help.' Her eyes shone in the moonlight as she looked back at him.

He fished out his keys; his parents had locked up with them still working. It was one of the reasons it was actually easy enough to be here at his age – none of them were in the house together long enough to really annoy one another.

The kitchen was quiet when they stepped inside and he flipped on the lights that illuminated the room and the work surfaces beneath the dark wooden cabinets. As well as a hint of spices from the mulled wine waiting in the pot on the stove, a faint smell of dough from the bread machine Heather used regularly hung in the air with the timer showing another fresh loaf would be ready in less than an hour. Benjamin retrieved the heavy box from where he'd left it on the porch and, back inside, pushed it onto the Welsh dresser before he took the container of leftovers from Tilly and slotted it into the fridge.

Time to heat up the pot of mulled wine. He took off the lid to check what was left and by his estimations, there was enough for a couple of glasses each if Tilly wanted to stay a while.

Tilly was already over beside the eight-foot Fraser fir in the corner of the room. 'This is beautiful.' She moved around inspecting the ornaments.

'You know, it doesn't matter how many trees are out there,' he said tilting his head in the direction of the fields that lay beyond the house, 'and it doesn't matter that all of us are surrounded by them all day, every day, there's still something special about selecting one and bringing it inside the house.' He checked himself. 'Where are my manners? Let me take your coat.'

She unbuttoned the burnt-orange garment and he slipped it from her shoulders. He hung it over the back of one of the dining chairs and although they didn't touch, it seemed intimate, a scent of her perfume on the item he'd taken from her. He watched her adjust the sleeves of her dress back down to her wrists. 'Harvey and Melissa came to choose a tree a few days ago,' he told her as he went back to stirring the mulled wine to get the spices circulating. Already they'd multiplied in their scent since the heat went on beneath the pot.

'Barney did, too,' she smiled. 'I'm surprised he hasn't started getting his tree in November – he threatens to every year.'

'He was a December 1st customer,' Benjamin grinned.

Tilly shook her head, back to walking around the tree to admire all the decorations. 'He'll be making it up here earlier every year, I reckon. I wonder if Harvey and Melissa might get married beside their tree.'

'Maybe.' He kind of liked that idea, too. 'And they're happy with Tumbleweed House?'

'Content is probably more the word.' She came over to peep into the pot and nodded her approval at the smell unleashed from the wine. 'The outside will have enough space for a marquee but it's a squash with all the elderberry bushes.'

'I hadn't thought of that.'

'Can't be helped,' she shrugged. 'And at least with some sort of marquee everyone will be gathered together to watch them say their vows. I think that's what they really want, everyone together – it's why the barn worked so well for them; it wasn't just that it was special.'

He cut a few slices from an orange taken from the fruit bowl before he took out a couple of glasses with handles and an etched swirly pattern on the side of each from the Welsh dresser ready to serve the mulled wine.

Tilly came over and crouched down to pick up a piece of paper. 'You knocked this off.'

'Clumsy,' he told her as he set down the glasses to take it from her but he paused when he saw a look of bewilderment pass over her face. 'What's wrong?'

'Nothing… I mean, none of my business.' Without looking at it again, she passed him the piece of paper as though it might burn her fingers if she held onto it any longer.

It wasn't until he'd moved the glasses over to the kitchen benchtop near the pan of warming wine and looked at the paper for himself that he realised why.

'Benjamin…' Tilly's voice penetrated his thoughts and he wasn't sure how long he'd zoned out for.

She wouldn't have needed to study the piece of paper hard. The black, boldface title gave the game away. *Application for a Divorce* would've screamed out to her as much as it did to him. What she might not have noticed was that the form had actually been filled in.

He slumped down on a kitchen chair. 'Well, at least now I know why I've felt like there's something off between my parents.' He rested his forearms on his knees, the form still in his hands. 'It wasn't all in my imagination.'

Tilly stirred the mixture on the stove and turned off the gas so it didn't spoil. She ladled out two generous servings and brought them both over to the table. 'Here, I think you need this.' She handed him a glass and sat down.

The odd creak from the house as it started to wind down for the day and the rattle of the back door that had a penguin draft excluder lying at the foot of it to stop the cold winter wind were the only sounds apart from the soft blowing from Tilly's lips as she tried to cool her drink. He closed his eyes and attempted to make sense of what he'd seen. His parents, divorcing – it was unbelievable. It felt unreal. And yet, it was one hundred per cent happening. It was all there in black and white, the form to set the wheels in motion. He left the table and put the form back where it had come from on top of the Welsh dresser.

'I'm sorry, Benjamin.' Tilly braved speaking before he did.

All he could do was give a small smile in acknowledgement of her sympathy before he sat down again and sagged back against his chair. His parents had bickered over the years – what couple didn't? 'I should've known.'

'How could you?'

He caught sight of their wedding photograph still in its Wedgwood frame on the wall at the far side of the room. He didn't need to get any closer to picture his mum's head against his dad's chest, his dad's chin resting on top of her head, both of them looking as though they were in a dream, they couldn't believe their luck.

Benjamin sipped the mulled wine that would've tasted better had he not seen that piece of paper. 'I wonder when they were going to tell me and Charlotte.' He raked a hand through his hair. Sometimes he forgot it was short now, it didn't tangle like it used to – it wasn't nearly as satisfying for taking out your frustration. 'And now I sound like a big baby.'

Tilly reached out and covered his hand with hers, the move making them both look up. 'You're not a baby, you're their child and always will be. I'd say it's a perfectly normal reaction and this clearly came out of the blue.'

Her sympathy was helping to cushion the blow and he found it hard not to turn his palm face up and hold her hand properly. Would that be too bold a move? 'I'm glad you're here,' he told her instead.

'Me too.' But she took her hand away and went over to the wall to look at one of the other photographs up there. It wasn't the traditional wedding shot but a more relaxed one of his parents with all their guests. Wine in hand, Tilly peered closer and then turned to Benjamin. 'Was this picture taken here at the farm?'

He joined her, his wine glass warming his palm that was wrapped around it. 'It sure was. Mum said it wasn't the official photographer who took that one, though, it was a friend, but they had it framed because it's so natural. Look at the way everyone's smiling.'

'It's lovely. It reminds me of those pictures in Barney's barn.'

The jointly appreciated moment between them made Benjamin realise how close he'd grown to Tilly. Heritage Cove's annual Wedding Dress Ball raised money for charity and Barney always put up a picture of the event on the wall of the barn so guests the year after could take in the importance of the occasion not only to raise money but to bring the community together. This summer Benjamin had danced with Tilly. It was only briefly and he'd danced with others, too, but his dance with her was the one he remembered. He'd never forget what it felt like to hold her close and wished he could do it right now, but her next comment jolted him back to reality rather than dreaming of what could be.

'Did your parents ever think of holding weddings here?'

He nodded. 'They did for a time, but I guess they never got around to developing a plan.' And it didn't look like they ever would, either. Benjamin frowned as a thought reared its ugly head again. 'I wonder if the business is in trouble. Dad said it wasn't when I asked him, but I wonder whether he'd even tell me if it was. I mean, divorce doesn't come out of nowhere, does it? Maybe they've had arguments about money, or lack of it. Perhaps I'm not around enough to have heard any disagreements.' He was clutching at straws but it was nicer to think that something had happened to cause a marriage breakdown than the alternative, which was simply that they'd fallen out of love with each other.

When he looked at Tilly she was still taking in the scene in the photograph but her lips were slightly twisted as though she was thinking about something very hard. 'You're frowning.'

She stopped doing it and told him, 'I'm thinking, that's all.'

'Out with it.' Her company at least numbed the shock of finding out about his parents.

'I'm thinking you could offer to hold Harvey and Melissa's wedding here.' Her eyes danced.

'You really are taking your bridesmaid duties seriously,' he said.

But she wouldn't be deterred. 'Think about it. It's such a romantic setting. I couldn't imagine anywhere more suited to holding a wedding – the smell of pine trees in the air, the lights strung across those closest to the house, and in this picture…' She looked closer. '…that's the veranda your parents and their guests are gathering on, isn't it?'

'It sure is.' Tilly was standing so close to him now that he felt almost overwhelmed by her exquisite feminine perfume, the scent taking him back to that dance in the barn in the summer, their bodies pressed close. He cleared his throat and tried to focus. You would think the shock of finding out about his parents' marital issues might dampen his feelings for Tilly, at least for a moment, but he was finding them increasingly hard to ignore. 'Dad said it was a beautiful day when they got married. They'd had the ceremony on the veranda and guests had either watched from there or the grass area beyond.' He began to laugh. 'Apparently the guests dispersed after the nuptials and most were happily chatting near the trees and drinking their champagne when they got caught out as the heavens opened. Heritage Cove hadn't seen rain for almost a fortnight but that day, according to Dad, Mother Nature made up for it.'

Tilly looked even closer at the picture. 'I didn't notice before, I think the smiles were all I saw, but you're right, some of the guests have wet hair, look!'

He'd forgotten about it too, having seen the picture so many times before that it had become a taken-for-granted part of their home. His parents had exchanged their vows right here at Mistletoe Gate Farm, the place they'd once described as their Forever Home. What would happen to the farm if they divorced? Would they sell it? What if someone bought it and demolished the business, turned it into an identikit housing estate?

'I don't think Mum and Dad will go for it,' he concluded miserably. He'd love to help his friends out, but with Danny and Heather planning a divorce, the last thing they would want was young love thrown in their face.

Tilly didn't say anything for a while, but then she came over to the table and rather than sitting opposite Benjamin as before, she sat next to him. 'If they are having financial difficulties then perhaps Melissa and Harvey's wedding could be the start of something new for them. If your parents considered holding weddings here in the past but never got around to it, what better way to show them that it could work? It could mean that form never gets posted in, the divorce doesn't happen.'

'I appreciate the optimism.' It would be easy to get carried away with it, too.

'Come on, stay positive. Mistletoe Gate Farm is stunning in the winter and this wedding really could turn things around. Isn't it worth a try?'

'So, if it was you, would you get married here?' he ventured.

'If I was lucky enough to fall in love, yes.' She didn't meet his gaze this time.

'And you wouldn't mind the mud?'

She harrumphed. 'Of course not. I'd tell all the guests to come in boots – way more comfy than wedding shoes, in my opinion.'

Benjamin admired her outlook and the hopeful spin but if whatever was going on between his parents had gone as far as filling out forms to file for divorce, it was going to take a lot more than a village wedding to save the day. Or perhaps they could double up and have not just a wedding but a divorce party at the same time. Cynical, but practical, wasn't it?

His scepticism was overshadowed by Tilly's optimism as she floated ideas about how many could comfortably fit on the veranda, where the groom could stand and wait for his bride, how they could decorate the space, and how guests could spill onto the grass amidst the magic of the farm. She talked catering, how they could serve canapés and simple finger foods rather than anything too formal with a sit-down meal, she thought about the signing of a register, car parking for guests.

'Were you a wedding planner in your former life?' he laughed, the mulled wine calming him down, at least. He ladled out a second serving for each of them.

'Nope, just a romantic.'

Had anyone else had the idea, Benjamin would've never said a word to either of his parents. But because it was Tilly, when Danny came in through the door, after a little nudge and prompt from Tilly, he blurted the whole idea out to his dad.

* * *

Benjamin had to admit it felt good heading out with Tilly again and not because they both now had a couple of glasses of mulled wine inside them.

'Come on,' she urged, 'the waffle shack will be closed if we don't hurry up, and I don't want Harvey and Melissa to write those invitations without listening to our proposal.'

He was glad it had been Tilly with him when he found that form. She'd certainly not let him wallow – not yet, anyway. They'd told Danny the idea and then when Heather came home fifteen minutes ago, they told her too. She'd come into the house and the first thing she said was that she'd seen Melissa and Harvey, who both looked to have the weight of the world on their shoulders. *The barn was so perfect*, Heather had said. *The house is practical but it's going to take a bit of decorating to really make it magical.* And that was when Tilly leapt in and blurted out their idea. She'd looked at Benjamin as though she might get in trouble for taking the lead but he'd just nodded to give his go-ahead. Neither of his parents had dismissed the idea at all and Danny in particular had been all ears. Would it be too much for Benjamin to hope that his father wanted to do anything he could to save the marriage and that was why he was so on board?

Benjamin and Tilly passed the village tree and field, walking at a pace that almost had them both breathless. And once they reached the Little Waffle Shack, bypassing customers coming out, they found Melissa and Harvey inside, pen poised ready to write another invitation.

'Stop!' Tilly alerted not only them but everyone else in the shack. 'Sorry.' She cringed, looking around and aiming her apology at Daniel as well as his customers. 'I meant Harvey and Melissa. Everyone else, carry on.'

'And why do we need to stop?' Harvey asked, although happily putting down his pen. There was a small stack of what Benjamin assumed were already-written invitations tucked into their envelopes and another, much bigger, pile of envelopes with cards sitting beneath the flaps, waiting to be written.

Tilly and Benjamin sat down with their friends and Tilly waited for Benjamin to take it from here. It felt odd enthusing about a wedding at the farm when what was once a family home might, in the not-too-distant future, be sold off to someone else to make happy memories there. But Benjamin ran the idea past their friends, conveying the magic they could both see already. He talked about his parents' wedding – what little he knew of the details – and explained how Harvey and Melissa could have their ceremony under cover, that the veranda was so enormous they could crowd all the guests onto it if the weather was that bad. And he was sure his mum would let people spill into the kitchen if they really had to, although he and everyone else knew the real allure would be in the outdoor location surrounded by Christmas trees.

'I don't know, it's a huge ask,' said Harvey.

Benjamin recapped how his parents had thought about hosting weddings years ago but had never got around to investigating it further. 'You could be the trial run, so it would be doing them a favour in a way. They were both really enthusiastic about the idea. Honestly. Talk to them – they said to tell you to go up there for a chat or call them as soon as you like.'

Harvey and Melissa looked at each other and seemed to be on board until Melissa hesitated. 'I don't want to put anyone out. I already feel terrible that Barney feels so awful about the barn being unusable; I don't want anyone else to be under unnecessary pressure.'

'It'll either convince them weddings at the farm are a possibility or put them off for life,' Harvey concluded.

Benjamin hated to tell them that although their own nuptials had been held there, Danny and Heather Doyle were heading for divorce.

'You don't need to decide now,' he said, pushing that thought from his head. 'Sleep on it, go over in the morning.'

Melissa and Harvey nodded their agreement and Benjamin and

Tilly left them to it. It was colder outside the waffle shack than it had been when they'd headed up this way, anxious to catch Harvey and Melissa and tell them about the new idea. 'I'll walk you home,' Benjamin offered, getting a smile of agreement in return.

'It'll be so much better than Tumbleweed House,' Tilly declared as they set off towards her cottage, 'and if this helps your parents see that the farm could have other ways to generate income off-season then it can only help, right?'

'It can't do much more harm.'

'That's the spirit.'

'Thanks, Tilly.'

'I only made the suggestion,' she shrugged, as though it was nothing.

'Doesn't matter, having your friendship and support means a lot.'

She didn't answer straight away but then from wherever her thoughts had gone, just for a second, she brought them back to the matter in hand. 'I'm busy with the shop but never too busy to help out with a wedding, especially for two such special people. So, anything that needs doing, let your parents know I'll pitch in. I can talk decorations, help set up for the day, whatever is necessary.' They paused before crossing over the road that would take them to her cottage.

And as he walked her all the way to her front door it was on the tip of his tongue to ask her out. But this time, what held him back wasn't the fact it hadn't even been a year since his breakup with Zoe, it wasn't because he worried Tilly would say no, it was because the only couple in his mind right now were his parents.

The couple he'd thought would be together forever.

5

'Mum, the house is fine.' Tilly was fielding yet another call from her parents. 'I bought four timer switches for lamps and they go off at different times, your neighbour is keeping an eye out and I gave her a key to the back gate so she can check around that side.' Tilly rolled her eyes at Jade, who was browsing the candle selection in Tilly's Bits 'n' Pieces, holding up a pale-pink, tapered, dinner candle for closer inspection and to see what it looked like in one of the pastel candle holders on the chest of drawers. 'Yes, the neighbour locks the gate afterwards. Now, go, enjoy your holiday. Your neighbour is already texting me twice a day; I have a job to do as well as being your security detail,' she laughed. 'Okay love you too.'

'I heard they were broken into.' Jade, dressed in jeans and a navy, knitted sweater down to mid-thigh beneath a slightly shorter jacket, set the candle and candle holder onto the counter ready to pay.

Tilly put her phone out of the way. 'They were, but no real damage done and not too much taken. I think we're all looking at it with the view that it could've been worse.'

'Still, not nice knowing someone's been through your things,' Jade shuddered.

'No, definitely not. But enough about that, these are beautiful – great choice,' she said, complimenting the purchases before she wrapped each item in tissue paper.

'They're for Celeste. She just painted a pink feature wall in her bedroom – it sounds a bit too much, but it's a subtle pink and this candle and holder will go really well on top of her tallboy.'

'Well, she'll love them. Do you have much more shopping to do?'

'This is the last gift I need to buy, thank goodness.'

'You must be busy with cake commissions in the run-up to Christmas.'

As well as owning and running the bakery with her sister, Jade had launched an additional extra, specialising in cakes. And she was very good at it. Her Christmas cakes were like nothing Tilly had ever seen before – there were two in the window now that attracted plenty of stares and apparently a fair few orders. One was a reindeer's face made out of tender sponge and covered in chocolate icing, with a sprinkling of gold dust across its chocolate antlers. The other was an alpine village complete with penguins, ice-skaters, skiers, and snow-covered fir trees.

'How's the wedding cake coming along?'

Jade wagged her finger after dropping her purse into her bag. 'Nice try, but no details – it's a surprise for everyone.' Jade's latest commission was for Harvey and Melissa's wedding and was to be a combination of a wedding and a Christmas cake. The details were for now between the baker and the bride and groom.

'Spoilsport.' She handed Jade her receipt.

'I've heard about the plans to have the wedding at Mistletoe Gate Farm. Melissa can't stop talking about it.'

'I did wonder if I'd overstepped the mark by suggesting it.'

Jade shook her head. 'Not by the sounds of it.'

Tilly had lain awake last night thinking about Benjamin – something she did often, contemplating their friendship and whether it would ever be more. But what had made her so restless in the small hours was thinking of his parents too, the form to file for a divorce that was completed already. This wedding idea could be what they needed, as she hoped, but what if it was something else that would cause tension and make things so much worse?

'Everyone loves Melissa and Harvey,' Jade went on, 'and Barney. And everyone knows how cut up they *all* are about the barn not being used for the big day. So, I'll bet Danny and Heather are delighted, and what a venue! I mean, Linc and I are nowhere near thinking of marriage – but I wouldn't say no to having my ceremony there one day,' she grinned. Jade had been dating local teacher Linc since his arrival at the Cove in the summer.

'It is going to be incredibly romantic.'

'I hear you and Benjamin came up with the idea together.'

'I suppose we did.'

'Has he asked you out yet?' She asked the question after lowering her voice when a man Tilly didn't recognise came in to browse. At the handmade card section, he'd be hard pushed to overhear what they were saying.

'I think we're established as friends,' Tilly shrugged. The discovery of his parents' marital issues the other night hadn't exactly ignited a romantic spark.

When Jade went back to the bakery, not far from the shop on the same side of The Street, Tilly tidied the jewellery tree at the counter. She was still aware of her male customer, who hadn't picked anything up yet and seemed to be watching her every now and then. Either he was about to pinch something or he was doing what a lot of men did when they came in here – they looked at everything because they had no idea where to start.

'May I help you find something?' she suggested to the man, who seemed nervous. He had blond, spiky hair, the kind that looked like it did its own thing after it was washed and he didn't attempt to tame it in any way. He smelt of stale smoke and Tilly stood back a bit from him.

'You can help me.' The confidence in his voice made her realise his hesitancy clearly wasn't nervousness as she'd suspected. 'But I don't need to buy anything.' He pushed his hands into a donkey jacket with sleeves that were slightly too long for him. 'You're Tilly, aren't you?'

'That's right, I am. And you are...?' She casually stood nearer to the door. Mostly, she didn't mind being in the shop on her own. There were plenty of people milling up and down the street outside all day, many of whom popped in to say hello or waved, and she glanced now to see whether anyone was loitering, just in case she needed them.

'I'm Scott.' Hand out of his pocket, he thrust it in her direction as though his name was the only explanation she needed.

She had no idea who he was but it seemed the polite thing to do to return the gesture. 'I'm sorry, do I know you?'

'Scott Baker.'

Baker? Her family surname. But she had to shake her head because she still had no idea who he was.

He made a noise that might have been *jeez* or something similar, his eyes roaming the room as if it might help him form a sentence. 'I'm Nigel's brother.'

That made no sense. Her dad, Nigel, didn't have a brother. He was an only child. 'I'm not sure I understand.'

He opened his donkey jacket and flapped at the collar. 'It's hot in here,' he frowned. Beneath the coat he wore a creased T-shirt, sea-blue, with a well-known brand printed across the front except part of the first word had begun to peel off.

Tilly wasn't sure what to make of this man, who must be confused. 'I'm not being funny but—'

'You've never heard of me.' He looked around the shop either in curiosity or to avoid Tilly's scrutiny. 'This place has changed.'

'You've been here before?'

'Well, it did belong to my mother.' He smiled at her then, ice-blue eyes showing a hint of emotion or amusement, she wasn't sure which.

Tilly couldn't believe it. How could her gran not have told her about another son? And how could her dad have kept it quiet all these years?

'It used to be called something else in those days,' he went on and she tried to ignore the way he sniffed and used the back of his hand to get rid of any drips that might be lingering. 'You changed the name.'

It took her a moment to think of anything in reply, she was so discombobulated by his claim. 'I had to – it was called the Candle Shop and when I started selling so many other items and the shop evolved, the name didn't fit any more.'

He moved towards the Welsh dresser along the far wall. 'This was on the other side of the shop, I think.'

'That's right,' she stammered. So much had changed since she'd been at the helm.

'It smelt different back then, too.'

'Not so many candles now.' Her words almost tripped over one another as they came out.

'Smells better now,' he said, facing her briefly before he walked around inspecting what else she had on offer. 'Back then the waft was too much. I always wanted to leave the door open when I came in here.'

She managed a hesitant smile as he moved around regarding the shop from all angles.

'This wall ladder,' he said, putting his hand across the rungs. 'It used to be black with yellow stars painted on. I should know, I painted it.'

Tilly had no idea what to say. Her brain was still grappling with this revelation, that her dad had a brother. And his brother was here. Not only that, he claimed to have painted the ladder that Grandma Shirley had kept and the one time Tilly had asked whether they should repaint it to something brighter, she'd said she liked it the way it was but never elaborated further. Tilly had only repainted it recently in a bright white.

'Nothing lasts forever, right?' Scott shrugged and she couldn't tell whether he was being wistful or facetious.

'I'm sorry, I don't know what to say to you,' she blurted out. 'This is all a bit sudden.'

'I apologise.' His demeanour changed and he seemed to remember she might be shocked at his appearance. 'Here I go, lumbering in here like a complete idiot, scaring you when you've obviously never heard of me. Me and your dad… well, we never did see eye to eye.'

Clearly not. Neither her dad nor her grandma had ever mentioned this man. Why?

He was flapping at his coat again now the buttons were open.

'You can hang your coat over the stool if you like,' she suggested. She wasn't sure whether he wanted to hang around, whether that's what she wanted either. But it seemed the right thing to do and she did want to know more about him and the claims he was making. What on earth had happened to cause her gran to keep quiet about one of her own children?

And then Tilly had a sinking feeling. Had this Scott done something so terrible it was unforgivable?

And if he had, here she was, alone in a little shop with him, trapped behind the till.

6

Benjamin had risen early this morning and was sitting on the veranda, jacket and beanie on to keep the winter chill at bay, coffee mug clasped between his palms. His dad was already giving out instructions to workers and it was all systems go, ready for another day selling Christmas trees at Mistletoe Gate Farm. Benjamin couldn't help feeling somewhat resentful that Danny was going about his business as though nothing was out of the ordinary.

He almost dropped his mug. Unless Danny didn't know about the divorce. Was this something that was going to be sprung on him by his wife?

But Benjamin swigged the remains of his coffee. Unlikely, given Heather had left that form somewhere not exactly hidden. It had gone from its position – he'd checked late last night – and he hoped he was wrong. He hoped at least they'd agreed on something and this wasn't going to blindside Danny when the papers came through.

'You're out early,' said Heather when he appeared in the kitchen.

'You know me, I like to enjoy a coffee before I get going, and what better place to do it?'

She seemed to relax entirely as she picked up her cup of tea. 'You're not wrong there.'

'I love this farm, no better place to live.' He thought he'd say it, gauge her reaction, but all he got was a smile and a nod of agreement.

'Knock, knock!' It was Barney at the back door and Benjamin went to open it.

'You're an early riser too. Come to get another tree?' Benjamin asked.

'No, but I am here on important business.' He pulled off his hat, which sent his grey hair on end with the static until he smoothed it down.

'Come in,' Heather urged. 'You're nice and wrapped up,' she smiled as he peeled off a scarf, his coat and a cardigan he had on over another jumper. Heather was all ready for the day but not in outdoor wear, Benjamin noticed. Usually she'd be in casual jeans, a big chunky jumper, and thick socks, ready to pull on her boots but instead she was wearing smarter, slim-fitting jeans and a blouse, and the fluffy socks she wore around the house instead of slippers.

'I've left Lois at home wrapping Christmas gifts,' Barney told her. 'I'm here to talk weddings,' he informed Benjamin, rubbing his palms together and accepting Heather's offer of a cup of tea.

Harvey and Melissa had leapt at the chance to have their wedding here at the farm and they'd come by to see Heather and Danny the morning after Benjamin and Tilly floated the idea to them. They'd all talked at length about how the ceremony would work, costs involved, the happy couple telling Benjamin's parents that they doubted this would be the last wedding here. It was the perfect place. Benjamin had merely kept quiet when he heard them saying that. He'd looked at each of his parents in turn, tried to see whether their faces gave anything away, but it was as though they were caught up in the romance of it all.

Involving Barney in the arrangements had been a given from the start and as Benjamin made himself a couple of poached eggs on toast for breakfast, he listened to Barney launch into wedding talk straight away. They talked vows, music, food, guest lists – in fact, they talked at such a rapid rate they covered everything from how they'd arrange decorations on the veranda to where exactly Melissa would walk towards the groom-to-be. Heather was scribbling it all down in a big notebook, making sketches here and there with Barney's approval. And Barney clarified that he had his suit all organised, ready to walk Melissa down the aisle and give her away.

Benjamin had washed everything up, dried it all, and put it away when Heather came over to put the kettle on again. She dropped more tea bags into the grey-and-white-spotted teapot she'd got from Tilly's Bits 'n' Pieces years ago that – apart from a tiny chip off the handle glued back on for her by Danny – was still going strong. 'This planning is quite something,' she said.

'You think you've taken on too much?'

'Not at all.' Her shoulders dropped slightly. 'It's actually a lot of fun. I just hope we don't disappoint.'

He drummed his fingers on the side of the sink but stopped in case she picked up on any tension. The best way to work out what was going on and to get answers would be to tread very carefully. 'They've seen your wedding photos, right?'

'Of course, they're the best advert.'

'Then if it's anything like your day, they'll be happy.'

'Barney mentioned having the wedding here to Lottie from the convenience store and her eyes lit up, apparently. She's not dating anyone but she said she's thinking of putting her name down at the farm for a date in the future – you know, just in case,' she laughed.

'She's already been asking me whether weddings will become synonymous with Mistletoe Gate Farm.'

'And what do you think?' He pushed his hands into the pockets of his jeans so he wasn't tempted to drum on the work surface again.

'It's something to think about, but the future is unpredictable.' She sighed as though the idea had been there, the enthusiasm building, but now she'd come crashing back down to earth.

'Fingers crossed for some dry weather,' he said, attempting to reignite the zeal she'd had moments ago. 'Although a bit of snow will make it more magical.'

'You're quite the romantic. You take after your father.'

'Dad's a romantic?' She seemed to be thinking of better times already. He wanted to get that look back on her face, the one that moments ago had told of all the promises she and Danny had made to each other, of how their special day at the farm had been just the beginning of their lives together.

'He always was.'

Benjamin couldn't quite pick up whether she meant that he'd been romantic and wasn't any more or that she knew he still was and longed for it to be like that again. It took all of his willpower not to pry about what had gone wrong after all these years.

'What sort of things did he do?' He had to keep her on the same trajectory, talking about Danny in a way that recalled the happier times. Maybe it was the only thing that would work and be a reminder that what they had was too special to walk away from.

Benjamin's attempts to get his mum talking more about Danny were thwarted when Barney got restless and came over.

'Can I do anything to help?' Barney didn't sit still for long – never had, as far as Benjamin knew – and he'd hate being waited on.

'Grab the biscuit tin.' Heather nodded to its position next to the bread bin. 'Take it over to the coffee table. I've got some more ideas we need to discuss.'

And just like that, conversation over. Barney took his position on the sofa again, setting the biscuit tin down next to their big notebook with all the wedding plans they'd been working on scribbled on the open pages. 'He seems happy with the wedding being here.'

Heather smiled. 'I could hug Tilly for suggesting it.' She was watching him, but like her, he had no desire to talk about his love life. 'Invite Tilly for drinks one night,' she suggested. 'Although you already did that with the mulled wine. It looked like you were getting along very well.'

'You get back to your planning,' he said, shaking his head before he left them to it and headed upstairs to take a shower and get ready for work.

When he emerged from his bedroom he got halfway down the stairs before he stopped at the sound of voices in the kitchen. Barney must have left because he could only hear Heather and Danny. He felt as though he was ten years old again, lurking, waiting until his parents moved from the kitchen to the sitting room so that he could sneak in and grab something extra to eat despite dinnertime being well and truly over.

He heard his dad speaking. 'I've left Parker and Jared in charge. I need to have something to eat.' When Heather didn't say anything else, their previous conversation clearly over, he added, 'I can make an omelette if you're interested?'

'No thanks, I'll eat something more later. I'm still full from my porridge.'

Benjamin crept down the rest of the stairs and hovered behind the door that led into the kitchen and the dining area. From where he was standing he could just about see through the door hinge that his mum had put down the big notebook she'd been using to make the wedding plans and his dad was asking more about it.

'Don't you trust me to pull this off?' Heather asked shirtily. 'It's not a frivolous idea, it's someone's wedding. It's a good business move – not that that really matters any more.'

All Danny did was sigh, a sigh loud enough to be audible even from a distance, and Benjamin realised they were both very much in the know about the divorce. He couldn't decide whether that was a good thing or a bad.

'Can you work this afternoon?' Danny asked.

'I said I would.' Again, she bit his head off as though she couldn't tolerate his annoying questions. 'I have a few things to do, but two-thirty p.m. I'll be there without distractions.'

Danny seemed to pick up on her defensiveness. 'Have we really reached the point where we can't have a civil conversation unless it's to keep up appearances in front of everyone else?'

His mum sounded exhausted when she told him he was being ridiculous. 'That's not the way it is,' she insisted.

'Isn't it?'

Through the crack between the hinges and the door Benjamin could see that Heather had spun around to face her husband. 'That isn't what I want.' She clutched her phone and a set of headphones that she proceeded to untangle when Danny didn't really answer.

Finally, when Benjamin thought he was going to have to creep away, he heard his dad say, 'I've been thinking, why don't you book a holiday after New Year? Anywhere – sunny, cold, whatever you choose.'

'So, you give me permission to take time off, is that it? You think a holiday is the answer to everything?'

'That wasn't what I said. You make it sound like I'm patronising you.'

Benjamin moved away quickly, into the downstairs toilet, as his mum pushed her headphones into her ears – a sure sign the conversation was over. She may as well have stuck two fingers up at Danny.

Benjamin had heard them bicker over the years. Everyone did it – no relationship was one-hundred-per-cent perfect all of the time. But the difference now was that they both sounded so defeated.

He heard his mum's footfall on the stairs, her repeating what sounded like Italian phrases. His parents had honeymooned in Italy – Verona – but it was probably too much to ask that she was trying to relive the good old days. From what he'd just witnessed she seemed more likely to be wanting to escape them.

7

Tilly still couldn't get used to it. An uncle, her dad's brother, a member of her family right here in Heritage Cove, sitting in front of her. The whiff of stale smoke was almost overwhelming – she'd seen him stub his cigarette out in the doorway before he came in – but she'd discreetly lit a scented candle beside the till and she'd go and pick up the discarded butt later.

When Scott had come in a couple of days ago, she'd been shocked – so shocked that he'd told her he'd leave her to it and he'd scarpered before she could even think of asking him for more information. Then curiosity had turned to suspicion and she'd wondered whether he was a random weirdo who'd known her grandma was no longer around and had decided for some reason to make up a story and cause trouble. Then again, he'd known about the ladder, hadn't he? Tilly had thrown herself into the busyness of the shop that day wondering how her dad and her grandma could've kept something so huge a secret. They had their faults as a family but dishonesty wasn't one of them.

And today, here was Scott again. He'd poked his head around the door fifteen minutes ago and instead of presenting him with the same flabbergasted expression she'd worn for most of his last visit, she'd offered him a hot drink and now here they were, sipping tea and talking at the counter.

'I put three sugars in, as requested,' she told him as he blew across the steaming liquid.

He held the cup aloft as though marking their meeting with a toast. 'I need the boost today.' He took a slurp before setting the cup down. 'You probably do, too – I'm quite a shock.'

She hadn't noticed the first time but now that he was opposite her, she could see he must dye his hair because the roots were grey. She wrapped her hands around her own cup. She'd thought about turning the sign on the door to *Closed* so they could talk properly but decided against it. She was happy to break off and serve customers as they came in. In fact, it might help her out in some ways, shifting her focus away from all of this. And she didn't feel entirely safe yet; he was still a virtual stranger to her and so locking herself away with a mysterious man probably wasn't the most sensible idea.

'I'm not sure where to start when you know nothing about me.' He slurped his tea again and when she offered him a biscuit, chewed noisily.

His habits were small things but they did make her wonder whether this man could really be related to her dad and her gran, who had both always been polite, with impeccable table manners. Then again, she had no idea what this relative of hers had been through if he'd been cast aside by his own family so maybe not all of it could be put down to nature or upbringing. What she could see were hints of a family resemblance – her dad's eyes were the same colour, he had the same bushy eyebrows, and Nigel had also had blond hair once upon a time although he'd never gone down the bleaching route like Scott. Her dad had let his blond hair fade into an ashy grey over the years, which suited him.

Tilly offered Scott another biscuit when he looked longingly at the packet. The stool near the till was often occupied by men who came in here with their wives and were waiting for the off, or by an elderly person waiting for whoever they'd come in with to make their choice. Tilly often found herself talking with whoever was sitting there – it was one of the parts of this job she quite enjoyed, and mostly she did it as she unpacked new items and refilled the shelves.

'Ask me questions,' Scott suggested, picking up a crumb he'd dropped on the counter and popping it into his mouth. 'Ask me anything. Well… not *anything*. Keep it clean,' he joked.

'How old are you?' She'd start with the simple questions.

'That I can answer.' His smile was kind and he had a pleasant demeanour now he'd stopped eating as though he was half-starved. 'I'm fifty-eight, so that makes me your dad's younger brother.'

She nodded in acknowledgement. 'Do you live nearby?'

'I've moved around a bit,' he shrugged. 'Right now I'm renting a flat in Lowestoft. Being so close by, I knew I had to come back and see the Cove and Mum's old shop.' He glanced over at the cabinet lined with a host of teapots – colours from slate-grey to pale pink, spots and stripes, gaudy floral on a navy background. 'Mum always did love her teapots. It's nice to see them on sale in here instead of only stinky candles.'

The shop had always smelt beautiful to Tilly but she supposed men thought of it differently. 'They're very popular,' she confirmed. 'Both the teapots and the candles,' she added for clarification.

'I bought her a teapot for Christmas one year. I was only a lad. I found it in one of those shops that sell everything, mostly junk, near the seafront up the coast. The bottom of it was a basket – black, or could've been navy blue – and the lid had a curled-up cat on top. I saw it and it made me think of Mum. I think I was trying to get back into her good books.'

Tilly didn't want to ask what for. People changed, didn't they? Tilly had been angry at Melissa when she left the Cove behind and didn't contact Barney for a long while, but Melissa had had her reasons and Tilly had forgiven her and moved forwards. Daniel and Harvey had had problems too until Daniel braved coming back to the village. Now, the brothers were as close as ever. Scott was in a similar position to the one Daniel had been in, now processing his emotions as he came back to revisit a bit of his past. And if he really was that terrible, surely he wouldn't remember the special things about Shirley, such as her love of teapots, and he definitely wouldn't remember a piece in such fine detail.

A customer came in and Tilly turned her attentions to the woman although she left without buying anything quite soon after, the open door blasting in cold air as she made her exit.

Tilly went back behind the counter. 'My dad never told me about you.' She lifted her mug of tea but it was only the dregs left and they were cold by now.

Rather than looking around the shop some more, Scott turned to face her. He had his hands clasped together on his lap and Tilly could see his thumbnails digging into his skin. 'I got into a lot of trouble over the years and I brought a load of problems Mum's way.' He cleared his throat. 'I didn't commit murder, don't worry, but petty thefts, joyriding, dabbling in drugs – a lot of things I'm ashamed of – and it all mounted up until Mum shut me out of her life and my brother did the same. I can't blame them, really.' His voice came out quieter than it had up until now when he admitted, 'I wish I'd made amends with Mum before she died.'

Tilly watched Scott, hands still clasped together, one leg bouncing up and down agitatedly. She wondered whether he was always this way or if it was because he was having to own up to a past he wasn't proud of. 'How did you know Grandma Shirley died?'

He seemed surprised by her question. 'A solicitor tracked me down,' he stammered, perhaps a little embarrassed. But then his confidence returned. 'How's that? After everything I did, she still thought of me in her will and left me some money. It was enough for me to get a car, to cover my rent for a while, and now I even have steady work.'

Part of her softened. Here he was fronting up to someone who could easily have known all about him and told him to get lost. Yet he'd still been brave enough to come. Perhaps being strong-willed ran in the family – maybe she didn't just get that from her dad but her uncle too. Tilly didn't have any brothers or sisters but she wished in many ways that she had. She did have close friends but it would've been nice to have someone who shared your childhood as well as the years since. She wondered, did her dad miss Scott? Or had he shut him away in a part of his life that no longer existed? She couldn't imagine ever doing that to a sibling. Even if they didn't get on, she liked to think she'd maintain polite contact and be there for them and vice versa. Or maybe she was being idealistic. She knew she could be dreamy, something she was pretty sure she *hadn't* inherited from her father.

Scott's presence here now served as a reminder to Tilly that she never wanted to fall out with her parents over anything, least of all her career choices and the fact she'd rejected the idea of going into law and favoured instead a life running a shop filled with pretty things, items people bought to add pleasure to their lives, things that some might see as frivolous. She still remembered the day she told her mum and dad of her decision and the conversation that resulted in her storming out of the house at the lack of support and understanding. She'd gone with a friend to watch a movie – she couldn't even remember what it was called – all she'd known was that she needed to get away before any of them said anything else they'd regret. Her dad had already run on and on about how she was giving up a world of opportunity if she didn't go on to study a proper subject rather than something fluffy like textiles. He'd told her retail was a dead-end job, too.

The conversation about Tilly not wanting to go to university had caused a bust-up with her parents that lasted almost a month. And when Tilly's best friend's mum died and Tilly saw her friend fall apart, she decided there and then that whatever the angst between them, life was too short to hold it against her mum and dad, or at least too short to push them away completely. And when Grandma Shirley died and the shop passed to Nigel and then Tilly, things slowly began to change for the better. They were far from perfect, but their relationship was certainly a lot more tolerable. Tilly had always wondered whether Nigel's change in viewpoint had come in part from losing his mother. He and Grandma Shirley were close and Tilly had thought later that perhaps her grandma had given him a bit of a talking to before she died, told him not to ruin his relationship with his daughter by being so stubborn. But Tilly and her dad had never talked about it.

'I left it too late.' Scott's words brought Tilly back to thinking about his estrangement from his family. 'I can't change that now. But I can try to make things right with Nigel.'

'That's why you're here?' Although, knowing her dad was the total opposite of a pushover and knowing he'd kept this man a secret, she wasn't so sure Scott was going to have much luck with his mission. 'Dad's away on a cruise. And he doesn't live here, they live up north.'

He nodded. 'I know, and I didn't expect to see him when I came here. To be honest, if there'd been any likelihood of him being around, I might not have come at all.' When she met his gaze he added quickly, 'Not that I think you're a soft touch, of course.' Actually, she probably was. Her gran had always said she had the most forgiving temperament.

'You can't make things right unless you talk to him,' said Tilly.

'I know, but maybe we could wait a while. I'd like to get to know you first.'

Perhaps what Scott really needed was for someone to give him a chance, and he wouldn't get that if her dad knew he was here. Tilly smiled. 'I'd like that, and I don't need to tell Dad just yet.' She was already beginning to enjoy having him hang around. Earlier they'd laughed together when a customer leapt back in fright at the big snowman in the entrance as though it was a real person, they'd been amused by the kid who pressed his face right up against the window to stare in and left marks on the glass. It felt easy with Scott, something she hadn't had with family in a very long time.

Scott moved from the stool to look at the few scarves looped over vertical poles on top of a rack in colours from pale lemon-yellow right through the spectrum to dusky grey and black. 'Mum always loved her fancy scarves, I remember – the brighter the better.' He looked around the shop. 'How's business going?'

'Great, especially this time of year. My only complaint is the lack of space. As you can see, it's pretty crowded in here.'

When a group of ladies came bustling through the door Scott kept his voice low. 'I've taken up enough of your time, Tilly. I'd better get going.'

'I don't mind at all.' Although perhaps it was better if he went on his way. It would give her time to process all this some more. And there must be a lot he wasn't saying – maybe in time he'd share and confide in her.

He put on his jacket and did up the buttons, his fingers trembling slightly as he pulled out his packet of cigarettes and a lighter. 'Can I come back?'

'I'd like that.' Her heart went out to him as she wondered how it would feel to be estranged from your family, thinking you had nobody in your corner. She hadn't noticed a wedding ring and he hadn't mentioned a girlfriend, either, which meant he likely had nobody on his side. Perhaps loneliness had forced his hand in trying to put right his mistakes.

With a small wave, he turned up the collar of his coat and left her to it. And on his departure Tilly felt something inside her melt. Was this man the source of her dad's pain, the reason why he wasn't very good at expressing his feelings? Could it be that her uncle had made such a mess of his life that it had made her dad want to control everything in his own?

And maybe if that was it, it wasn't too late to work things out with her dad, the way Grandma Shirley had probably hoped for.

8

'So, let me get this straight...' said Benjamin to Jade as they stood in the kitchen at the house on Mistletoe Gate Farm. 'You've come here to hand out cake tasters but you don't want to share other details about the wedding cake.'

Jade's apron was sticking out beneath her coat. She'd come over because Melissa was here talking through plans with Heather while Harvey was at work. The flavours had been decided on some time ago but apparently Jade wanted to make doubly sure Melissa was happy with the choice. 'It's my business, I don't want to make mistakes,' she said.

'I'm sure they didn't want red velvet cake,' he said, puzzled. He was pretty sure he'd heard murmurings of elderflower and lemon.

'I brought you cake so how can you complain?'

'Hey, not complaining, promise,' he said, lifting up the piece of red velvet cake and taking a generous bit.

'Couples don't always share the intricate details of their cake before the big day,' she insisted. 'You've got to keep some surprises back.'

'Okay, keep giving me the sweet stuff,' he said between mouthfuls, 'and I won't ask any more questions.'

'Thank you.'

'Thank *you* for the cake,' he said demolishing the last of his piece of red velvet cake. 'How are the orders going for Christmas?'

'I thought you said you wouldn't ask any more questions,' she teased, but, laughing, she said, 'Very busy – lots of orders for Christmas cakes, of course, but I've got another wedding to cater for, a ninetieth birthday party, and a New Year's cake.'

'And how's Linc?'

Demurely she told him her boyfriend was very well, thank you, enjoying his teaching position and they were talking about her moving in with him soon.

'That's great, I'm made up for you.'

She smiled her thanks and with a wave to him, Heather and Melissa, she was off.

Benjamin put his empty tea mug into the dishwasher and gathered his things ready to head to the pub for work. Jade was a good businesswoman, much like his sister – and he had the sudden realisation that Charlotte wouldn't have any inkling about what their parents were planning. She'd be devastated when she found out, not only because of their separation but because this surely meant things with the farm were about to change. And Charlotte had dreamt of running this farm herself one day. Had their parents even given any thought to what this would mean for her?

Melissa and Heather were talking twinkly lights and how many sets they had arriving later today, soft white versus bright white, and Heather assured the bride-to-be they'd have plenty for the entire row of trees opposite the veranda. Usually positioned in front of those trees were the netting machine and tables arranged to make the buying process easier, but all that would be moved and it really was going to be an incredibly romantic backdrop. They talked about bridesmaids, too – Tilly's name was mentioned, how she looked at her final fitting in her dress. Thinking about her rather than the state of his parents' marriage definitely did the trick and Benjamin set off for work, pausing outside to talk to his dad as he stood at the netting machine having pulled another tree through and sent a contented family on their way. By the looks of things Danny had just polished off a piece of cake before sipping from the flask of coffee he often took outside with him.

'Did Jade give you cake?'

'Whatever gave you that impression?' There was no sign of cake now, after all, only an empty plastic container.

'The icing on your cheek.'

He wiped it away. 'Busted.'

Danny greeted another family and netted the tree in the machine for them, talking through the process with two young children who were fascinated at how a tree could be "wrapped". Benjamin could remember having that same sense of marvel as a boy. He and Charlotte would follow their dad around the farm helping him plant new seedlings, clearing piles of debris and taking it away in their mini wheelbarrows, handling shears carefully and helping shape the trees. They'd stood at the till and taken cash alongside their parents, too. It had always been a family business and Danny and Heather were as much a part of this place as the trees were. How could it possibly all be coming to an end?

'Do you need me to help out later?' Benjamin asked his dad before he left. Whatever could be done to lighten the stress, he'd do. 'I'm at the pub until three and then I'll have a couple of hours.'

'You don't want to spend your free time here. You work too hard.' Danny, the tree standing tall in his grasp now and wrapped tightly in the netting, waited for the parents to take one end each. The kids dutifully supported the middle with their tiny hands as they all walked away back to their car.

'And so do you.' He watched his dad grab a broom and sweep around so needles and branches didn't mount up too much underfoot. 'Business is going well, isn't it?'

'Of course, why do you keep asking?'

'No reason, just wondering,' he sighed. 'I'll be on my way, then.'

'Bye, son.' And Danny greeted a boy with a tree that his dad was suggesting might be too fat for the machine, at which Danny laughed before proving him wrong.

Benjamin walked between the holly bushes close to the farm and down the pedestrian path to the gate surrounded by mistletoe that seemed to flourish the instant it was cut back. Over the years Benjamin had often heard customers as they came through the gate and headed up to the farm chattering about the smell of mistletoe in the air, how they adored mistletoe-scented candles or room sprays that made them feel all festive. The truth was, mistletoe didn't have a scent. It was a winter evergreen with no discernible smell and while beautiful to look at and evocative, particularly here at the farm, it was widely misunderstood. It was actually poisonous as well as romantic. The mistletoe that had given this place its name was also only sold right here at the farm and not online as well like many places offered. Heather and Danny had made that decision by reasoning that if they opened up sales online they might sell so much that supplies here in the Cove dwindled – and not only would that take away the beauty of the on-foot approach through what was referred to as the mistletoe gate, it would limit an important food source and habitat for wildlife, which would be damaging to the local environment.

Lost in his reveries, Benjamin didn't spot a man coming the other way and apologised when he bumped into him. 'I'm so sorry, I didn't see you there.'

But the man grumbled and continued to stamp out his cigarette.

'Would you mind picking that up?' he said, eyeing the butt on the ground.

The man harrumphed, shook his head, ignored the request and began foraging in the bushes.

'If you cut fresh mistletoe, just take it to the kiosk.' Benjamin could just about get over the butt – he'd get rid of it later rather than upset a potential customer – but he felt it his place to advise what to do about the plant. His parents were pretty trusting and there was a small wooden sign with the sales procedure right next to the man so he had no excuse not to see it, but Benjamin thought another reminder might be needed here. He wanted to add 'go gentle' when he saw the way this guy was manhandling the bushes.

'I don't want mistletoe, don't get your knickers in a twist,' the man sneered.

Benjamin frowned. 'There's no need to be rude. And this is a farm, a business, so whatever you're looking for has to be paid for.'

'I only want some holly to cut and take away. The stuff grows everywhere, can't see any here though.'

There was some, closer towards the farm, but he wasn't about to tell the man that because he suspected this stranger wasn't going to put his hand in his pocket for anything unless he was explicitly told to do so. 'I'm afraid whilst holly is plentiful, if it's on private land then it would be up to the owner whether you could cut it and take it away.'

'Are you the owner?'

'Not exactly, but my family is.' And the people of Heritage Cove were honest enough to cut their own mistletoe and holly and pay a fair price at the kiosk. Heather also made holly and mistletoe bunches that she tied with red, satin ribbon and sold as decorations. People like this man who assumed they could take, take, take didn't impress Benjamin one bit.

'Forget it.' The man gave up looking and wiped his hands on his jacket as though rooting around in the bushes had left something unpleasant on them. 'I'm sure I can find it elsewhere. For free.' He said the last words with particular emphasis.

'Good luck. I'm sure you will.' Benjamin hoped he'd find it far away from Heritage Cove, too, and he lingered just to make sure the man, who looked vaguely familiar, moved on.

* * *

At the Copper Plough, Benjamin didn't even have to reach the kitchens to know that the roast chickens were already in, with the comforting smell of their lemon-and-herb seasoning and garlic rub filling the air.

Henry had made a good start on the onion gravy that all the punters loved – the thicker the better, they said – and Benjamin now pulled on his apron ready to get on with the sticky date puddings. He was allowed to play with the menu whenever he liked and he'd chosen to do these because, old-school and comforting, served with a butterscotch sauce, they were a winter favourite around here. He preheated the smaller oven – the pub kitchen wasn't massive but somehow the owners had designed it in such a way that it worked well. There was one cooker that had a traditional six-burner range on top and a main oven beneath, as well as a second oven. At the end of a long stretch of benchtop was a totally separate, free-standing cooker, not quite as large as the first given the space constraints but it meant flexibility. And it was in this oven and on this cooktop that Benjamin could work on the dessert of the day.

As Benjamin weighed out ingredients before brushing a muffin tray with melted butter so the puddings wouldn't stick, Henry told him he'd got his tree. 'Every year I swear I get a better one,' he said.

'I don't doubt it,' Benjamin smiled, proud of the family business.

'The wedding will be amazing. My other half had Melissa come and quote to redecorate our bedroom,' Henry added by way of explanation. 'Do you think your parents might run more weddings after this one? I mean, I know this is a favour with the barn being out of action, but...'

Benjamin cottoned on. 'Are you thinking of popping the question to Sophie?'

'Maybe,' Henry grinned. He looked more of a surfer dude than a kitchen hand with blond hair that was bleached by the sun, even when the sun hadn't been out for months, tied out of the way.

'Who knows what my parents have planned,' said Benjamin. And that was the absolute truth. It didn't bear thinking about that the farm could be sold on when his parents divorced and might not even be a farm in the future. Imagine someone destroying all those trees, turning the farm into something else entirely. He wondered whether his sister would want to make a plan to buy it herself when she found out what was happening but he wasn't sure her financial position was good enough just yet, and if their parents wanted rid of it and to go their separate ways, there wasn't much she'd be able to do.

Benjamin, Henry, and Marnie when she joined them, worked flat out. Roast dinners were ferried from kitchen to table, jugs of thick, luscious gravy poured across the meat, potatoes and seasonal veg, and although the sticky date puddings had all gone within an hour, customers who missed out didn't seem to mind getting the New York cheesecake as an alternative. By the time Benjamin had finished up, ready for a few hours off before round two tonight, he more than welcomed Tilly's arrival at the pub.

'I've come to see Nola,' she beamed. It was always nice to see her smile, it felt comforting even though she did it to everyone. Today, she seemed extra happy.

'And there I was thinking you'd come to see me.' It was a flirtatious remark that he rarely made – he wasn't that smooth – but it was out before he could stop himself and Tilly obviously picked up on it straight away because she blushed just as Nola appeared from the other side of the pub, where she'd been collecting empties from what looked like a Christmas party. It was a table of eight revellers, all with paper hats on, and Benjamin was pretty sure none of them would be capable of driving home in their merriment.

Tilly avoided his gaze by turning her attention to Nola – something about borrowing outdoor heaters, from what he could hear – and then, satisfied she'd done her bit for now, she turned back to him. 'It's for the wedding,' she explained. 'Your mum and dad only have a few heaters and Melissa was worrying that with guests being outside, even on the veranda, they'll get cold. Nola is happy for us to use the ones from here as they've got so many for the gardens.'

He loved the way she was flustered talking to him again – it showed she cared, or at least that's what he hoped. 'What's the forecast for the big day, do you know?'

'No idea, so we're planning for every eventuality.'

'You're doing a good job helping out so much.'

She shrugged. 'I'm quite enjoying myself, really, and I know if it were me getting married, any bit of stress taken away would be a blessing – so much to organise, and that's without a storm taking away your venue.' She began to smile. 'You look really hot.'

He'd been flapping his top without realising. But he didn't tease her about her unfortunate choice of words – he didn't want to make her any more uncomfortable. 'I honestly forget it's winter when I'm in the kitchen.'

'Are you leaving?' She eyed the coat in his hand.

'Yep, that's me finished until tonight's shift.' He gestured for her to lead the way outside.

He hadn't even reached the end of the path out front before he pulled on his coat, the temperature unforgiving. Winter really was setting in and this morning his dad had been out sprinkling grit over the pathways at the farm to make sure they were safe.

'I'll walk your way,' he told Tilly as they stood between the iron lamp-posts that marked the end of the path stretching from the entrance of the four-hundred-year-old pub to The Street that wound its way through the village. To go home he'd have to go left; to go to Tilly's Bits 'n' Pieces, which sat between the convenience store and the Heritage Tea Rooms, it was right. 'I could do with a decent walk so I'll go all the way out of the village and double back past the inn and across the fields.'

'Watch out for icy patches – it was slippery outside my cottage this morning.'

'I'll bear it in mind,' he smiled before they lapsed into work talk, about the festive season and the busyness it brought. 'I've got time off between Christmas and New Year and already I can't wait.'

'I can't afford to close the shop for long but I'm thinking of taking a bit of a break too. Trade drops off with everyone's wallets having a breather from Christmas but then come the new year I usually get people looking for something unique as they're redecorating or restyling something or other.'

'Good old New Year's resolutions,' he chuckled.

'Exactly.'

'Well, when I eventually buy my own place I'll be sure to stop by the shop. Mum said the other day that my bedroom needs a feminine touch. Not sure what that means but maybe you can help me out.'

'I'd be happy to.' She adjusted her scarf so it sat much higher on her neck and swished her hair away from her face. The wind was whipping round again and reminding everyone that winter was here and Christmas wasn't too far away. 'I don't think it's necessarily a feminine touch, though.'

'How do you know?' He nudged her. 'You haven't seen my bedroom.'

She briefly looked at him but hid a smile as they walked on, waving at Lottie who was behind the till in the convenience store. 'I haven't but I'll bet you don't have accessories.'

'Accessories?'

'You know, things…'

'You mean junk. Nope, don't have that. I'm oddly tidy. I have a lamp by my bed, a few pictures on my walls, not much else. Oh, and an alarm clock.'

'You don't want to sort your room now?'

'No chance, that implies I'll be staying.'

'At least the house is big,' she said encouragingly.

'You're right. I have plenty of my own space so shouldn't complain.' And if he hadn't been living there, hadn't found that form, the divorce could've been finalised before he even had any idea. At least this way he had a chance to get his head around it, the same for Charlotte when he told her. 'Come the spring I should have enough savings to make up a deposit and be in a position to look for a place of my own.' And if they sold the farm, he might be looking a lot sooner than that.

'Well, come and see me when you've found somewhere.' They'd reached her shop and as she let herself in, she bent down to pick up the post from the mat.

He spotted something new on the wall just inside the door. 'I like this.'

'It came in yesterday.' She shrugged off her coat as he admired the shabby-chic chalkboard perfect for hanging in a kitchen.

He ran a hand across its border. It was the sort of chalkboard you might see in a bistro and exactly what he could imagine in his own kitchen one day.

Tilly was already getting on with dusting the countertop next to the till. 'I'll leave you to it,' he said.

'I don't mind the company.'

He took that as a sign she wanted him here and he wasn't going to argue. 'In that case, I'll hang around before I go on my walk.'

'Have you said anything to your parents yet?'

He didn't have to query what about. 'I wouldn't even know where to start with that conversation.'

'I wouldn't either.' She took out a pile of cards from a small box and, over at the display shelves, slotted them into the available gaps. Each card looked handmade with an intricate design. 'You must be torn between wanting and not wanting to open that particular can of worms.'

He smiled at her intuition. 'Spot on. And it's their busiest season so whatever is going on between them, I've decided not to mention it until after Christmas. They need to focus on the business. Whatever happens, having a good season always means a lot to everyone.'

'Every time I go to the farm it's packed full of customers and from what I've overheard, some have driven for miles to visit Mistletoe Gate Farm.'

'I've noticed the same.' Yesterday he'd got talking to a man from Cromer, way up the coast, who'd heard about the farm when he was in his local wool shop – he'd been advised about a farm in the quaint village of Heritage Cove and told it was the most idyllic setting and *the* best place to buy a Christmas tree. Hearing that had made Benjamin feel proud and sad all at once, and whenever he thought about how devastated his sister was going to be when she found out what was going on with their parents, he wanted to hide away until whatever change coming their way was done and dusted.

'Talking of family,' Tilly began, back at the counter and folding down the cardboard box she'd emptied, ready to put in the recycling. 'I have news in that regard.'

'I take it it's good news and not of the burglary variety.' She was smiling so it had to be, but her smile wavered a little.

'It's good news... I think.'

'That's too cryptic for me, you're going to have to spell it out.'

'The other day I met my uncle for the first time. Dad's brother.'

'Your dad has a brother?' He remembered when Shirley died and the wake had been held at Barney's he'd met Tilly's parents but couldn't remember meeting another son. As far as he'd been aware, Shirley had only had one child.

'Something I only found out when he showed up here.'

So, his memory hadn't failed him. 'And your dad never let on? Your gran never mentioned her other son? I know he wasn't at the funeral.'

'Nobody ever said a word about him.' She briefly filled him in on some of her uncle Scott's back story. Younger than Nigel, he'd got into a lot of trouble, he'd stolen from Shirley – made her life a misery, by the sounds of it – and his own family didn't want anything to do with him.

'Families, eh?' he said. 'The secrets they keep.'

'I'll say.'

They stopped chatting when Celeste came in with Lucy, who was delivering more items for the shop. Both women glanced his way and Benjamin wondered, was Tilly the only one who didn't really know what his feelings were towards her? Or was she aware and uninterested? Perhaps that was it – she didn't know how to let him down gently.

'Is he coming back?' Benjamin asked when they were alone again.

'He popped in earlier to give me a gift. He didn't stay long – I get the impression he's nervous about messing up with family again, the same way he always has.'

She was a nice person; there weren't likely to be many people she wouldn't give the benefit of the doubt to. 'How do you feel about him being around?'

'I'm not totally sure yet. And I feel awkward that I haven't told my parents, especially Dad. It feels underhand to keep this from him but Scott deserves a chance and I wanted to get to know him first, make up my own mind.'

'Is that wise?'

She seemed taken aback by his unspoken suggestion that she might be a little too forgiving with someone she didn't know. 'I know how hard Dad can be on people, that's all.'

Locals here knew only too well about second chances or hasty judgements – Melissa had fled the Cove and been out of touch with those who cared about her for years and coming back had been hard for her when not everyone had welcomed her with open arms. Tilly had been protective over Barney, worried Melissa would hurt him by running off again, and Harvey had himself been wary of his former love making an appearance. But now, Melissa was at home in the Cove and nobody could imagine her living anywhere else. Daniel was another person who'd been through the wringer with his family, with trouble he'd got into, and when he first returned, he and Harvey hadn't spoken in years. Now, you'd never know they were once estranged. Perhaps the Cove really was the place for new beginnings.

'I suppose it couldn't hurt to give the guy a go,' said Benjamin.

Tilly softened. 'He does seem very sad about how things worked out. It's too late with Grandma Shirley but I know he'd like to try again with Dad.' She looked at the door when another customer came in to look at the candle holder in the window. But before she went over to help, she beamed another smile at Benjamin. 'I'll show you the present he brought for me earlier.' And she reached down beneath the counter and pulled out a carrier bag that was folded over at the top to show a decent haul of holly bundled inside. 'I'm going to decorate the shop with it – you know, put sprigs in the corners of mirrors, on shelves. It'll go nicely with the twinkly lights I've got.'

It could be a coincidence but Benjamin had a sudden sinking feeling in the pit of his stomach. Could the stranger he'd had words with earlier be the mysterious Uncle Scott that Tilly was talking about?

Benjamin began to think that maybe there was a good reason for her dad keeping him out of their lives.

9

Tilly had seven separate sets of fairy lights and after she'd positioned holly around the shop – on shelves and mirrors, on the Welsh dresser, the chest of drawers and beside the till – she strung the lights around as much of the space as she could. When Scott had brought the holly into the shop as a gift for her she'd been incredibly touched and, thinking he might like to hear a special memory of his mum, she'd ended up talking about how Grandma Shirley had always loved having holly in the house at Christmas time, how she'd string up ribbons and hang cards from them along with sprigs of holly at either end, how she'd put sprigs on picture frames, at the base of ornaments, beside the television.

'Now it feels like Christmas,' Tilly said out loud with a smile as she finished decorating the shop and the rain continued to teem down beyond the window. She'd spend the last hour of her working day basking in the cosiness of it all.

The rain had finally let up by the time Tilly turned off all the lights ready to set off for Mistletoe Gate Farm. She was meeting Melissa and Tracy up there to work on decorations for the wedding that could easily be made in advance and kept somewhere dry until they were needed.

Lois was hovering just outside the shop when Tilly opened the door, all set to go out and lock up behind her. 'Are you waiting for me?' Tilly asked.

Wrapped up in an emerald-green coat, her grey hair tucked beneath a woolly hat and with her usual coral lipstick in place, the woman always looked elegant and perfectly in place in the Cove. 'I have dinner for the lot of you – save you getting a takeaway.' That explained the big container in her arms. 'It's a chicken casserole with dumplings and there's enough for eight generous portions.'

'Lois, you're so kind.'

'It's my way of sidling into the group... if I may?' She was just like Barney – well into their seventies, both of them liked to get involved in whatever was going on in the village. Lois, however, was still sometimes tentative about overstepping when she hadn't lived here all that long.

'Lois, you don't ever need to ask for permission if you want to be involved – and with this wedding, I'd say the more help we get the better. The farm's veranda is big and it's going to take quite a lot to decorate it the way Melissa has envisaged.'

'Well, it's a good job I'm here then.'

'And it's very kind of you to bring some dinner along. Barney is forever raving about your cooking.'

'Between you and me, Barney is struggling with the wedding not being at the barn and he's determined to chip in every step of the way. Right about now he'd have been finalising decor, so me cooking for you all up at the farm and volunteering to help out while he's on his way back from meeting with someone who supplies boards for the grass is something I can do to make him happy.'

Barney's closeness to Melissa and Harvey was never in doubt. 'I don't know many parents who'd want to be this involved in wedding planning.'

'You know Barney and weddings.' The annual Wedding Dress Ball raised money for White Clover, a charity that helped bereaved parents cope with their grief after the loss of a child, a cause that held significant meaning for Barney and Lois.

'Dare I ask what boards for the grass are?' Tilly said, already grateful a warming dinner was on the cards tonight. She'd had a bit of a headache this afternoon and had sneezed a few times in quick succession. With any luck, if a cold was brewing then she could scare it away with some hot, wholesome food before it developed into anything much at all.

'Melissa was fine about not having dancing seeing as the venue has changed but it was Harvey who was really disappointed. He wants to dance with his bride. And, of course, Barney wants to make it happen for him. So, he got on the phone to Danny first thing this morning and the two of them remembered about the fair that had set up one year on the grass behind the village bus stop. Both of them had watched it being installed – they'd been much younger then and you know what boys are like, wanting to know how everything works. Anyway, they thought there had to be a solution and Danny said that the grass at the farm is always something that needs attention come spring after visitors have traipsed all over it through the winter, so he's not worried about it suffering if we lay down wooden boards like they had at the fair to make a dancefloor.'

'It sounds like a marvellous idea.' The wind whipped at them as they walked and Tilly hunched her shoulders, closing the gap between the top of her coat and the warmth of her hat.

'I wonder if this will set off a trend,' said Lois. 'Maybe Danny and Heather might start to host more weddings at the farm. It's a beautiful venue, after all.'

'Hmm.' Tilly didn't add much more; it wasn't her place to

discuss anything about the tension looming at Mistletoe Gate Farm between its owners. Instead, she brought up the subject of Melissa's dress, which was all Lois needed to take the conversation off in a different direction entirely.

Up at the farm, Lois and Tilly were soon pulled into the action. Heather had already brought in huge swathes of holly, which now lay piled in the centre of the long dining table. Next to it and on chairs were enormous clumps of mistletoe, rolls of red ribbon and garden twine, ready to fashion the arrangements that would be dotted around the veranda. They were using fresh foliage and once they'd made everything, they'd stand the stems in water and store them all in the equipment shed until the big day, which was creeping ever closer.

'Ouch,' Tilly winced, shaking out her finger. 'I've lost count of how many times I've pricked myself with this holly.'

'They're such pretty arrangements I think they're worth a few injuries,' Melissa grinned.

'Easy to say when you're not bleeding.' Tilly grabbed a tissue to stop the flow before she carried on.

'I appreciate you helping.' Melissa looked across at Heather, Tracy and Lois to include them as well. 'I'd already scheduled time off in the run-up to the wedding but that was before it was relocated from the barn. There's been so much to reorganise and I couldn't have done it without you all. I can't thank you enough.'

'How is your work going?' Tilly asked.

Melissa had left her job as a flight attendant to throw herself into the long-term plan she and Harvey had to set up a full-time business together, her side of the partnership being interior design and his being renovations. She'd taken a course and had already got a few jobs by word of mouth and was busy setting up an online presence for their new venture too. And when Harvey had a job to strip out an old fireplace at a cottage on Tilly's road, Melissa had been tasked with giving the rest of the sitting room a complete makeover. Apparently, the owner had been thrilled with the results.

'I'm enjoying it and business will grow, slowly.'

'But you have other things to focus on right now,' Tilly smiled. 'Is Harvey taking much time off?'

'Not apart from the honeymoon – he's been working overtime to cover the period he won't be paid.'

'I have another decorating idea... for the wedding,' she elaborated in case Melissa thought she was talking interior design.

'Tell me – always happy to hear more!'

Tilly described the recent delivery of glass bowls at the shop. 'I thought I'd ordered two but it seems I ordered twenty. And while I think customers will love them, I don't have the space to put them on display all at once so they'll be stocked upstairs doing nothing. I thought we could fill them with water and use floating candles.'

'I love that idea.' They agreed Harvey should go to the shop later and pick them up to bring back here and Tilly would add candles to the boxes so they'd be ready to go.

Danny bundled in through the back door bringing the earthy smell of the outdoors in with him as he delivered two large, shallow-sided cardboard boxes and set them on the floor. 'Here you go, put whatever arrangements you make into these and I'll transport them down to the shed, where I'll have buckets of water waiting.' He'd already told them when they'd discussed these decorations that both holly and mistletoe would stay looking at their best if they were kept cool and in water so, with less than two weeks until the wedding, they didn't need to worry that these arrangements wouldn't look just as good on the big day as they did now.

They took a break for dinner, eating on their laps with the table out of action, and Lois's cooking was exactly what Tilly needed. Then between the five of them they had the dishes done in no time at all.

'Lois, don't forget to take this when you go.' Heather patted the top of the container Lois had used to transport the dinner. There were two portions already sitting in bowls waiting to be warmed up for the men when they were ready to eat. 'I need to leave you ladies to it, go outside and help make sure everything is cleared up for the day, but shout out if you need extra greenery – I can grab more, even in the dark.'

'I think we're all set,' said Tracy, taking in what they had left.

Tilly put yet another bunch of holly and ivy together with mistletoe and tied it off with a length of red satin ribbon before taking it over to place with the ones Lois had already begun to load into the cardboard boxes Danny had left.

The door opened again and this time it was Benjamin who brought in a real blast of cold. Tilly still got a quickening heartbeat whenever he turned up, expected or not.

'You look hard at work.' He addressed them all but smiled directly at Tilly before heading for the sink to wash his hands.

'It's been busy,' Tilly told him, trying to sound nonchalant as she added, 'There's a bowl of dinner for you.'

'Great, I've worked up a real appetite.' He dried his hands and put the bowl into the microwave to warm its contents through.

'Not at the pub tonight?' She grabbed a tissue just in time to catch a sneeze, which was quickly followed by another.

'I have a rare evening off. And you've got a cold coming.'

She blew her nose as delicately as she could. 'It seems that way. I had a bit of a headache earlier but I thought a few hot drinks and a good dinner would stop it in its tracks.'

'An early night should do the trick.'

Lois called over. 'Benjamin, make yourself useful. Come and help us finish these decorations.'

The microwave pinged just in time and he pulled out the bowl, cradled it in one palm and picked up his fork. 'Sorry, got my hands full.' He gave Tilly a wink.

She wished he'd linger close to her for a bit longer. She wanted to lean her head on his shoulder and snuggle against his chest. And she knew the reason she wanted to do that wasn't just because she was sick.

* * *

The following day Tilly realised she'd been kidding herself that she didn't have a stinking cold. Her eyes and her nose were streaming, she had a dull headache, and all she wanted to do was close her eyes. But business wouldn't let her have a day off and so she simply had to keep going, thankful it appeared to be a head cold at least and not the flu – which would have given her no choice but to close Tilly's Bits 'n' Pieces and take to her bed.

When the door to her shop opened for the umpteenth time she mustered up a smile, quickly relieved that it wasn't yet another customer but Uncle Scott. It felt odd using that name when she'd only just discovered his existence, but she quite liked it. She still hadn't mentioned to either of her parents that he'd turned up in the Cove, not even this morning when she spoke to them and felt so rubbish that she'd almost let her guard down and forgotten it was to be a secret for now, until the time was right. She'd been making a cup of tea with her phone on loudspeaker so she could talk to them at the same time and when her eyes fell on the teapot she'd kept of her grandma's – a teal piece with ducks around the bottom half – sitting in the cupboard, rarely used given Tilly's preference for teabags, which were so much more convenient, she'd almost blurted out about the characterful teapot Scott told her he'd once bought Grandma Shirley.

Scott surveyed her as he came closer. Dressed in baggy jeans and the same donkey jacket he always wore, he hadn't shaved this morning and a mousy-coloured beard was starting to show through with little spikes on his chin. 'Oh dear,' he grimaced. 'You look rough.'

At least it made her laugh. 'Thanks. I seem to have caught a cold and I've been pretending to customers all morning that I'm fine.'

'It's the red nose that gives it away.' He pulled a face. 'Sorry, I'm being rude. I hope I'm not offending you.'

She swished away his worry. 'Not at all, and I know my nose is red. Unfortunately, foundation doesn't cover it up after you've wiped at it a thousand times in one hour.' She indicated the stool for him to sit down and wait while she put a proper smile on her face to serve a lady who came in looking for a card for her husband, whose birthday was on Christmas Eve. They spent a good ten minutes talking about how every year she liked to make sure he had as much fuss around his special day as she got around hers in the middle of the year. And that fuss meant a birthday cake on Christmas Eve, with nobody allowed to save their appetite for the feast the next day, and a birthday stocking for his presents.

'Got to hand it to you,' said Scott when the woman left. 'If you feel as bad as you look, you deserve a medal for making polite conversation for so long with your customers. Some of them rabbit on and on – I wonder whether they'll ever shut up.'

Tilly bashed her shin on the box of glass bowls she'd left ready for Harvey to come and collect as she went to grab another tissue from the box out back. She blew her nose, got rid of the tissue and stuffed a few more into her pocket for later before returning to the other side of the curtain. 'The talking is a part of the job that I really love. I enjoy hearing snippets about their lives.'

'Even though you feel like sh—'

She smiled that he'd stopped himself from saying the word. 'Yes, even when I feel rubbish.'

'See, that's another reason I'm glad I came here to meet you first, Tilly. You're easy to talk to, I get the impression you're fair.' She liked to think so too. 'I had breakfast up at your waffle shack.'

It pleased her that he was hanging around the village he'd avoided for too long. 'I've had many a breakfast up there – what did you go for?' She liked this. A member of her family, popping in, casually. It gave her a feeling of belonging, a link to her family she hadn't always felt when she first lost her gran, at least not until her dad handed the shop down to her and trusted her to run it the way she saw fit.

'I had waffles with bacon and maple syrup.' He pinched his fingers and thumb together on one hand and kissed them. 'The perfect way to start my day.'

They talked some more about what was served at the waffle shack – the sweet, the savoury, the celebratory waffles for Christmas, Easter, Halloween.

'You've got your pick of food places here,' he approved. 'I'd almost forgotten that about Heritage Cove. I went to the pub once when I was here years ago, but the menu was crap. The tea rooms weren't much better either – the woman who ran the place was miserable.'

Tilly, holding a tissue over her nose ready to blow again, was disappointed to hear her uncle talk about anyone in the village that way when she'd been feeling so good about having him here. But then again, he didn't know people like she did; it was easy to form opinions without the benefit of community and friendship, neither of which she suspected he'd ever been lucky enough to have experienced.

'The pub has changed a lot. A good friend of mine took over the cooking and he totally rejigs the menu whenever he feels it needs a bit of a push. And Etna, who owns the tea rooms, is quite lovely.'

He sighed. 'I've been rude again, haven't I?' He tugged a hand through his bleached-blond hair. 'I need to work on that. I'm very sorry... am I forgiven?'

'You are forgiven.' She wondered how many times he'd used the same smile on the rest of the family before they gave up on him. It certainly had the power to change your thinking. 'All you need to know is that Heritage Cove is a wonderful little community and we're no strangers to giving people a second chance. You might find you've come to exactly the right place.' Perhaps given his history with family he was bound to say the wrong thing now and again. At least he recognised he was doing it.

Tilly hoped she wasn't the one driving him to bite his nails down the way he was doing now. Or was it a habit? Nerves, even? 'Could you please watch the shop for me while I nip upstairs?' she asked. Letting him know she wanted him around could only help. 'I keep my cleaning supplies up there and it's high time the glass in this place had a bit of attention. I didn't have the energy earlier but now the sun has shifted position I can't bear to look at all those marks on the windows.' There were plenty of them from where customers had tried to peer in at the window display to get a closer look at items and prices.

His chest puffed out. 'I'd be delighted to, Tilly.'

Upstairs she grabbed a fresh cloth and the glass cleaner and back in the shop she found Scott standing at the counter as if on guard. 'You'll scare the customers off looking that tense.'

'I was trying to look like someone responsible rather than someone up to no good.'

Tilly sneezed three times in a row on her way over to the glass and gave up on the idea of wiping anything. 'Here, let me.' Scott plucked the cloth and spray from her hand. 'May as well put me to good use.'

Scott insisted Tilly sit on the stool for an extended break while he cleaned the glass and, as she sat there, she realised that no matter how rough she felt, it was nice to have him here. So what if she wasn't entirely comfortable with him yet, or that sometimes he could look shifty if she caught him unawares?

Perhaps in time things would become a lot easier and her dad might even see the way to letting him back into his life.

10

'Could you do me a favour and be me for a couple of hours?' Danny, coat on over a smart shirt and trousers, had an envelope in his hand as he came out onto the veranda, where Benjamin was chilling out with a bottle of beer after working from early morning right up until mid-afternoon at the pub.

Benjamin did his best not to groan. 'Can't I enjoy my beer?'

'Bit cold for one of those, isn't it?'

He shook his head. 'Not when you've been hard at it.'

'I'm sorry, son, it's just that there's something I really need to do.'

Benjamin necked his beer, put the empty bottle on the floor, and slowly stood up. He did his best to get a look at the address on the envelope his dad had a hold of but Danny clung to it like the closely guarded secret it most probably was. More forms? Perhaps his signature to join Heather's.

'I promise I'll be back in under two hours,' said Danny, giving nothing away.

'You'd better be – I'm due out with the lads tonight.' He checked his watch.

'I'll be back, don't worry.'

Danny went on his way and Benjamin helped customers find their ideal tree, cut down more to line up for his mum to sell to those who weren't fussed about trailing up and down the rows to find the perfect specimen. He ran down to cut clusters of mistletoe for customers upon request, for others he cut ivy, he took payments, netted trees, and all the while he tried his best not to think about his parents and their impending divorce or why they thought keeping it from him and Charlotte might make it any easier to bear. Maybe they were waiting until after Christmas; they didn't want to spoil the big day – but already it was ruined. Given what he knew, how could he sit and smile, open presents, and pretend everything was just fine?

* * *

Danny returned and took over helping a family fix a tree to the roof of their car. Benjamin headed inside for a shower and once he was dressed, he found his mum in the kitchen with her headphones still on, every now and then uttering phrases in Italian as Benjamin pulled on his boots. When he'd asked her earlier she'd told him she was learning a new language to keep her brain active. He harrumphed now – she wouldn't hear him anyway – thinking perhaps she was plotting some kind of escape, although quite what that entailed he didn't know. Maybe her plan was to split up from her husband and flit off to Italy to live in a ramshackle house. And if she did that, where would that leave the rest of them?

The cold night air made him feel better at least as he started walking and he got all the way down to The Street, where he stopped outside the pub to chat to Nola as she assembled three glow-in-the-dark reindeers she'd apparently bought from Tilly's shop.

'She sells those? Where on earth does she find the space?' He hadn't seen her for a few days; she was likely recovering from her cold and he'd been so busy.

'She didn't really have to.' Nola's cheeks were as rosy as the wine she sold behind the bar. She switched on the lights of the third reindeer and patted him on the head as though he were real. 'These were delivered this morning and I fell in love with them before Tilly even had a chance to think about where they could be displayed.'

'Have you chained them down?' He had visions of another storm and these guys taking off, making the whole village believe that maybe reindeers really could fly.

'Of course.' But she was thinking of another reason they might move from their spots. 'I've spent enough time around inebriated people to know these will go on a walk come closing time, probably end up on someone's roof.'

Benjamin went on his way and smiled at Lottie, who kept the local convenience store open nice and late for those who needed it. But his smile was quickly replaced by a frown when he saw that awful man coming out of Tilly's Bits 'n' Pieces again, and the frown only deepened when he saw Tilly lock the door behind them both and start walking alongside him.

'Benjamin!' She beamed his way and there was no avoiding the introduction. Even now the night had cast its shadow across The Street, and despite the twinkling and colourful decorations strung from one side of the road to the other, suspended in the air for the rest of the month, he was going to have to deal with it.

Benjamin, hands rammed into his pockets ready to walk past and on up to the Little Waffle Shack to meet Harvey, Daniel, and Linc for a boys' night, took a deep breath before he put on a forced air of welcome for the newcomer. Perhaps he'd judged him too hastily. 'Hey, Tilly.'

'Benjamin, this is my uncle, Scott.' Tilly, whose hair flicked out from beneath a purple hat pulled tightly over her head, looked as though she'd got an early Christmas present with this man's company.

Benjamin nodded and said hello but thankfully Scott didn't go in for a handshake. Benjamin had only met this man fleetingly but he didn't trust him in the slightest. He looked shifty, and it was bugging him that he still couldn't recollect where he'd seen him before that day at the farm. Benjamin suspected Tilly was confusing his demeanour with shyness or awkwardness, but he wouldn't mind betting it was neither with this man who had a smile that looked fake from a mile off, deep wrinkles in his forehead, blond hair that had obviously had a helping hand with a bottle of dye given the greying roots, and yellowing teeth when he flashed a grin.

'I was taking Uncle Scott for a drink at the pub,' Tilly explained.

Benjamin smiled. 'I was admiring the reindeer moments ago.'

'You liked them? I couldn't resist buying them and I was thinking I'd squeeze them into my window display with a bit of rejigging but Nola took them off my hands.' She turned to Scott. 'Benjamin is the chef at the Copper Plough.'

Scott looked as though he was thinking up something insulting to say but even he seemed to be affected by Tilly's smile so perhaps he did have a heart after all. 'I look forward to trying the food.'

And paying for it, Benjamin hoped.

'Join us?' Tilly asked.

'Can't. I'm due to meet the lads up at the waffle shack.' Damn, he shouldn't have said that. What if Tilly and Scott changed their mind and decided to go there instead?

'I'm gasping for a beer,' Scott put in, to Benjamin's relief. 'I've been helping her in the shop,' he announced, as though it was the toughest thing anyone could ever do, as though he'd dragged a stranded rowing boat that had lost its oars all the way to shore to rescue its occupant. Did he want an award?

'I'll see you tomorrow, then,' Tilly smiled. 'I'm having dinner at the pub with Lucy.'

'Can I get in on that?' Scott jumped in. 'I'd like to meet more of your friends here.'

Tilly hesitated but – being the kind, generous and whole-hearted person she was – she said, 'Sure, I don't see why not.' And she waved goodbye to Benjamin.

If anything, Tilly seemed thrilled this new man in her life was demanding more of her time and, as he carried on towards the end of The Street, Benjamin made a mental note to watch the guy carefully when he was at work in the pub tomorrow night, and also to check with Lucy that he'd paid his way, because Benjamin had the distinct feeling he hadn't misjudged Scott too hastily at all. He was up to something.

* * *

After a good helping of waffles followed by beers with the boys after Daniel closed up for the night, Benjamin felt brave enough to make the call that he was dreading, to tell his sister what was going on with their parents. They'd always got on well, still did, but he'd been avoiding doing this for too long.

When Charlotte answered he took a deep breath and blurted it all out. It took her a while to digest what he was telling her because it wasn't just their parents separating that was sad, it was the splintering of their childhood memories. All those happy times on the family farm, from hauling in a Christmas tree every year to Heather ladling out mulled wine for the adults as the kids started with the decorations. It was the shattering of the fond recollections of barbecuing on the veranda in summer, with Charlotte and

Benjamin running up and down rows of trees as though they were in a maze to the calls of *Don't tread on the saplings!* when they went near the beds with the newest plants that were yet to grow into trees.

Benjamin had walked from the shack as he talked on the phone and he stopped when he got to the village Christmas tree. He looked up at it, the lights against the night sky, nobody around but him. He would've sat on the ground if it was summer but not only was it cold, it was damp after this morning's mist and then the drizzle that followed before it cleared to let the sunshine through. 'Mum's walking around with her headphones in her ears,' he told Charlotte. 'Learning Italian, although I suspect it's to avoid talking to Dad. Dad is throwing his time into the farm, but nothing new there.'

'Is Mum still working, too?'

'Yeah – apart from the form I found and a bit of tension you'd never know anything had changed. She's still making garlands, helping customers, cutting mistletoe, ringing up orders on the till, and arranging tree deliveries, helping get ready for Melissa's wedding. She's so excited about the wedding that you'd never know anything was amiss.'

'Do you think they just got bored with each other?'

'I suppose that could be it.' Charlotte had only just heard the news so she was starting along the same thought process that he'd been through since finding the divorce papers. Now, though, he'd given up trying to guess their reasons, and he didn't want to admit that he wondered whether they were in financial difficulties because there was no point in speculating.

'I'll be home for Christmas soon,' Charlotte sighed.

'And there's Melissa and Harvey's wedding to look forward to,' Benjamin injected in the hope it would lift her from sounding so despondent.

'You're right. I was looking forward to it in the barn, but having it at our farm is extra special.'

Neither of them had to say it. They'd both seen enough photographs of their parents' wedding day, including the one still fixed to the wall, to know that Mistletoe Gate Farm was incredibly romantic when it came to wedding venues.

'Are you bringing your boyfriend home with you for Christmas?'

'We broke up.'

'Oh, sis, I'm sorry.'

'Don't be... turned out he was a bit of a jerk.'

Breakups were never nice but listening to the light-hearted humour back in her voice as she told Benjamin she'd known he wasn't for her when he suggested a fake Christmas tree, Benjamin was relieved. The news about their parents couldn't have been easy to hear and he hated being the bearer of bad tidings to anyone, especially Charlotte. He'd never forgotten the day her bunny rabbit died and he'd had to break the news. It wasn't an experience he'd ever been keen to repeat, seeing her face pale and hugging her as she cried. As much as she had a solid business head on her shoulders, she was sensitive, too.

'And what about you?' she asked. 'Do you have a plus-one yet? Have you actually asked Tilly out?'

'How do you know about Tilly?' She hadn't been home this side of the summer months.

'Lottie may have mentioned it when we last spoke.'

His sister was good friends with Lottie so he might've known any local gossip could get wings and fly off wherever it wanted. 'I think everyone knows I like Tilly apart from Tilly.'

'You sure about that?'

He frowned. 'Maybe she does know, although that's not a good sign if she hasn't said anything.'

'Maybe she's being a traditionalist, waiting for you to make the first move.'

'Hmm...'

'So, go ask her.'

'She's got something else going on at the moment.' He spilled the details about her uncle turning up in the Cove all of a sudden, clearly making it his mission to get to know her.

'Why the jealousy when he's a relation?' Charlotte had picked up on Benjamin's disapproval from the get-go.

'Remember Mr McArdle?'

'The guy who owned the allotment next to Kenneth's?'

'That's him.' Local man Kenneth Soames had owned and run an allotment for a good few decades and Mr McArdle had tended the adjacent plot. 'Do you remember how Kenneth never liked him from the day he secured that allotment patch? Everyone in the Cove told Kenneth to give the poor guy a chance, said that he was charming, very friendly.'

'Until he wasn't,' said Charlotte.

'Exactly.' Mr McArdle had been sweetness and light until he revealed his true colours and was caught sabotaging Kenneth's prize cauliflowers in a fit of jealousy and sprinkling chemicals over his sprouts to kill them off.

'Are you trying to tell me you think this uncle of Tilly's is playing games? Why would he want to do that when he's family?'

'I don't know.'

'But you intend to find out.' It was a statement rather than a question. She knew her brother very well.

'I can't ignore it, Charlotte.'

After a pause she said, 'It's clear how much you like Tilly and for that reason I'd love you to get together. From what I know of her, she's lovely – and much better than Zoe.'

'Hey.'

'Sorry, but she and I never got on, you know that.'

They'd clashed once when Zoe borrowed Charlotte's favourite French Connection shirt after getting drenched in the rain when Benjamin had her help him in the farthest field when the winds and rain had come and his dad needed assistance to ensure they covered a row of new saplings that would otherwise be destroyed. She hadn't wanted to help but they needed all hands on deck that day. Afterwards he'd come out of the shower to find his sister yelling, demanding Zoe take the shirt off, asking her why she thought it was acceptable to go into her room and help herself. Benjamin hadn't understood why his sister was overreacting until he realised it wasn't an item from Charlotte's wardrobe, but Zoe had taken the item from a bag in his sister's bedroom. The shirt was brand new and Zoe had snapped the labels off and put it on, just like that. She'd admitted later that she'd done it to annoy Charlotte because Charlotte didn't like her. Benjamin had insisted she was wrong about that but he knew she wasn't – his sister had always thought Zoe prissy with the way she wouldn't go outside to the fields if she could help it in case her hair got ruined, or the way she refused to sit on the bench on the veranda without laying down a towel first as she said it looked dirty.

Sometimes Benjamin wondered how he and Zoe had stayed together for so long.

'Tell me one thing,' said Charlotte. 'Does Tilly own a pair of wellies?'

His laughter boomed as he began to leave the village tree behind and head back to the farm. 'She most certainly does. Bright red ones – I think you'd approve.' And he knew exactly why she'd asked the question. She'd asked the same of Zoe once and Zoe had told her she'd never buy something so unflattering.

'Then she's good enough for my brother. But be careful,

Benjamin. You can't interfere when it's her family. I know women. Tilly won't thank you for sticking your oar in if you're wrong.'

'No, I don't suppose she will.'

'But also...' Charlotte warned, 'make sure you're there to catch her when she falls if you turn out to be right about this man.'

11

Uncle Scott had been back to the shop every day for the last three. He'd lifted the heavy boxes in from the delivery van, he'd repaired the sideboard and fixed the door that was almost off its hinges, he'd made cups of tea, swept the floor, and had generally kept Tilly company.

Today, while she ran to grab a sandwich from the bakery Scott kept an eye on the shop and when she got back he told her, 'Just the one customer. She paid cash and is coming to pick up the dressing table with the mirror in the morning.'

'You sold the dressing table?' She beamed at him. 'I've had that for almost a year; nobody has been interested in it before now.'

He showed her the little stool he'd positioned in front of it. 'I told her to take a seat, try it out for size, and she was sold.'

Tilly hung her coat out back and let him serve the next few customers at his insistence while she ate her sandwich before making a cup of tea for the both of them.

When she emerged from the back with two mugs she found him charming Etna, who left all smiles. It felt good to see him trying, especially after he'd described the owner of the tea rooms all those years ago as miserable – Etna had owned it for so long that in all likelihood that woman would've been her.

Benjamin was wrong to doubt Scott. She knew he did because of the attention he'd paid them when she went for dinner at the pub the other night with him and Lucy. Benjamin had looked over more than a few times as though he was waiting for Scott, at any moment, to put a foot wrong. But he hadn't. In fact, he'd even paid for dinner for all three of them, insisting he treat Lucy too since she was such a good friend to Tilly.

Scott thanked her for the tea and clinked his mug against hers in a toast. 'I can see why you like working in here, always people to talk to,' he said now they were alone again and Etna had gone on her way.

His comment rankled a little – she didn't *work* in the shop, she *owned* it and ran the entire business, but she supposed it was just wording, she shouldn't be bothered by it.

He slurped his tea. 'Mum always liked a good chat. I think she felt like she was providing a service half the time.'

'That sounds like Grandma Shirley,' she smiled.

'You were close?'

'We were. She always seemed to have my back.' When his face twitched, she wondered whether he felt she hadn't had his so she steered the conversation towards calmer waters. 'I loved coming in here and smelling all the candles – spring flowers, forest floor, I'm sure she had a fragrance called treehouse once. They all had such fun names.'

'They were definitely popular. Bit too stinky for me,' he grimaced. 'Mum had them all over the house, too.'

'I love the turn of the seasons here at the shop, when the new stock comes in and I can pick out my favourite scents. I treated myself to one recently, something called alpine cabin.'

'Now, that could smell of anything.' He was biting his nails again but when she looked at him he stopped.

'I'm pretty sure they don't always smell like what it says on the label,' she clarified, 'but the cosy-sounding names sell the candles to customers, for sure. As soon as I get Christmas stock in here I see a huge uptick in sales.'

As she went out back to refill their empty cups, she stubbed her toe on a cardboard box full of the same festive-scented candles they were talking about. They'd been waiting to be unpacked but there wasn't enough room on the shelves yet, especially not now they'd sold the dressing table – she was a surface down.

'You need more space,' said Scott. 'You've got so much stuff now that you sell more than just candles.'

'When I first took on the shop I thought I'd keep everything the same but then, gradually, I added more and more – cards, cushions, items for the home, jewellery. The furniture came later. Grandma Shirley had this gaudy, gold, buffet dresser with pink and red roses painted on it.'

'Sounds delightful.' She hadn't noticed before but he had a gold filling in one of his teeth that could only be seen from a certain angle.

'I used the dresser in the shop as a surface for candles and when a lady came in one day she wasn't looking at the candles, only the dresser itself. I explained it wasn't for sale, it was part of the shop, and she was devastated. She ran her hand across its surface as though she'd found a piece of treasure. And then she offered me several hundred pounds for it.'

'She wanted it that badly?'

Tilly shrugged. 'She said it was hard these days to find anything unique, everyone wound up having the same furniture pieces. She gave me the money and came back that afternoon with her son and a van and took it away. That was the day I realised I could do so much more with this place.'

'You've got a sound business mind, Tilly.' He was looking around the shop, admiring one of the iron shelving units on the wall. It wasn't for sale but on the floor were three more like it, made at Lucy's Blacksmithing.

Tilly picked up the straw basket of handmade cards she'd noticed was running low. She grabbed another box from upstairs and, back at the counter, unwrapped a collection of pretty designs, each unique – one with a snowman, a bright-blue scarf drawn as though it was being lifted by the wind; another with a group of children having a snowball fight; others with various different Christmas scenes.

'I'd love to sell so much more,' she confessed, relishing how interested he was in what she was doing. 'I'd love to go to antique fairs, craft fairs, car-boot sales, and garage sales to hunt down items like the buffet dresser I told you about. House clearances are an option, too, such as deceased estates – sounds morbid, I admit, but elderly people hold on to real treasures for years and while their family think they're junk and want to get rid of them, there are other people who are desperate for a bit of individuality and snap them up.'

'Have you tried eBay?'

She pointed to the distressed white armoire in the corner with a twisted-rope decoration in the shape of a heart looped over its rounded handles. 'I got that from eBay so it didn't cost much at all. I think the owner just wanted shot of it and nobody else bid apart from me so I was lucky. I never pay over the odds or anything as I can't afford to and also, I don't have the space to buy too much. Until that armoire is sold and perhaps a few more items, I can't buy more.'

He brought up a website on his phone. 'I went to this car-boot sale yesterday and thought of you.'

'Wow...' She looked up at him. 'Where was this?'

He handed Tilly his phone so she could take a better look. 'About ten miles from here.'

'Look at the side table... and the tallboy.' She scrolled enthusiastically. 'If only the shop could fit in more stock. I mean, it's one thing *me* tripping over – quite another if a customer does it. I could be sued.' Yesterday she'd caught her foot on the slightly protruding base of the armoire as she'd reached into the window display to rehang the robin-redbreast ornament that had been weighing down a branch on the tree so much it was about to drop; she'd almost gone head first into the window. And then on the way back to the counter she'd narrowly avoided knocking over the candlestick holders on the shelf nearest the till and in trying to catch them had whacked her hip bone so hard it made a loud knock.

She scrolled until she came to a picture of a two-piece luggage-trunk set. Its beautiful workmanship and dark façade had her almost able to smell the wood and the leather used on the buckles. There was a photo of a vintage trunk, too, with a curved top – the sort she could imagine might in the olden days have been taken from home to a boarding school like those she'd read about in books as a girl.

'I feel as though I'm missing out.' Her spirits sank and she handed him back the phone. The only extra space she had was upstairs and if she put things up there, customers would never see them and they wouldn't sell.

He downed his tea and plonked the mug by the till. 'What you need to ask yourself is *why* you're missing out.'

'That much is obvious.' Her tea, still hot, warmed her palms as she clasped her mug between them and glanced around the space –

or lack of it – in the shop. 'I don't have the room in here, and I don't have the funds to refurbish the upstairs.'

'Is that what you'd like to do?' He was biting his nails again but as she didn't know him all that well she didn't feel like she could nag him. She smiled inwardly; perhaps that could come in time.

'When I took over the shop, I wanted to find my feet. I didn't have time to think about anything other than getting from one day to the next. There was learning about stock reordering, keeping the place clean and tidy, insurance, formalities, security. It was all a very steep learning curve.'

'It sounds as though there's a *but* coming.'

She set down her mug in front of her. 'I feel like I need to take the next step with the shop but the risk is too big.'

'Financially?'

'I only just managed to get a mortgage to buy my cottage. And this is my catch-22, I suppose: I know I'll make higher profit margins if I do out the upstairs of this place and buy more stock, particularly unique, bigger items that would turn a quick profit, but I can't do renovations without the bigger profits in the first place.'

'Is there much to renovate up there?' His eyes shot heavenward to indicate the upstairs.

'Don't you remember it?'

'It's been a long time since I was here last.'

The sadness lacing his voice had her picking up her key and a sign she kept beneath the counter. She held up the sign, which said *Back in Five...* 'I'm putting this on the door and locking up – we'll nip upstairs and I'll show you.' A simple discussion was all it had taken to ignite her passion again, her dream of a renovation, of developing this place and taking the next step, and it felt like a gift to be able to share it with someone else at last.

In the rooms above the shop Scott took it all in – the original wallpaper still on the walls although faded in the bits where it was still intact, peeling off in others; the musty smell she'd long associated with upstairs that hung around even with the windows open; the stain on the floor on the landing by the radiator that had once leaked and left its mark. She'd already warned Scott about the wobbly post at the top of the staircase that she always made sure to avoid – it was just another thing that needed attention. He laughed when she showed him the bathroom in all its glory, salmon-pink bathtub included. She had a downstairs cloakroom at the shop in what had once been a cupboard under the stairs until she'd had it converted to house a toilet, sink, and vanity unit, and so she'd left the bathroom under the heading of things she should do one day when she had the funds. It was dark up here, as well – they needed all the lights on – but back when this space was habitable, big windows hadn't really been a thing.

'It needs a bit of work,' he said.

'That's the understatement of the year.' She tilted her head to indicate they should head downstairs again and once they were back in the shop and she'd removed the sign from the door, she said, 'It'll take thousands to make the improvements and I don't have thousands. Unless Father Christmas is very generous this year,' she laughed.

'It's good to have a clear idea of what you want to do with it.'

'Yeah, I suppose it is.'

And as Tilly began to talk some more, Scott encouraged her all the way. She told him about her vision to make the area around the counter downstairs less cluttered so that she could move some of her things from the crowded shelves behind the curtain, making a thoroughfare for customers. The stairs would need to be seen to, repaired in the places that were dangerous, and the old bathroom suite upstairs could be ripped out. She could use one room just for stock, with wall shelving – 'I'd have the other couple of rooms set out as proper rooms of a house so customers can wander through.

I'll keep the smaller, easy-to-shove-in-your-pocket items downstairs so I don't have to worry about leaving the upstairs unattended. Then bigger items like cushions can go on furniture I'm selling, blankets and throws too.'

'I like the idea of setting up the rooms as though they're part of a home. That's what they do in posh furniture shops.'

'It could look really amazing.' She could have sofas stretching along walls, side tables with vases and flowers on top, mirrors or pictures on walls, candles and holders dotted around.

'You never know, someone might even come in and love the entire rooms up there so much that they insist on buying everything at once.'

'I guess I can dream!'

When Scott's phone rang he said he had to go, he was meeting a mate for fish and chips. 'I've been helping him paint a big house by the sea. Back-breaking work but it's earning me a bit of cash.'

'Good for you.' She liked to think he was sorting himself out.

'I won't be in tomorrow, it'll be more painting for me, but how about I stop by the day after?'

'You don't have to ask. Stop by anytime.'

He rapped his knuckles on the counter then raised his hand to wave and he was off.

Tilly closed the door behind her uncle and sighed. It was wonderful to finally tell someone about her ideas. She still didn't talk much business with her dad but she liked to think he'd be proud if she did eventually renovate and expand, take the shop to a whole new level. Or was it all just a pipe dream? One minute she thought it could really happen, the next it was as though it was almost within her grasp – she could just about graze her fingers along the edges of the dream that was there waiting for her – but she couldn't quite reach it.

Benjamin came into the shop as Tilly was on her hands and

knees trying to prise out a greeting card that must've been knocked off the display and floated to the floor and somehow got wedged beneath the chest of drawers.

'Ouch.' She put a hand to her head when she banged it as she stood up.

'You need more space.'

'Tell me something I don't know.' She repositioned the card on the display rack and straightened others. 'Sometimes I feel as though I spend more time tidying or shifting things around to make room than anything else.'

They both turned when hailstones began to pelt the glass. 'Where on earth did they come from?' Benjamin asked.

'No idea, but I'm glad I'm inside.' She put her hands together. 'Please don't let any of them break my window. Oh, my snowman!' The four-foot snowman standing beside the front door was right in the line of fire, his felt hat covered in white balls.

'Want me to fetch him in?'

She thought about it for a second. 'No, he's seen tougher days than this.' She could remember Grandma Shirley fussing about him if the rain slanted in his direction and she'd almost brought him inside the shop more than once before deciding his job really was to be outside. And he'd seen Tilly through every Christmas that she'd owned the store – she figured he was strong enough to go on for years yet.

'Mum said you had a couple of signs for me to pick up,' Benjamin said when they lost interest in the weather and the hailstones had eased off enough that there wasn't quite so much din drowning out their conversation. 'Does that make sense?'

'Perfect sense. Wait there.' She went upstairs and came back with two wooden boards. 'I spoke with Melissa and Heather the other day and we decided that because the wedding is at the farm we'll need some kind of signage on the gate, and I suggested these.'

She pulled away the paper that had been wrapped around them. 'I found them for sale online.'

Benjamin held one vertical. 'These are cool.' On black slate were the words *Welcome, friends and family, to the wedding of* written in white and, beneath, Harvey and Melissa's names as well as the date. Sprigs of mistletoe had been drawn around the top-left corner of the sign and across the top, more at the bottom right, along with flourishes of the enchanting Christmas plant around the happy couple's names. There was an arrow in one corner of the sign and it would point guests through the gate, prompting them to follow the path. Unless you knew there was a farm at the end it would be easy for anyone on foot to think that path led to nowhere. The other sign would go near the entrance for cars, with that arrow also pointing ahead.

'Do you really think they're cool enough for Melissa and Harvey?'

'Are you kidding?' he grinned. 'They'll be more than happy. I'll take these up to the farm.' He picked up the signs.

'Everything seems to be coming together. It's going to be a winter-wonderland wedding.'

He adjusted the boards so he could hold them better. 'Yeah, it sure is.'

'Did you find out anything more about what's going on with your mum and dad?'

'Unfortunately, I'd say it was obvious.'

'I'm really sorry, Benjamin.'

'I told Charlotte.'

'How did she take it?' Charlotte had moved away a long time ago but, as with everyone from the Cove, she always considered herself at home when she came back here and liked things to stay relatively the same around the place.

'Hard to tell on the phone. Shocked, I think.'

She showed him to the door and pulled it open now he had his hands full. 'At least the hail has stopped.'

He smiled but turned to her rather than walking away. 'I came past here earlier and saw your uncle with you.'

She brushed away the hailstones that had gathered on top of the snowman's hat. The roads beyond were still wet, puddles lingered, and cars slowed as they drove through the village, eager not to drench anyone on the footpath. 'He's been helping me out. I'm enjoying having him around.'

'I'm sure you are.'

'Come on, I know there's a *but* coming.'

'I'm worried that you don't really know him.'

His blunt answer took her by surprise. She'd expected denial of her suggestion, assurance that he felt sure she knew what she was doing. 'I don't know him well, but I do believe everyone deserves another chance.' When he said nothing, she added, 'Daniel, Melissa – there are two examples.'

He nodded. 'You're right. Ignore me. Just looking out for my friend.'

And there it was: the friend reference. And it bothered Tilly almost as much as it bothered her that he clearly didn't approve of her uncle. But if he'd been there earlier and listened to his encouragement and enthusiasm, he'd see for himself that Scott had good intentions. The only niggle Tilly really had was that she'd asked Scott again earlier today if she could tell her dad about his arrival in the Cove now – she didn't think keeping a secret was the best way to improve her relationship with her parents and the longer she kept quiet, the worse she felt – but he had insisted it wouldn't be fair to spring it on Nigel when he was away on holiday. And she supposed he was right, it wouldn't be, so she'd keep it to herself for a while longer and perhaps get to know Scott some more first.

'I'll take these up to the farm.' Benjamin still had the signs hugged against his body so gave her a smile rather than a wave goodbye.

Back in the warmth of the shop Tilly wrapped a vase for the customer who came in when Benjamin left, she sold a dozen Christmas cards to Etna from the tea rooms and a beautiful festive cushion to Hazel from the riding stables. And when all was quiet for few moments she leaned against the counter and thought again about the upstairs of the property and the possibilities it held. Her mind drifted to paint colours – she was thinking pale ivory or even a very soft pink might work to give the two main rooms a welcoming yet fresh feel. She pictured the furniture she could arrange, the items that really would make those rooms look like something out of a catalogue. She could get rid of the ugly strip lights and replace them with fittings that were much more stylish.

She took out an A4 notepad from beneath the till. There was nothing wrong with jotting down ideas, was there? She made notes about her customer base, competition in other villages, existing expenses and cashflow, the savings she'd got in the bank. And rather than lingering on the doubts that Benjamin clearly had and was somehow managing to project onto her without even trying, she chose to believe in Scott, in family.

You never knew what might happen – perhaps in the new year she'd be hosting her parents and her uncle, together, with designs in hand, to show them all how much potential the shop had to be even bigger and better.

12

Barney had always had an open house; he welcomed visitors whenever they turned up at his cottage, and it was no different the following afternoon when Benjamin knocked on his front door before heading to the pub for the late afternoon and evening shift. He was immediately welcomed in and offered a cup of tea.

As they talked and the kettle boiled, Benjamin looked out at the barn damaged by the storm – the tarpaulin secured on the roof, the temporary wood used to hold the dislodged doors shut. The low-lying mist across the fields beyond the barn made for an eerie scene much like the one up at the farm when Benjamin had woken this morning, the beauty of each and every pine tree shrouded in grey.

'I can't believe another Christmas is almost upon us.' Barney topped up each mug with milk and Benjamin shook his head to the offer of sugar.

'The years turn around too quick.'

'Even quicker when you get to my age,' Barney quipped. 'Be warned.'

'I'll try to remember that.' Benjamin picked up his mug of tea as they moved over to sit at the table.

'The farm seems as busy as always. I'm not sure how Heather and Danny manage it all.'

They did usually manage it well but clearly something had gone wrong this year. 'Mum knew I was walking this way so asked me to let you know that the wedding plans are all in hand, there's nothing to worry about. Tilly made some signs, too – did you see them?'

'She sent me some pictures and I wholly approve. Not that it's my wedding, of course.'

'It's not, but you're an important part of it.' His mum had asked him to stop by Barney's on his way to work this afternoon to make sure the man who was to all intents and purposes the father of the bride wasn't fretting about anything. He was always apologising for showing up at the farm unannounced and Heather wanted him to know it wasn't a problem at all. 'Mum says anytime you have questions or want to check things, go up there, you're always welcome.'

'I appreciate that. I may wander up later, get out of Lois's way when she's making dinner.'

'She likes her cooking; I can understand that, it's soothing.'

'I checked the long-term weather forecast this morning and it's predicted to be a dry day for the wedding. At least we don't have to worry about the bride and groom being pelted with hailstones like the ones yesterday. Some of those were like golf balls.'

'They were shocking. I was at Tilly's shop and I think she was worried one would come through the window.' When Barney gave him a look that suggested he was going to ask him about his visit with Tilly, Benjamin changed the topic. 'When you go up to the farm, take a look at some of the decorations the girls made – they're stored in one of the sheds. The veranda is going to look amazing.' He was waffling now to deflect attention from himself.

'I don't need to check every detail.' Barney swished a hand through the air. 'I know it's all in hand. I just had a bit of a tantrum that I couldn't throw the wedding myself but I think it's working out even better than I could've imagined. Melissa and Harvey certainly both seem happy and that's all I can ask for.'

'How bad is the damage inside the barn?' Benjamin went over to the doors at the back of the house from where he could see the rolling hills of countryside beyond Barney's property, the courtyard where vehicles could easily park and the beautiful barn that didn't quite look itself at the moment.

'The internal damage is mostly from water,' Barney sighed. 'It could've been a lot worse. And I've placed the order for extra timber for the doors. Unfortunately, at this time of year and with the terrible weather, demand for supplies and repairs has gone up. And I understand there are plenty in greater need of rebuilding jobs than me – our home is intact, not like for others.'

'One of Hazel's stables is unusable,' Benjamin confirmed, 'and part of the roof of her house was damaged.'

Barney nodded. 'The roof above the kitchen. Not the best place, not with Christmas dinner fast approaching.' He seemed pragmatic until he looked over at the barn again. 'I can't wait to see it fixed. I know the farm is a beautiful venue but the barn just means so much to the kids.'

Barney didn't have children of his own yet he was so close to Melissa and Harvey that he often referred to them as *the kids*. 'It does, and so do you, Barney. As long as you're there with them and you walk Melissa down the aisle, that's all that matters. It's all Melissa will be worried about. Well, that and the million other things a bride and groom have to think about in the lead-up to a wedding.'

Barney recalled Melissa's distress when the company she'd hired the white linen tablecloths from said she couldn't cancel with such late notice. 'I took over the call and diverted her booking to the ball next summer. I need those tablecloths every year; I usually use a different firm but it was easier this way. Honestly, anything with the word "wedding" attached to it is overpriced. Want flowers? Sure. Here's a price and then you can add on ninety per cent since you let slip it's a wedding. Good job Harvey and Melissa's catering is being organised by Etna, Jade and Celeste – at least they're not upping the costs by an eye-watering amount.'

Benjamin smiled. Anyone getting married in the Cove had their pick of food types so why would they ever go anywhere else? They could have baked goods from the Twist and Turn Bakery or from the Heritage Tea Rooms, they could employ his skills as a chef or they could have waffles from Daniel's shack.

He took his cup over to the sink to rinse it out. 'The barn will be up and running again in the new year, Barney, but for now, don't worry at all. The wedding plans are well under way at the farm and it'll be a great day. A real winter-wonderland wedding.'

Barney began to laugh. 'Does Tilly know you're an old romantic?'

He pulled a face because without realising it he'd just used the exact phrase – a winter-wonderland wedding – that Tilly had used yesterday. And by the look he was getting now, Benjamin could tell that Barney knew all about his feelings for the woman. With a groan he asked, 'Does everyone know how much I like her?'

'I think they might do.'

'Does Tilly know?'

'Of course she does, but if I know Tilly, she'll be waiting for you to make the first move.'

Charlotte had said exactly the same thing, so maybe there was something in it, Benjamin thought. He had both hands planted on the edge of the sink as he contemplated how everyone was waiting for a development that had to come from him yet he still hadn't had the nerve to say anything to Tilly. He didn't want her to think he was on the rebound, and apart from that, her uncle was in the picture and creating tension between them the more he hung around and raised Benjamin's suspicions.

'Come on, you.' Barney put a hand on his shoulder briefly. 'Lois brought back some oatmeal-and-raisin cookies from the bakery. Can I tempt you?'

'Do you really need to ask?'

Barney not only welcomed visitors, he was always there to listen to their troubles, and as the two men sat at the kitchen table with their cookies and another cup of tea at Barney's insistence, instead of taking a really long walk as planned, Benjamin ended up talking frankly.

'Zoe and I were together for a long time and I think people here got used to us being a couple.'

'You don't regret separating, though.'

He loved the way Barney phrased it. 'Not at all. To be honest, it was over a long time before it officially was, if you know what I mean. I always thought I'd be devastated if we ever broke up but things had got so difficult and miserable that I think it was mostly a relief when it finally ended between us.'

'I'm sure Tilly hasn't been serious about anyone since she split up with her boyfriend a long time ago now. He broke her heart and I know she was wary for a while, but you two have been friends for some time – it's a good sign.'

'Hmm... sometimes it might not be a good thing,' said Benjamin, adding an explanation that sometimes friendship stayed just that and developed no further.

'You don't know until you try.' Barney picked up a stray raisin that had fallen from his cookie and looked carefully at his house guest. 'What is it that you're not saying?'

'Very astute, Barney.'

He tapped the side of his head. 'Still got all my faculties. Not much you can get by me, lad,' he laughed.

'You were friends with Tilly's grandma, right?'

Barney nodded. 'Very good friends we were.'

'So, you know about Scott?'

Barney shook his head. 'Not a name I've come across. Why?'

'Scott is Tilly's uncle, on her dad's side.'

It took a while for Barney to process it in his head. 'Shirley had another child… other than Nigel? Wow.' He blew out his cheeks.

'They've been estranged for many years – something to do with things he did in his past.'

'Shirley never said a word, not in all the time I knew her.' He was shaking his head in disbelief until he looked at Benjamin. 'Then again, I should understand it. I kept things quiet about myself when I first came to the Cove.'

Barney had arrived in Heritage Cove decades ago to start over and it was only when Lois showed up the summer before last – prompted by a bit of delving on Melissa's part - and they reunited that his friends in the Cove learned of their painful secret, their previous marriage, and the loss of their baby son.

Barney handed Benjamin another cookie but didn't take one for himself. 'I'm watching my sugar levels,' he said.

Benjamin doubted that was true – Barney had always been a lover of the bakery and went there most days, although how much of that was for the products and how much was for the chatter Benjamin didn't know. 'It's not that nobody here knew about Scott,' he went on, 'it's that I've met him and there's something about him that just…' His whole body tensed at the thought of how Scott looked as though he was up to no good, at the niggling suspicion he'd seen him somewhere before.

'Do you think you're worrying because you're so close to Tilly?'

'I'll admit that's part of it.' He recapped on their first encounter at the farm when Scott had been after some ivy. 'He sneered at me, he was really very rude, and when I asked him to pick up the cigarette butt he'd dropped, he was having none of it. You know when you get a first impression and you have a feeling it says it all about a person?'

'I do know what you mean. And that's a worry.' Barney frowned. 'Has Tilly told you anything about why he's suddenly come here after all this time?'

'She thinks he deserves a chance to prove himself.' Benjamin picked up the crumb he'd dropped and put it in the bin. 'Call it paranoia but I'm just waiting for him to do something and show his true colours.'

When Melissa left the Cove and didn't return for years, Tilly had got close to Barney, something Benjamin suspected came from both sides. Barney would've been missing Melissa and worrying himself silly, wondering why she hadn't been in touch, and Tilly had stepped into the void. Without family here for Tilly, she'd turned to Barney when she had her own troubles along the way.

'I suppose all we can do at this stage is sit back and trust her judgement,' said Barney after pausing for a moment to think. 'She's always been independent, never one to admit she needs help, but I've made sure to keep an eye on her and I won't stop now. So that's two of us on the lookout.'

He was right, it was the best way forward. With both of them watching the stranger who was hanging around the village, surely nothing bad could come Tilly's way.

This man may think he deserved a second chance and her trust but Tilly deserved happiness and Benjamin wasn't about to let anyone ruin that.

* * *

The next day Benjamin found himself working at Mistletoe Gate Farm right through until dark despite having another late shift up at the pub to get to afterwards. He'd woken early in the morning to help out and found both his mum and his dad outside nursing stinking colds. He'd known then that each of them needed to rest for a few hours at least. Heather had eventually gone back to bed and, after some persuasion, Danny had finally gone back inside to lie down on the sofa.

Throughout the morning and well into the afternoon Benjamin got the type of workout he suspected his dad was more than used to. He hauled trees, netted them, led families in the direction of what they wanted, he juggled break times for himself and the other staff. And as he worked, he felt as though an awful lot of people had only just realised it was Christmas with the influx of cars, excited families charging up and down the rows to find the perfect tree. Danny had already cordoned off the trees in the rows nearest the house ready for the wedding, the plan being to weave lights through their branches as a romantic backdrop, but there were still plenty of other trees for customers to choose from.

'You okay manning the till?' Benjamin asked Parker as daylight began to fade, before checking with Jared that he could handle the tree netting and delivery arrangements while he helped a couple find a Norway spruce that was the right height for their hallway. He had on a bright-yellow beanie as well as a yellow bib with *Staff* written across the back so customers could identify him as the member of staff who could come and chop down a tree should they want to do that now rather than tag it for later delivery.

He heaved the chosen tree back to the netting area and there was no time to rest; he was immediately accosted by a father and young son who'd found their ideal tree in the end row of Fraser firs. He followed them, cut it down, and took it to be netted, by which time the skies had darkened and Danny had reappeared, insisting he'd had a Lemsip and was fine to work.

'Don't give everyone your germs,' Benjamin whispered,

knowing it would take a lot more than a head cold to keep Danny down. 'Sniffing and nose-blowing is really bad for business.'

'Thanks for the concern, son, but I'll stick to the jobs that don't involve customer contact.' He winked and it reminded Benjamin of being a little boy, when any troubles you had were instantly lifted by a few reassuring words from your mum or dad.

Heather was next to appear. It seemed she couldn't be struck down for long either and declared the long sleep had done her the world of good. Whatever was going on between them, at least they weren't about to let this year's business suffer. Benjamin supposed he should be grateful for that.

A few minutes later Heather called over to Benjamin to tell him she'd had a call from the Heritage Inn asking for a six-foot Fraser fir to be delivered this evening. They already had a tree in reception but this was for a guest's room, apparently.

Benjamin whistled his way along the rows of the great, green beauties until he found a tree he knew would be perfect. He crouched down with his saw, ready to start cutting.

'I approve.' Tilly was standing beside him.

He stood up tall and smiled. 'I wasn't expecting to see you here.' His breath came out white on the air and even though it was almost totally dark now, they had enough floodlights dotted around that he could see her eyes twinkling away. He liked to hope it was because she was feeling the same way as he was at the sight of her.

'I needed to get out for a walk after a crazy day in the shop. It's busy here,' she added, looking around them.

'I think this is our busiest night yet. And I've still got my shift at the pub to get through.'

'You can rest once Christmas is over,' she smiled. 'I came to get a couple of fresh wreaths for the shop,' she said when neither of them knew what to say next. It had been awkward at the shop the other day when he'd expressed concern about Scott and it seemed they were back to that again. He hoped she wouldn't get wind of his conversation with Barney – it could make matters worse. But Benjamin knew that despite Barney's love of a good gossip, you could always rely on the man to be discreet when it mattered so he doubted he had anything to worry about in that regard.

'I thought you had one on the door already.'

'Your mum asked if I'd put a wreath in my window – which I did, and it was snatched up straight away. The customer also wanted mistletoe so I sent her up this way and I thought I'd grab more than one wreath this time since they're so popular. It's amazing how many people seem to leave decorating their homes until the last minute.'

Benjamin wondered whether his hunch that the business was in financial straits might be correct if his mum had taken to recruiting the locals to drum up business, although looking around tonight it was hard to believe there was any kind of cash-flow problem. He got back down on the ground to saw the tree when Tilly offered to hold the top steady for him. If he was on his own he could manage it well enough but it was easier with two people.

When he stood up again he asked whether she'd heard anything more from her parents.

She frowned as he took charge of the tree. 'Why do you ask?'

'I noticed you closed the shop earlier,' he said by way of explanation. He'd nipped to the bakery to grab a sandwich for his lunch and to have a bit of a break himself. 'I hoped everything was all right, that their house hadn't been targeted again. You know, burglars sometimes return to the scene of the crime.'

'Yeah, if they're dumb.' She was smiling now as she explained how the neighbours were keeping watch and how one of them apparently had a baseball bat on hand.

'Good for them, defending what's theirs.'

She twisted her wellington boot in the dirt as though she was nervous. 'I closed the shop so I could go out with Uncle Scott. We went to an antiques fair to buy furniture. I had to grab the bargains while I could. I don't really have space but I didn't want to miss out.' She was rambling, probably because she knew he disapproved of anything involving Scott. He did his best not to react, especially because she seemed to want to confide in him. 'There were so many beautiful items, Benjamin, there really were. I bought what I could fit into Scott's truck and I can find a place for the vases I found, the lovely wooden tray will sit on the chest of drawers in the shop, the small side table can stay right near the counter – I'll just warn people it's there. I found a gilt-edged mirror, too, and Scott has already put that up on the wall for me.'

He really was getting his feet under the table, so to speak. The question was, why?

'You sure you're not buying too much for that shop of yours?' His attempt to sound unconcerned didn't quite come off that way.

She pouted. 'What makes you say that? It'll sell.'

'I'm sure it will.' He was making a mess of this. Charlotte had told him Tilly might not thank him for interfering.

'You don't like Scott much, do you?' she said before he could try to talk his way out of sounding like a total arse.

'I don't know him.' He shifted his grip on the tree, his hand beginning to cramp from holding it too long.

'He's been really kind to me, he's helped out in the shop, he turned up and took me today without question even though he was meant to be helping a friend with some painting. And he haggled for a better price on a couple of the items for me.'

'I'm glad.' And he really was. It was great to see her so animated and full of excitement.

'Scott thinks expansion at the shop would really work. I didn't think I had the funds to convert the upstairs but we discussed it again today and he had some more ideas. He helped me scribble out a bit of a plan and I think the bank might well lend me the money.'

Well, things really had moved fast. 'Take it steady, Tilly. Don't rush into it.'

Clearly affronted by his suggestion that she wasn't in control, she told him, 'This is a good thing. Be happy for me. It could take Tilly's Bits 'n' Pieces to a whole new level.'

Maybe it would, maybe it wouldn't. Had she really thought this through? His hesitation was enough to put her back up a little more. She stood up straighter, hands pushed deep into her pockets. 'He told me, you know. He told me you and he had a run-in at the farm.'

Of course he did. Of course Scott would've come clean. What better way to make him seem like the good guy and anyone else involved the villain? 'It wasn't really a run-in, I just explained about the holly being available for purchase and he wasn't keen on that idea.'

'You can get it anywhere, you know.' She'd taken Scott's side, defended family like so many people did, blinkered to any faults they may have.

'I know you can.' Falling out with her was the last thing he wanted.

'I don't have much family in my life, I like that he's here.' Her voice hinted at doubts and his heart went out to her.

He lost the edge to his voice. 'I know you do. It must be really nice. What did your dad say about him being here?'

'I haven't told Dad yet.' She wasn't looking directly at him any more. 'I know what Dad's like from personal experience – he can be a harsh critic. I want to give Scott a chance.'

But not telling her dad about his brother being in town set off the alarm bells for Benjamin and they were almost deafening. 'I'd better get this tree to the inn or Tracy will wonder whether it's coming at all.'

'See you, then.' She looked hurt, put out that he wouldn't talk more, and as much as she was defending Scott, she gave Benjamin the impression that perhaps she actually wanted someone on her side, someone challenging his presence just to make sure she was doing the right thing in letting him into her life.

But Benjamin couldn't be that person if his interference would turn Tilly against him.

He watched her walk away in front of him as he carried the tree at a pace a lot slower than hers. Her red wellies were the last thing he could see as she faded into the distance, the half-light of the moon not quite enough to make the vision last for long.

As he loaded the tree into his dad's truck ready to drive it to the inn he thought about what else his sister had said. Yes, Charlotte had told him not to interfere, but she'd also told him to make sure he was there in case Tilly fell.

Benjamin's challenge now was going to be striking that balance, because he felt sure Scott hadn't revealed his true self yet and that he had more surprises in store for all of them.

13

Tilly pushed open the door to the shop the next morning, shoving the post on the mat out of the way with her foot. She'd got back from the farm last night feeling frustrated, upset that Benjamin wasn't even giving Scott a chance to prove himself and even more disappointed at his lack of enthusiasm about her dream to expand the shop. His opinion mattered more than he realised and she'd thought he would've been willing to let her confide in him about her worries when it came to the shop and also any concerns about her uncle. Because it wasn't as if she didn't have any at all. She trusted that Scott was on the right path but not telling her dad about his presence in the Cove was beginning to really play on her mind.

She was about to close the door when she jumped. Hand against her chest, she looked down at the slate-grey cat. 'Shadow, you scared me half to death.'

His arrival was followed soon after by Lucy's. 'Did my—'

But she didn't need to ask whether her cat had come into the shop.

'He's all right, aren't you, Shadow?' And, in her arms, he

warmed Tilly up from the grey and murky day outside, the sort of weather that made you wish you could hunker down beneath your duvet all day long. Shadow was a regular visitor to all the businesses along The Street as though he wanted to be a part of the community just like Lucy.

'I saw him run across the road – he's getting far too brave for my liking.' Lucy's overalls were filthy from her job in the workshop using the forge and other tools to make such beautiful things from what could best be described as pieces of scrap metal. She scooped her cat out of Tilly's arms. 'There was a time he would at least stick to the one side of the road or the grassy area up towards the waffle shack.'

'It's always nice to have a cuddle.' Tilly stroked the top of Shadow's head and he purred contentedly as though his only mission this morning had been to garner as much attention as possible.

But Lucy's attention wasn't on her cat, it was on the mirror Scott had hung on the wall. 'This is new.' She handed Shadow over to Tilly again so she could inspect it further. She ran her fingers along the edge. 'It's beautiful.'

Tilly told her about the antiques fair she and her uncle had been to the previous day. 'I could've bought so much more but I haven't got anywhere to put it.'

'How much?' Lucy asked before Tilly could say anything else, let alone point out the chip on one edge.

Tilly floated the price she'd considered, knocking off a bit for the damage.

'I'll take it,' said Lucy. 'I've been looking for a mirror for a while and this is it. I don't have the biggest bedroom but I'm thinking this would go on the wall next to the wardrobe. Can I bring the money by later and collect it?'

'Of course you can.'

Lucy, being a business woman herself, asked Tilly whether

she'd seriously thought about making items like the mirror more of a feature as well as the smaller things. 'I know you don't have a whole lot of space but if this is the sort of thing you find reasonably locally, imagine what you could pick up farther afield.'

Tilly admitted, 'Expansion has been a dream of mine for a while.' It just felt like too much of a risk right now.

Lucy took Shadow back although he seemed reluctant to leave Tilly's arms. 'So, why don't you?'

Simple as that. Why don't you?

It was the reaction Tilly had wanted from Benjamin last night and hadn't got. He'd reacted as though it might be the stupidest idea she'd had yet.

Yesterday morning Tilly had worked in the shop as usual and Uncle Scott had come in, taking her by surprise because she'd thought he was busy helping a friend with some decorating. 'Check this out,' he'd said, thrusting a newspaper at her as soon as her customer went on his way. Tilly had taken the folded-over newspaper and seen a photograph of an old manor house with a big parcel of land and a headline advertising the fair.

'It's less than ten miles away,' Scott had enthused, chugging on in his excitement, 'It's the second day of three today so some bargains might be gone but there may be more up for grabs. I can take you in my truck. Close the shop for an hour or so around lunchtime, I'll grab us something from the bakery to eat on the way. Come on, what do you say?'

'I don't know, it's my busiest time.'

'Tilly this could give you a chance to buy some unique pieces, get more of a vision of what you can do for the shop.'

It felt so good having someone there, a member of her own family, encouraging her to leap in with both feet rather than criticising decisions she might make. And it was only a couple of seconds more before she said, 'Let's do it.'

Tilly thought about it again now when Lucy and Shadow left and she leaned against the counter by the till. Benjamin shouldn't interfere when he knew nothing about Scott's situation – she didn't know all that much, either, but her instincts had surely been proved right because he'd cancelled his plans to take her to the vintage fair and moments ago Lucy had snatched up one of the items that Tilly had found there. It had to be a sign – a sign that Scott was on her side and that maybe an expansion could really work. It might take a while to save up or arrange a bank loan but as she and Scott had talked and she'd heard his belief in her ability to grow the shop to what she wanted it to be, she'd found herself feeling more driven than ever.

* * *

By mid-afternoon, after a rush of customers, Tilly looked up and smiled when she saw her uncle come in through the door with a tray of takeaway coffees from Etna's.

'Thought you might want some sustenance,' he boomed in a voice that was probably more suited to the pub than her shop.

It was then that Tilly realised that the raven-haired woman who had followed him in wasn't another customer with a dulled sense of smell given the cloud of perfume that came in with her but someone Scott knew, who was about to be the recipient of the third cup pushed into the cardboard tray.

Scott told the woman to grab the stool out of the way. 'Not much space in here,' he said with a smile before introducing her to Tilly.

The woman, Selena, had just disposed of chewing gum in a piece of tissue and pushed it into her bag. 'Good to meet you,' she enthused, extending a chilli-red-manicured hand to shake Tilly's. 'I've heard a lot about you. I haven't met any of Scotty's family before.'

Tilly couldn't quite place Selena's accent – perhaps Yorkshire, she wasn't sure. It certainly wasn't from around here. Scott hadn't mentioned a girlfriend before, either, not in all the time they'd spent together, but her calling him Scotty suggested these two had been together for a while. Tilly waited for her uncle to offer more information but they were too busy extolling the virtues of Tilly's shop, which she had to admit felt rather good.

'You've got some wonderful stuff.' Selena reached out a hand to touch the silk scarves and Tilly hoped she didn't have sticky fingers from the chewing gum.

Scott leapt forwards and plucked out the electric-blue scarf, draping it around Selena's neck. 'This complements your eyes.'

It was odd seeing Scott with a woman. Tilly almost felt jealous, a bit put out, which was silly when he was family. She pulled herself together. 'The electric blue is a very good choice and Uncle Scott is right, it suits you. Plus, I can give you a discount.'

'I'll buy it but only for full price,' Scott said firmly. 'You have a business to run.'

Tilly rung up the sale and a happy Selena wrapped the silk scarf back around her neck. She went on to admire the jewellery, which she described as exquisite, bought a couple of handmade cards to send to friends, and when Scott asked whether he could take Selena to show her the upstairs and the changes he and Tilly had discussed, Tilly didn't see why not.

'He's been going on about this shop for days,' Selena said with a roll of her eyes as she followed after him while Tilly stayed on the shop floor.

From downstairs Tilly heard the tell-tale creak above her position at the till meaning they were in the room at the front, the one that still had an old fireplace, and she imagined Scott telling Selena how Tilly planned to furnish the rooms with items so they resembled a home.

When Scott and Selena came downstairs again, Selena had finished her coffee and already popped in what Tilly hoped was a fresh piece of gum. Chewing away again, she announced, 'This place has potential,' and then, with a squeeze of Scott's arm, she added, 'Scotty is glad he found you. Family is so important, don't you think?'

'It really is.' Tilly thought again of her dad and her increasing discomfort that he still didn't know Scott was around. She hadn't done anything wrong but the longer she left it, the more she began to wonder whether she'd be in trouble. She hoped not, but there was so much she didn't know about what had happened in the past.

Tilly took the empty cups off their hands and went to add them to the recycling pile upstairs. She wanted some time to gather herself because her emotions were about to get the better of her. It was good to have some family by her side, but was she getting carried away with it all? She wasn't totally sure about Selena and she couldn't quite put her finger on why. All she knew was that the woman's presence was suddenly making her question Scott being here in the first place. Perhaps it was just that she'd got used to spending time with her uncle and having his attention but, now, here was someone muscling in on what she'd grown to think of as their getting-to-know-you family time.

'Tilly!' Scott's voice came from the bottom of the stairs. When she appeared at the top and brought down the box of recycling ready to go into the bins out the back, he told her she had a customer waiting who was interested in the side table she'd put near the counter, almost out of sight for fear someone might trip over it. Tilly couldn't believe it. She'd had a chance to dust the table but she'd assumed it would need a good polish as well before she got any interest.

When she'd sold the table and the happy customer left the shop, Tilly realised Selena had gone.

'She had to take off,' Scott explained. 'But more importantly,' he said giving her a nudge, 'you sold the table already.'

She beamed at him. 'Items I found at the fair have barely hung around for five minutes.'

'I told you. Old stuff is all the rage. People pay a fortune for one-of-a-kind.' He clapped his hands and rubbed his palms together before he noticed something at his feet and bent down to pick up a piece of paper that had fallen to the floor near the counter. 'What's this?'

She took it. 'It's nothing.'

'It's not nothing – it said Business Plan at the top. May I take a look?' When she hesitated he seemed offended. 'I'm interested, Tilly. I suppose with this once being Mum's shop I kind of care what happens to it.'

'It's just ideas,' she said as she handed him her scribblings. She wasn't sure why she felt embarrassed; it wasn't as though she hadn't told him her dreams.

He looked through the sketches, the jotted ideas, the sums she'd done, before Tilly took the plan back and pushed it under the counter enough that it wouldn't get blown to the floor again next time the door opened.

'The finances are the real sticking point,' she said.

Scott, still standing at the customer side of the counter, leaned his forearms onto its surface. 'But you want the expansion.'

She sighed. 'I *really* want the expansion.'

'Then let me help.' He looked over his shoulder to make sure their discussion was private, but the customer who'd just been browsing the cards had left without purchasing anything.

'You want to help?' Shocked, it took her a while to realise he meant it.

'I have some money put by. I could loan it to you.'

'I couldn't do that, it's too much to ask.' And if he had money, why wasn't he buying some place to live rather than renting? Was it because family meant more to him than anything else and he wanted to sort things out with them first? She felt it only fair to be completely honest. 'I'd need quite a few thousand, it's not a small amount.'

'I know, I saw your finances and your calculations for what you might need.'

'I think this is something I have to do for myself.' She'd prefer to have a formal agreement with a bank, keep everything above board and transparent.

'Tilly, your dreams for this place are spot on. And look at the sales you've made in just a day since you went to the vintage fair. With extra space you'd be able to buy in more furniture. Profits would soar.' It was what she'd always wanted and his enthusiasm was hard to extinguish. 'When Mum died, she left me some money. Even though we weren't in touch, she still thought of me.'

Tilly gulped to think of the pain Grandma Shirley must've endured, not knowing her son at the end but still thinking of him in her last days.

'I felt guilty about Mum so I put all the money into one of those fancy accounts – you know, the sort that gets you more interest than point one of a per cent.'

Tilly laughed. Interest rates were pathetic – it was almost better to stuff money under your mattress. 'You mean a term deposit account?'

'That's the one.' He clicked his fingers to acknowledge her nailing the name. 'It's coming up to the end of the term – a couple of months and I'll have it.' He revealed how much he had invested and it was a few thousand more than she needed.

'Maybe I'll take my ideas to the bank first, see what they say. That way I might not need to use your money at all.'

'Are you crazy? The bank will charge you a ton of interest. I won't. We're family. Let me do this for you and you can pay the loan back monthly.'

She wanted to ask what was in it for him but, looking crestfallen that she might not accept, he came out with it before she could find the right phrasing. 'This is my chance to prove myself to my brother. Perhaps then he might not mind me being in his life.'

Tilly's heart lurched. She didn't have a sibling but she could well imagine what it must be like for him. Daniel had faced the same with Harvey when he returned to the Cove, with Harvey thinking he was nothing other than bad news, and look at them now – brothers in every sense of the word, who got on as though nothing had ever happened. She wondered whether this was why her dad had been so resistant to her following a career path he was unsure of at first, whether he was worried she'd go down a route leading to nowhere, choose a path that was all wrong just like Scott seemed to have done.

'Tilly, come on, what do you say?'

'I suppose it could be an option... but I don't even know who I'd get to do the work. I'd need to have someone reliable.' Harvey would be her first choice but not only did he have work with his loft-fitting firm, she'd heard him talking about plenty of jobs of his own he had lined up for the new year. It seemed she wasn't the only one keen on a renovation.

'I've been working odd jobs for a long time,' Scott persisted. 'I've made contacts all over the place – builders, plasterers, plumbers, electricians. I've picked up skills here and there, too, so I can help, it'll keep costs down.' She had to admit it sounded tempting, it sounded doable. 'This is what you want, I know it is.'

And when he looked on expectantly, before she could change her mind she found herself nodding.

Scott balled his fists and held them up tentatively. 'That's a yes?'

She hesitated only a moment longer. 'It's a yes!'

He raised his fists in the air, cheered and raced around to her side of the till to give her a hug. It felt a little awkward, he smelt a little smoky, but it was a nice gesture.

'Selena is an interior designer.' His eyes dazzled as though on a high. 'I was a bit sneaky bringing her in here but I wanted to show her the shop and the upstairs and see whether she thought she might be able to help. She says she could do the work for a really good rate and she has some great ideas for colours up there.'

Tilly didn't know what to say. She loved her uncle's eagerness, but did she really want a stranger to be responsible for major changes in her shop, involved with decisions that were so personal? In her head she'd envisaged Melissa being the one to help her when it was time to do the place up and expand. Then again, Melissa was crazy busy these days with jobs in the pipeline, not to mention the wedding and honeymoon. Could this be the best option all round?

Scott had already brought up more vintage fairs online, details of car-boot sales where Tilly could find unmissable bargains, and Tilly tried to push away her misgivings and instead took a look for herself.

Perhaps she should go with it, trust in the process.

Was it too much to believe that very soon she could be well on her way to having the shop she'd always dreamt of? And in doing so, her dad would finally be able to see that she didn't just work in a shop or even just own one; she ran a business all by herself, and a successful one at that.

14

Benjamin had spent the first part of the morning helping to load trees into his dad's truck ready for delivery. Now, he was lying on his bed looking up at the ceiling, the same place he'd been for the last hour. And all he'd been able to think about was their family and how they'd gone from being solid to breaking apart. When he saw his mum earlier as she stared into her mug of tea as though it might tell her the right way forward, she looked like she'd given up. And it destroyed what he'd admired about his parents ever since he was little – they'd always had a dogged determination to soldier on through tough times and come out the other side.

Luckily for Benjamin the family home allowed him plenty of space, otherwise he might be camping out on someone's floor just to avoid his parents' bickering. Yesterday it had been a disagreement over whether Heather should've gone to pick up a few last-minute things for Christmas when the farm was overflowing with visitors. Earlier today it had been an argument about the heating bill. This place, being old, had never been cheap to heat but what usually would have fizzled from a row to a discussion and a compromise wasn't reaching that level of sensibility these days. And now, he had no idea what his parents were arguing about. But he could hear the tension in the murmur of voices that reached him even from the other side of the house and he knew he couldn't stay a moment longer. Sometimes when he had a day off he'd lounge around, maybe have a coffee on the veranda in the afternoon, perhaps read a book or watch a movie, but suddenly he felt the overwhelming need to be far away. God knows what the staff here thought of it all – it hardly made for ideal working conditions. Then again, if this was it, marriage over, the farm would be the next casualty and they wouldn't have to worry about workplace etiquette for much longer.

He left via the front door rather than the back so he didn't have to pass them by, the collar of his jacket turned up against the cold, one foot in front of the other at a pace that meant it was unlikely he'd be spotted. The last thing he wanted was to be roped in to help again. Usually he didn't mind but today he simply couldn't do it any more.

His head switched to thinking about Tilly as he made his escape. When he'd dropped the hint that she might want to be wary around her uncle she hadn't reacted well but, then again, if someone told him how to think he wouldn't like it one bit. He made up his mind to go into the shop and apologise even though he still had plenty of reservations. He just wanted Tilly to know that he was there for her if she needed him.

When he reached the convenience store he ducked inside to buy a bottle of orange juice. He was gasping and hadn't wanted to go anywhere near the kitchen with his parents around. He sipped at it as he walked on but when he came to Tilly's Bits 'n' Pieces he saw Scott in there and knew he couldn't go in. His shoulders tensed, his brow furrowed as he watched him and Tilly laughing about something. But when his eyes fell on Tilly and he realised how happy she looked, he felt guilty that all of his efforts seemed designed to thwart that. The last thing he ever wanted to do was dampen her spirit so perhaps today, steering clear was the best idea.

Etna was outside the Heritage Tea Rooms talking with her close friend Kenneth as he replaced the bulb in one of the lights surrounding the doorway. When he'd finished she hung a garland tied with a metallic-gold bow on the door.

'What do you think?' Etna asked, spotting Benjamin. She hooked her grey hair behind her ear when it blew against her cheek in the wintry breeze. A chunky, long, charcoal-coloured cardigan kept her warm as she hugged it around herself while Kenneth, tweaking the garland's position, had her stand back and tell him when it was straight. She nodded her approval that it was just right.

'It looks good. Why didn't you put one up earlier?'

'I thought I had enough decorations and with the door opening and closing all the time it would get knocked and damaged.'

'Fingers crossed it doesn't.' He finished up his orange juice and Etna took the bottle for him and told him she'd pop it into her recycling. 'You could always use Blu Tack behind to hold it down.'

'Good idea. I'll do that.'

Barney came out of the bakery armed with two baguettes. 'Late lunch for Lois and some of the family over from Ireland,' he said by way of explanation for the long pieces of bread. 'They've been doing the rounds and catching up with relatives all over the country and it's our turn today.'

Etna smiled as she held the door and frowned at the garland that was already slightly out of position. 'I'll bet you can barely get a word in edgeways. I remember them from the wedding.'

So did Benjamin. The Irish relatives had descended on the Cove. All of them were great fun, but they were a talkative bunch.

'I'd have thought you'd love the chatter, Barney,' he said as Etna disappeared inside on the hunt for some Blu Tack.

'I do, but they all need some time to catch up and I needed some fresh air. I've got time for a cuppa before I leave, if I can interest you?'

'I could probably use a pint,' Benjamin laughed, 'but I'll take the tea instead.'

Etna offered to keep the baguettes safe and fresh in the store room out back while the men settled at a table after placing their order.

They talked about the upcoming wedding as they waited for their tea and Barney seemed to be slowly accepting that it wasn't such a bad thing to have it up at the farm. 'It might not be in the barn, but a family venue is more than special. Let's hope it snows, too.' He leaned forwards as he said it as though if anyone overheard it might jinx it and they wouldn't get the frost that would make everything sparkle and the day take on a romance of its own.

Benjamin's previous girlfriend Zoe had told him he was far too romantic. He'd never known there was such a thing but evidently for her there was – she hadn't even liked it when he cooked her eggs Benedict for Valentine's Day because she said it was all a big commercial con. He hadn't pointed out that he wasn't buying cards and balloons, he was cooking for the woman he loved. But looking back now, he could see she'd probably been ready to end things anyway at that point whereas he was trying whatever he could to save the relationship. And it was only when they were finally over that he realised they hadn't really been right for each other and his friendship with Tilly began to blossom, so much so that his feelings did too as they grew closer.

He wondered whether Tilly was a romantic. He suspected she probably was – what with the items she sold in the shop, the pretty things, the little touches she added, the ardour with which she talked about customers' preferences. She was sensitive yet strong; passionate and fiery yet able to be fair. And he'd always loved the way she dressed as though she didn't have to make excuses to anyone, wearing bold colours, out-of-the-ordinary outfits well suited to a personality that was vibrant yet always down to earth.

Barney talked more about the decorations that would adorn the veranda since he'd been up to see them for himself. They talked about how the mistletoe gate was the most romantic way to welcome friends and family to the nuptials. And when they'd exhausted wedding talk – they were men, after all – Barney said, 'I saw Tilly in her shop on my way to the bakery.' There was nothing new in that but Benjamin understood the point of the comment when he added, 'I take it that was her uncle I saw in there with her.'

'You haven't been introduced yet?'

'I'm afraid I avoided going into the shop when I saw him. Ever since you told me you were worried, I haven't wanted to seem as though I'm poking my nose in. There's a fine line between looking out for her and interfering.'

'You're telling me.' And Benjamin appreciated the choice of words, similar to those his sister had used when she tried to advise him. He briefly described Tilly's reaction at the farm the other day. 'She was very defensive and I ended up feeling bad for saying anything.'

'She would like having family around her.'

'She doesn't get on with her parents all that well, does she?' Benjamin finished the last of his tea and nodded at Etna's offer of another.

Barney tilted his head this way and that. 'They're better than they used to be. Tilly was always around her grandma when she owned the shop; anyone could see how much she fitted in with it all. Her parents pushed her academically, which is what every parent does to some extent. But Tilly felt they took it too far and then they fell out when Tilly decided on a change of direction. Nigel thought she was throwing away an opportunity to have more in her life. It was only when Shirley died that he started to come around. I wonder if it made him think that life was too short.' Barney's brow creased. 'Given none of us had ever heard that Nigel had a brother, perhaps the family rift was something her dad wasn't keen to repeat with his own daughter.'

'You might be right.' It certainly sounded like it was a possibility.

Barney shrugged. 'I might be. I think maybe that's why he passed the shop to Tilly when Shirley left it to him. But I get the feeling Tilly is constantly trying to prove herself.'

'She doesn't need to.'

'You and I know that, her dad probably knows that, but does Tilly?'

Benjamin sighed and sat back in his chair. Every time the door to the tea rooms opened it brought with it a rush of cold air that made him shiver until it closed again and the heat of the inside wrapped around him once again.

'I spoke with Tilly's parents at great length after Shirley's funeral,' said Barney. I wanted them to know that Tilly would always have a home in the Cove and that I and everyone else around here would look out for her. And I knew that no matter their disagreements along the way, her parents would never turn their backs on her.'

Benjamin made a face at Barney and luckily Barney wasn't slow on the uptake, he knew to stop talking, because Tilly was the latest customer to bring the outside air rushing in when she entered the tea rooms.

'I've come for takeaways,' she beamed, briskly rubbing her hands together as she walked over to say hello. 'It's freezing out there today.' She'd thrown her orange coat over a long, brown, corduroy dress and wore laced-up Doc Martens on her feet. In that moment she looked unequivocally Tilly and if her parents couldn't see how wonderful she was, Benjamin knew it was their loss.

'Three hot chocolates to go, please,' she smiled over at Etna.

'Three?' Barney queried. 'All for you?'

'No.' Coyly she added, 'I've got family. My uncle and his girlfriend.'

'That's nice,' said Barney, 'although I didn't know you had an uncle.'

Benjamin was thankful he didn't let on that they'd talked because Tilly would likely take it as gossiping given the way she'd reacted to Benjamin's worries.

'It's a long story.' She ducked over to the counter to use her credit card to pay for her drinks before coming back to stand with Barney and Benjamin while she waited. 'I'm going to expand the shop,' she announced excitedly, looking mostly at Barney.

Barney patted the chair beside him. 'Come on, you've got a few minutes while Etna makes those hot chocolates.' He placed a hand over hers on the table as she sat down. 'I want to hear *all* the details.'

She launched into what everyone knew – that the shop was overflowing with her finds. 'I don't have enough space any more and while I can keep things upstairs, I can't have customers going up there. It's not safe, it needs a lot of attention and a bit of a refurb, and an expansion could really take the business to a new level. My grandma never really talked much about making the shop bigger, but then she only sold candles. I've found so many beautiful furniture items, Barney.'

'You've got a good eye for it.'

'And I want to buy those items, sell them on.'

'You could even do a bit of furniture restoration,' Benjamin put in, anxious to let her know he was on her side.

'I could.' The way she smiled back at him suggested they were okay, that she didn't hold a grudge about him questioning Scott's presence.

'Scott's girlfriend is an interior designer,' Tilly went on and Benjamin did his best to bite his tongue at the mention of the man. 'She has a lot of enthusiasm for what I could do with the shop, colour schemes and the like. Selena can even get supplies at wholesale prices, which is brilliant. I've drawn up a bit of a plan, worked out my finances, and I was about to go to the bank to discuss whether they'd agree to a loan when Uncle Scott told me he'd lend me the money. I think he feels connected to the shop even after all these years.'

Benjamin tried not to let his gaze lock with Barney's because he felt sure he wasn't the only one who'd spotted a big red flag waving on the horizon.

'Did you really never know anything about my uncle Scott?' Tilly asked Barney. 'I know you were good friends with my grandma.'

'She honestly never said a word.' He looked at Tilly and asked, 'So, your uncle will finance the expansion project?'

Barney had to be wondering exactly what Benjamin was. What was in it for him?

'He'll loan me the money, so I won't need to sell the idea to the bank at all. I can get going with our plan.' She was full of excitement about her dream.

'I must say, that's wonderful.' Barney didn't have anything to add as Etna handed Tilly the cardboard tray of beverages.

'And thankfully I have enough cash to make a start now. Selena can get supplies while we wait for Uncle Scott's money to be released from the term deposit account. Then in a month or so, when the funds come through, he'll be able to finance the rest of the job. They've done some wonderful sketches.' She used her free arm to hug Barney. 'You'll love it when I show you.'

And there it was, the whole story, the story that made alarm bells ring in Benjamin's ears. And judging by the look Barney gave him as Tilly took her hot chocolates to go, he had heard those very same bells loud and incredibly clear.

15

'You're soaked through!' Tilly met her uncle at the door to her shop and ushered him inside. The rain had unleashed itself like a tropical storm rather than the drizzly efforts they frequently saw on the east coast.

'I really should invest in an umbrella. Selena had a pink one to lend me,' he shrugged, 'but wouldn't do much for my street cred.'

Tilly took his coat, at arm's length, out to the back and hung it on the hook farthest away from hers. She put an old towel below it so it could drip to its heart's content and took another, smaller, towel to Scott. 'I wasn't expecting to see you today.' She tried not to worry about the puddle on the floor as he plonked a soggy black canvas bag down by the counter.

He rubbed at his blond hair with the towel until it stood up in tufts. 'My outside job helping build a garage was rained off.'

'Build a garage?' He really was a jack of all trades. But she couldn't ask more because it was time to serve the lady who had come in to peruse the Christmas cards and had now made her selection.

Tilly put the cards into a paper bag, wished the woman a merry

Christmas, and opened the door for her so she could thrust her umbrella up the moment she stepped outside. 'Where's Selena today?' she asked when it was just the two of them again.

'She's been working this morning – another client. But she should be here very soon.'

'Interior designing?'

'She's very talented.'

Tilly nodded. 'I'm sure she is.' She'd certainly been animated talking colour schemes, anxious to buy in the supplies as soon as they could. Tilly had wanted to say she doubted anyone was redecorating at Christmas but Selena seemed worried that's exactly what might happen and it would limit their choices.

Tilly regarded the leather folder Scott had with him. It must've been tucked beneath his coat and she hadn't noticed it until now. 'What have you got there?'

'Something you're going to like... a lot,' he grinned, showing her some rough drawings. 'Now, I know neither me nor Selena are what you might call artists, and Selena will do proper plans – you know, on a computer – but she always likes to hand-sketch first so her clients can see what she has in mind.'

Tilly was touched that they'd done this regardless of whether it was professional or not. She looked at the drawings showing what they'd discussed, including the obliteration of the bathroom suite and the dividing of the bathroom in two to accommodate a small toilet facility with sink as well as a spacious storage cupboard for stock to help clear those rooms that would become display suites. One of the other upstairs rooms would be storage for bigger items so that if Tilly sold a piece of furniture she'd have a replacement at the ready.

'What do you think?'

'It all looks good.' Mind you, she wasn't sure what some parts of the drawing were, but she got the general gist, and the proper drawings would make it clearer later on. 'Does Selena have a website so I can see what else she's worked on?'

Before he could answer, a pink umbrella bobbed past the window and stopped at the door. Scott went to open up for Selena and made a fuss over her, taking her coat, leaving her umbrella in the bucket provided behind the door.

Tilly felt strangely ruffled that they now came as a team. She'd quite enjoyed spending time with Scott and the atmosphere shifted slightly whenever Selena joined them, as though Tilly was the outsider.

Selena was chewing that gum again although this time it wasn't bright pink to match her lipstick but a tangerine colour that looked capable of staining anything it landed on. 'Did you like my pictures?' she asked, unconcerned that others might not want to see what was churning around inside her mouth.

Pictures, not plans. But Tilly guessed it didn't hurt to be informal. 'I do. And I was just asking Scott about your website so I can see more of your work.'

'Selena isn't entirely convinced she needs one, but it's in hand, don't you worry,' Scott said when Selena didn't answer, as though she didn't understand the question. 'A good website takes time, doesn't it, babe?'

Babe? Tilly wasn't sure she'd go out with a guy if he changed her name to Babe, but each to their own. 'Maybe I could just see photos, then – you must have taken some of your previous jobs.'

Selena pouted – not an attractive look on anyone, let alone her. 'I can bring some another time. Don't you trust me?'

Scott looked devastated that this might be the case so Tilly leapt in quickly. 'It's not that – I'm interested, that's all. I want to see colour schemes.'

'She'll bring photos, won't you, babe?' He kissed her cheek as though she needed placating every few minutes.

'When do you think you'll have a chance to draw up the proper plans and give me a formal quote?' Tilly asked.

Scott's brow furrowed. 'We already discussed price.'

'I know.' Tilly's cardigan sleeves came down over her wrists and halfway down her hands and her fingers toyed with the woolly material. 'I thought a breakdown would help me get things sorted in my head.' She would've needed it for the bank if she wanted a loan and it didn't feel right not having all the details. Anyone who had their own business had a duty to understand exactly what they were getting themselves into.

'I can scribble a breakdown onto the back of the drawings,' Selena offered, although by her tone you would think she'd been asked to sacrifice her last piece of gum.

And so Tilly became all the more determined that she needed it. 'Yes please, it would be useful for me and to keep on my records.'

Selena lifted up the drawings. 'We don't have much time before Christmas so, as I said before, I don't want to delay getting my orders in. Things go crazy with the sales from Boxing Day – if we order things now it might cost a little more but we'll get exactly what we want rather than dribs and drabs that are marked down because nobody really likes them and because there isn't quite enough. I mean, take wallpaper, for example – we're going to need twenty or so rolls for the front room upstairs. The last thing you want is to only find nineteen available of your top choice.'

'I definitely wouldn't want that.' Tilly had hoped they'd get going with the renovations right after New Year since she was usually quiet for most of January and February, so Selena's urgency to get the supplies made sense. This timing would be the least disruptive to her business and meant the work could be completed well before footfall picked up again. She turned to Scott, deliberately excluding Selena for a moment. 'I'd really like a formal agreement.'

He put his hands on the tops of her arms. 'We're family – there's no need.'

But it wasn't so much him as Selena who made her feel as though something wasn't quite right here. In fact, she was beginning to wish Selena didn't come as part of the package at all. But how was she supposed to say that she wanted to be careful without offending her uncle? The last thing Tilly wanted was to frighten Scott away before she'd even given him a chance to prove himself.

Tilly served a family of four who were visiting from North Norfolk for the weekend. They'd had dinner in the pub last night and asked her whether she thought the chef would be willing to relocate to their neck of the woods because they'd loved the sticky date pudding so much. One described it as decadent, the other as outrageously indulgent. 'I'll let the chef know,' Tilly chuckled, sending them on their way. A small tug in her belly told her that as much as Benjamin frustrated her at times, she'd hate it if he was ever headhunted and left the Cove. In fact, it didn't bear thinking about at all.

Tilly closed the door on the rain again and Scott handed her the towel he'd used earlier so she could mop up the pools of water that had come in. Selena's red-painted fingernails were tapping away at a calculator as she stood in position at the counter, so Tilly was hopeful that meant she was working out some approximate costs.

'I wish you'd let me get some official paperwork drawn up,' Tilly said again to Scott, ignoring the roll of Selena's eyes she saw reflected in the mirror to one side of the shop. She was beginning to wonder what Scott even saw in this woman.

'I won't hear of it, and that's final,' he said, before bending over to pick up the bag he'd put down earlier which Tilly now realised must've been a cooler bag. Selena let out a little squeal as she saw what he was taking out of it.

'What's that for?' Tilly was a lot more collected at the sight of a bottle of sparkling wine and wondered whether she'd missed some grand announcement as Selena took out three plastic glasses from the side pocket of the bag.

'Too presumptuous?' Scott pulled a face, hesitating, bottle still in his hand but unopened. 'I kind of thought we could toast to expansion.'

'It's eleven o'clock in the morning,' Tilly laughed. She supposed he was trying.

'So it is,' he grinned before pulling off the foil, twisting the silver muselet, and opening the bottle with a pop.

Between customers they drank the sparkling wine and flipped through wallpaper designs online, although when they discussed paint colours and Selena seemed transfixed by the white-with-a-hint-of-peach emulsion, it made Tilly wonder how many of her clients would actually give the thumbs-up to that one. It was a little on the wrong side of the fresh shade she was going for and not at all classy in her opinion.

Tilly was a little relieved when Selena said she had to meet someone, grabbed her pink umbrella – red nails clashing impressively with the material – and left Tilly and Scott to finish their sparkling wine.

'To the Candle Shop!' he said as he got to his last mouthful. He lifted his glass in the air.

Tilly realised the bottle was empty; she'd only had one glass, Selena just a splash on account of her pre-Christmas figure-watching, and so it was hardly surprising Scott was on the tipsy side and forgot the name of the shop had changed.

Tilly held up her glass. 'To Tilly's Bits 'n' Pieces,' she corrected.

He slapped a hand across his forehead. 'Sorry,' he grimaced, 'I apologise. To Tilly's Bits 'n' Pieces.'

'Not a problem,' she replied. 'It must've been weird to see it change in name as well as style.' Not that she was actually sure he'd been here too many times. When he first appeared in the Cove, the way he talked suggested he'd spent a lot of time here. But over the last few days, some of the little things he said made her wonder how much Grandma Shirley had driven him away whenever he came near, wanting to keep him firmly in the past. Tilly had a hard time imagining her grandma being able to do that – she'd been so warm and caring – but maybe things had been very different back then and the only way she could've kept a son out of the picture was by making sure that not another soul around the village knew about him.

'I'd better make a move,' said Scott, zipping up the cooler bag with the empty glasses inside.

'I'll get your coat for you.' She grabbed it – still rather wet – from out the back and when she came through to the shop again he'd just finished looking at something on his phone.

'I'll have the money through in thirty days.' He put his thumb up as he shoved his phone into his jeans pocket. 'It's still a bit of a wait.'

'It'll pass in no time,' she assured him. He was helping her out, the last thing she wanted was for him to feel bad about how long it might take.

'The problem is, Selena's keen to get buying so you don't miss out.'

'Some of those wallpaper designs she showed me were gorgeous.'

He tugged a hand through his blond tips. 'I'm afraid we don't have the money without those savings so we can't even get started.' He harrumphed. 'I hate being on the scrounge with you.'

'You're not on the scrounge.' She was sorry that he felt that way when he was the one doing her a favour. He didn't have to take time out of his day to come here and help her with the ideas for expansion, he didn't have to cash in his term deposit and lend her any money at all. 'How much do you need to get started?'

'Oh no, it's me lending you money not the other way around.' With a shake of his head he added, 'I knew putting my money in that account would come back to bite me.'

'It was a wise investment.' She got the impression he'd had serious financial struggles over the years, so to have managed all this time to keep the money he'd inherited from his mum in savings really was admirable. 'Thirty days is a long time if we want to get going and make the most of the quiet period after Christmas. I have enough money to make a start.'

'I can't, Tilly. It wouldn't be right.' When his phone pinged again he took it out and looked at it briefly. 'It's Selena, she's at the wall-paper wholesalers for another client.' He turned his phone around to show her a photograph of the most exquisite wallpaper, the one Tilly had fallen in love with already when they'd looked at it online – blush-pink with butterflies. 'They have twenty-five rolls left,' he told her.

'We need twenty.'

'I'll ask if she can put them on credit card. Should be fine.' He keyed his reply to Selena but when he received a text back from her he growled in frustration. 'She's worried about doing that – she thinks she's dangerously close to her limit and doesn't want the interest charges if she can't repay straight away. She's been spoiling her nieces and nephews,' he added with a roll of his eyes. 'She has a lot of family and a lot of heart.'

Tilly loved that wallpaper and she didn't want to miss out. 'I can phone and pay with my card; Selena can take the rolls with her. Call her back.'

Scott disappeared behind the curtain so he wouldn't disturb Tilly or her customer, who had plucked out a red silk scarf and was already fishing in her bag for her purse. Tilly complimented her on her choice, telling her it was very Christmassy. The lady told her she'd be wearing it to church on Christmas Eve. When she left, Scott emerged but he looked edgy.

'She only went and bought the wallpaper on her card.' He shook his head. 'She shouldn't have done that. I didn't mean to pressure her but she knows you're the first member of my family to show an interest in me in years. I need to make sure she pays the card quickly or the interest will be brutal.'

'I can get the money to you and she can pay the card straight away,' Tilly leapt in. He looked distraught, as though he'd known he'd mess up somewhere but he just hadn't realised how or with who. 'Then there's no harm done.'

'You'd do that for me?'

'Of course.'

'Then I would be in your debt. Thank you, it really would be a weight off my mind.'

She took down his bank details so she'd be able to make the transaction as soon as she'd served the couple who'd already selected two festive candles and holders to go with them.

Tilly wished Selena had never appeared on the scene. That woman was trouble, she was sure of it – even if it was only because she added to Scott's stress levels when she made decisions he felt he had to take responsibility for. The only reason she was using her for the interior design in the first place was as a favour to Scott, and Tilly could only dream of having Melissa do this work for her rather than someone who got under her skin, and not in a good way.

Was she going to regret her decision to involve a woman she was disliking more and more as the days went on?

* * *

Tilly's shop was a hive of activity for the rest of the day and she had little opportunity to think about much else than the business. She transferred a sum of cash to Scott's account to pay on to Selena and was thrilled to get a photo back from him of the rolls of wallpaper she adored. Already she was picturing it on her walls upstairs before she filled the rooms with unique finds from antique fairs near and far. She wouldn't have minded seeing the wallpaper for herself, feeling the textures, but for now she'd have to be content with descriptions and pictures. And if she wanted the shop to be finished by spring when business usually picked up along with the sunshine, they couldn't waste any more time so she was glad Scott seemed to be thinking along the same lines. All Tilly wanted to do now was get to those vintage fairs she often saw advertised, discover hidden treasures, perhaps do restorations as Benjamin had suggested, using the smallest room upstairs as a workspace that could stay messy because it wouldn't be open to anyone other than her. It's where she could work her magic. She could work long into the evenings bringing the most beautiful pieces back to their former glory or making them even better.

Barney came in before closing time and handed Tilly a paper bag adorned with the Twist and Turn Bakery logo on the front.

'Whatever's inside it smells divine.' Tilly had had a small sandwich at lunchtime but she'd been so busy she hadn't had a chance to have a snack since and, with all the racing around, she'd worked up an appetite. She took out the cinnamon-and-raisin puff-pastry twist and grinned. 'Barney, you are my hero.'

He took off his coat and sat on the stool. 'Don't mind me, enjoy it, and if you're busy eating I'll deal with any customers who come along.'

'On one condition...' She pulled out Selena's designs that she'd left, the unofficial sketches. 'While I eat, you check these out.'

'It's all very exciting, Tilly.' He was interested, eager to know more as he looked at the drawings. 'It's lucky your uncle has a girlfriend who does interior design.' Barney turned one of the drawings the right way up. 'What colour schemes do you have in mind?' But he swished away the question as soon as he'd asked it. 'Colours are not my forte – Lois will vouch for that. She's in charge of any decoration or furnishings from now on. I don't think I've much of an idea at all. I picked up a paint colour I thought would look great but when I painted one small square on the wall, I had to agree with Lois's first opinion – it was hideous. Olive green.'

Tilly pulled a face. 'I don't need to see it to know that unless it's only a small area you're painting, that might not be the best choice.'

'Lois and Melissa have already discussed more appropriate colours and between them have planned how we'll decorate the hallway in the new year, how we'll bring it into the modern day.'

'I would've used Harvey and Melissa for this.' She felt awkward that she hadn't. 'But it all happened so suddenly.' And with her uncle financing this she could hardly turn down the offer of his girlfriend do the work. He'd assured her she'd get a family discount as well.

'Nonsense. Harvey is far too busy with his day job and preparing for the wedding and honeymoon – Melissa too, for that matter. They wouldn't have been able to commit to this until well into January. And it seems as though you're keen to get moving quickly.'

She reiterated Scott and Selena's suggestion that post-Christmas sales might result in her not getting exactly what she wanted. 'I would hate to have less choice. I want this renovation, this expansion, to go well. I don't want to cut any corners. And then when spring and summer get really busy I should have a full inventory from all the fairs I can go to and buy up stock from between now and then.' Tilly popped the last of the twist in her mouth and sighed. 'Thank you,' she said, covering her mouth.

'My pleasure.' He waited for her to finish. 'And you did get another couple of quotes, I take it?' When Tilly pulled a face at his question he shook his head. 'Tilly, you know—'

'I do know.' When she'd had work done at the cottage it had been before Harvey did many of his own renovations so she'd used people she didn't know. She'd got four quotes, evaluated all of them before she made her choice. It struck her that this time she'd leapt straight in because it was family.

'I'm sure Harvey wouldn't mind coming over to look at the drawings and the list of changes you've got here.'

Tilly had made a list of all the changes required, partly to ensure Selena didn't forget to include them in her plans or Scott didn't miss any out when he got quotes for the work from tradesmen he knew. She'd written down everything from dividing a room into two smaller ones to adding a couple more electrical sockets here and there and changing up light fittings. Perhaps she should've got another quote just to see how it compared.

Barney seemed able to tell exactly what she was thinking. 'You don't have to say anything to your uncle, so you won't offend him, but it may help you see whether these prices are fair, give you some confidence going forwards, give you peace of mind.'

She smiled, totally onto him. 'You mean it would give *you* peace of mind.'

'I admit I'm looking out for you.'

'Is that what the treat from the bakery was about?'

'That was out of the kindness of my heart,' he smiled.

She bristled, putting two and two together. 'You've been talking to Benjamin.'

'Not at great length.' She knew he was lying but Barney, father figure whenever she'd needed him to be, was a man it was not easy to be angry at. 'All right, busted. We have been talking. He's worried

– don't give him a hard time for that. And if Harvey sees this as a fair quote then I promise not to make any more fuss.'

'Deal,' she smiled. 'I'll ask Harvey to pop over, I promise. And thank you for being on my side.' It worked out well, too, that Scott wouldn't be around for a few days as he had a job on. Got to take the work while you can, he'd declared. She could get the quote without him even knowing and be reassured, ready to move forwards.

Barney pulled on his coat. 'I'd better get going. Dinner at the pub tonight – it's roast pork with all the trimmings for me.' He patted his tummy but on his way to the door he stopped. 'I meant to ask, what's this lady's name?'

'Scott's girlfriend? It's Selena Curtis, why?'

'Just wondering. You never know, if she does a good job here, maybe Lois could get her in to do other rooms in our place if it proves to be too much for Melissa on her own.' With an eye roll he added, 'First the hallway, then it'll be the bedroom, then the kitchen, you mark my words.'

Tilly waved her goodbyes. She wasn't sure she'd be recommending Selena for her people skills but that didn't mean she wouldn't do a good job.

She tidied the shop a little, gave any glass a good squirt with cleaner and an even better rub with a cloth – grubby fingers around the three-foot mark were a tell-tale sign they'd had some little visitors earlier who had been more fascinated with squishing their faces up against their reflections than by anything sold in Tilly's Bits 'n' Pieces.

At the end of a long day Tilly put on her coat, grabbed her bag, and switched off the lights out back. She was heading towards the door when she got another text from Scott, this time with some stunning photographs of the most beautiful carved walnut armchairs – two of them, both with ruby-red, velvet covers that were torn and faded but didn't stop her seeing the beauty if they had a bit of care and attention.

Found these at a garage sale around the corner from me! he said in his message. *They're perfect, just what you're looking for!*

She bashed back a text to say they were, to ask how much, and to ask whether he was still at the garage sale now.

He replied that he was, and another lady was vying for position and talking price.

Tilly called him straight away. 'Buy them, please! I don't want to miss out, they're gorgeous!' Finding these sorts of items was addictive but missing out on them didn't bear thinking about. 'How much are they, roughly?'

'Too much,' he whispered.

'More than a hundred?'

'Way more.'

Damn it. It was a garage sale so usually the person just wanted rid of the stuff and at this stage she wanted to keep her costs right down. She'd thought fifty quid or a hundred at most and would've grabbed the chairs at that price. If she recovered them and cleaned them up, used polish to get the most out of that wood, they'd sell for a good profit. She'd seen some like them online at one of those fancy interior places for almost eight hundred pounds apiece.

'Let me see what else is here,' he said dejectedly. 'Wait, there are actually four chairs in total,' he whispered. 'The same colour, same wood.'

Someone might want these when upholstered for a dining table at home. They could be beautiful as a set or could be sold off individually, each uniquely covered with a different material. Her mind was running away with her, ideas coming from all directions. She closed her eyes and asked, 'How much, Scott?' And when he reluctantly told her the price, she did the calculations in her head. It wouldn't cost much to restore their beauty and she could still make a significant profit on them. Displayed as part of a room upstairs at the shop rather than shoved in a corner out of the way, they'd look stunning.

'Go up to a hundred and fifty apiece,' she said before she could change her mind. She had to buy in stock at some point so why not when she saw it? 'Although for a garage sale this guy is charging way too much,' she added nervously.

'Couldn't agree more,' he said in a low voice. 'Garage sales have changed... a lot.'

She began to laugh. They certainly had. 'Much else there?'

'I'll send you a photo.'

As soon as she'd looked at the picture she put her phone back to her ear. 'How much longer is the guy running the sale?' She returned to the back of the shop and took off her coat again, sitting down behind the curtain as she saw the future of Tilly's Bits 'n' Pieces taking shape.

'I'll ask.' Muffled sounds came down the line until Scott was back and told her, 'Last day today before he takes it all with him over to Wales. He'll have to sell it there in his new place.'

For the next half an hour she had Scott go round and send pictures and prices of what was available and found a free-standing mirror, another beautiful wardrobe, a coffee table – none of which was in perfect condition, all of which could be improved and all of which were reasonably priced, or at least not so expensive that she wouldn't turn a profit.

'I'll transfer a thousand to your account,' said Tilly. 'I can do it now, online, on my phone.'

'You want me to buy the chairs and the coffee table *and* the wardrobe.' He began to chuckle. 'Didn't expect that. But great, I'll do it. And I'll knock another thousand off the loan when my money comes through in a few weeks.'

She murmured her agreement, buzzing on adrenalin and

looming possibilities. And if she kept finding items like this and did a good job restoring them, repayments weren't going to be a problem. Plus, it was such a relief not to have to go to a bank and convince them to lend her the money.

As soon as she hung up, she made the transfer.

This was what she had her savings for. And this was her chance to prove herself. Because while on some days she thought everything she did was for herself, on others she knew that deep down she still wanted her parents to be proud rather than disappointed.

When Tilly finally locked up the shop she patted the snowman on the head, giggling as she said goodbye to him.

She was about to make some wonderful changes and Uncle Scott had backed her every step of the way. Maybe it was time she repaid the favour. It was time to tell her dad that his brother was here and perhaps it would trigger the process of showing her dad that Scott had changed, give him a chance to repair the damage.

Maybe it would help her dad see that family was all that mattered in the end.

16

'She doesn't exist,' Barney told Benjamin the moment he stepped over the threshold at Mistletoe Gate Farm.

'Slow down... who?' Benjamin hadn't even had a chance to wonder what Barney was doing here.

'That woman, Selena.'

Benjamin was well aware of who Selena was and also well aware that Tilly could show up at any minute. As Melissa's bridesmaids, she and Tracy were due over here to finalise wedding details, practise where they would stand, where they would walk on the day itself. 'What do you mean she doesn't exist?' he asked Barney as he took his coat. The man was getting into a bit of a state, worry etched on his brow.

Barney looked around to check they were alone. Satisfied it was safe to talk, he said, 'Selena, this so-called interior designer, doesn't have a website, no Instagram—'

'Wait, you know Instagram?'

'Lois told me all about it and it's a must for sharing pictures. I've searched all other social media channels, used search engines and the only thing I've been able to find is a vague Facebook headshot that may or may not be Selena.'

'Have you told Tilly?'

'Not yet.' His concern clearly hadn't faded either. 'I've got a bad feeling about this.' They both turned when there was a *knock, knock* on the back door and Melissa poked her head in. 'A very bad feeling,' he added quietly.

Benjamin ushered Melissa and Harvey inside. It turned out Barney had come here to meet the girls and discuss music choices for the big day – something Melissa and Harvey had sorted out a while ago until last week the band cancelled. But perhaps it was a blessing given that the veranda here and the grass space beyond weren't really geared up for a big band ensemble.

Heather came downstairs looking as though she didn't have a care in the world. Make-up on, her face gave away nothing of the tears from earlier. Benjamin had heard her in her bedroom; she was crying and he'd paused, about to go in and check on her, when he realised perhaps the reason she'd hidden away was that she didn't want anyone to know. It hadn't been easy to walk away like that but she deserved her privacy. He wondered, was his dad hurting as badly?

But, now, there was no trace of those tears. And so Benjamin would get on with doing as much around here to help out as he could. He'd do anything to take away any additional stress for his parents even though he suspected it was too late to make a difference. He'd spoken to Charlotte last night and because she was still working she wouldn't be here until a day or two before the wedding so it was up to him to offer any practical assistance and just wait for the divorce bomb to drop, which surely it would do any moment now. Every time he walked into a room he expected his parents to sit him down saying they had something to tell him. And then he'd become one of those kids he'd felt sorry for at school, whose parents lived in separate houses and had separate lives.

Barney had taken charge of making the cups of tea but sidled over to Benjamin while Heather, Melisa and Harvey chatted at the table. 'You look tired.'

Benjamin harrumphed. 'I live on a Christmas tree farm. Goes with the territory that this is our busiest time.' He pulled on his work boots. He was due at the pub by late morning but before then he was going to cut back the bushes along the track and cut some more mistletoe.

'You're a chef, Benjamin, and a very good one. Maybe you need more staff here.'

'It's a family business,' he shrugged, because Barney was perceptive when it came to anyone in the Cove. He wasn't nosy but he was always there should any person need someone in their corner.

'Come here, Barney,' Melissa called out. 'I've got some soundtracks on my phone – we'll have a listen.'

Over at the table everyone was smiling as they played the first bit of music. Heather had gone to cut slices of the pear upside-down cake and to everyone else she looked fine but to Benjamin she just looked sad.

And with that unhappy thought, Benjamin ventured into the freezing outdoors.

By the time he reached the bushes along the path, having forgotten his gloves, his fingers were numb. He lifted the shears to trim the sides, lumped debris into the wheelbarrow beside him, breaking off now and then to blow into his palms or onto his fingers and warm them up. He went up one side of the track and down the other, greeting visitors as they came and went, and when he'd finished the cutting back he picked up the secateurs he'd brought with him to tackle any overhanging branches as well as cut some more mistletoe to take back to the house. His mum had suggested having extra sprigs tied to the beams in the kitchen to make it look romantic and he'd make sure he did the same with these pieces as they'd done with the decorations that had already been made, spraying the mistletoe with cool water and keeping it cold in the shed.

Benjamin had just climbed up onto the second rung of the stepladder intending to cut some more mistletoe when he looked up to see Tilly coming through the gate.

'Are some of these pieces for the wedding?' Tilly wanted to know.

'Mum wants extra.' He handed her some mistletoe and indicated to put it in the plastic tub that wasn't the home to debris. 'She wants to decorate the kitchen so it looks just as good as the veranda.' The house would be mostly off-limits for the guests but anyone who really suffered from the cold could at least find relief in the kitchen, especially when it came to enjoying the canapés.

'It grows so well.' She marvelled at what he'd cut and what still grew plentifully.

'Mum's been cutting from the back of the bushes whenever she can and she gets customers to do the same, so it's kept an impressive view around the gate, but it's time to trim some of the greenery back – otherwise visitors might not be able to get through.'

'Can I help?'

'Aren't you due at the house to confer about the music and practise your walk?'

She pulled a face. 'I've already had a text from Melissa to say they've agreed on most of the tracks. It sounds as though Barney has been great with suggestions so I'm not sure I'm even needed. And I don't think it'll take me long to master the walking. Melissa will tell me where to start from and I'm pretty sure I can make it to the end of my designated route without too much trouble.'

'I don't know, it can be tricky,' he teased. 'You might need to come over and practise some more. I'll help you if you need me to.'

'I think I'll manage,' she demurred, blushing from the top of her head to the toes of her red wellies that already had mud on them given the amount of rain lately. Last night at the Copper Plough Melissa had been panicking that the rain wouldn't stop and that the grass at the farm would turn into a bog, although Benjamin had overheard her say that Tilly suggested every guest bring wellies in that case. Typical Tilly, willing to see the adventure in everything.

'You due up at the pub?' Tilly asked as she took another clump of mistletoe from him and deposited it in the same plastic tub.

'Later on,' he answered.

'Still trying to do all you can to help.' It wasn't a question. 'You're a good man, Benjamin.'

He handed her another sprig of mistletoe. 'I like to think so.' It was why he was worried, especially now Barney had told him he couldn't find any trace of Selena and her so-called business. An online presence was a must these days and it was weird not to have one. But he wasn't going to say anything, not when Tilly seemed in no rush to get away from him.

He moved the ladder along and over to the other side, Tilly taking the mistletoe each time, and when he'd handed her the final sprig he collapsed the steps. 'Could you take the plastic tub of mistletoe up to the house while I put away this ladder?'

'Of course.'

There was a cluster of mistletoe right next to her and all he wanted to do was lift it higher into the air above them both and kiss her there and then. He didn't think he'd need words to tell her how he felt, he knew by the time he kissed her it would be obvious.

And although he couldn't tell her how worried he and now Barney were about what she was getting into, he would make sure he was there to catch her if she fell when Scott let her down. Which Benjamin had no doubt he would do.

It was just a matter of when.

17

At home in her cottage that sat back from the road with a small garden in front as well as a bijou green space out back, Tilly dragged herself out of bed and made a mug of tea to take and enjoy next to her Christmas tree. The aroma of pine was a welcome way to wake up despite the cold and the dark before she went to open the shop and she was convinced that without this tree here, getting out from beneath her duvet would've been a lot harder.

All it took was the flip of a switch to see the tree illuminated with fairy lights and it had the power to wake her up that bit more. She sent Scott a quick message to find out what time he was coming to the Cove. She couldn't wait to see those chairs he'd bought a few days ago, to put them upstairs out of the way and assess what they needed apart from new material to cover the seats. She picked up her iPad and put it on her lap, scrolling through the website she'd found last night while she drank her tea. She'd come across an amazing fabric supplier for her reupholstering needs with everything from durable plain colours that could be cleaned time and time again to the more decorative fabrics she might use if she found old armchairs. For those she envisaged bright colours, velvets, materials full of texture and plush.

Her tea almost finished, she was still fizzing at the idea of new projects when Scott's message came back on her phone and extinguished the joy. 'No way,' she groaned. She dropped her phone onto the coffee table along with the iPad before she went to tip the dregs of her tea away. Scott's van wouldn't start and he was stuck the other side of Lowestoft until he could get the breakdown service to come to his rescue.

Tilly messaged back that he wasn't to stress about it. *It's not like I have time to reupholster yet*, she told him, adding in a laughing emoji, deciding that making a joke was the best way to make him feel better about letting her down. She messaged him again to check that the things she'd had him buy weren't in his way – she could ask someone to go and get them if they were – but he said they weren't, he had access to a garage and so plenty of space. He encouraged her to keep looking for notices of more fairs, enthused about what they might find next, and, feeling a little better, she got ready for another day at Tilly's Bits 'n' Pieces.

* * *

Tilly spent the first hour at the shop helping a little old lady find a birthday gift for her husband who was in Aubrey House, the residential home that sat just outside the village past where Barney lived and the roaming fields that surrounded his house and the barn. The lady ended up selecting a gorgeous silver-plated photo frame, as well as a handmade card.

When she at last had a quiet moment before lunch, Tilly decided to message her parents. Here goes, she thought to herself. She was going to tell them she had something she needed to discuss and ask that they call her as soon as it was convenient. She had no idea which country they were in right now or whether they had any reception to receive the message, but it didn't matter – what was important was that when they called she could tell them that Scott had come back and wanted to reconnect. And if they took the news well, if they saw Scott's appearance as an opportunity for peace and harmony, it could be the perfect way to go into Christmas as a family.

She shouldn't have been surprised when her phone rang only a few minutes after sending the message. They must've been in an area with good mobile reception. 'Is everything all right?' was the first thing her dad asked, even though she'd told them in her message not to panic, that everything was okay, they needn't worry.

'Yes, it's fine.' A small flame of gratitude flickered that he still cared. Of course she'd always known he did really, but sometimes it was nice to have the reminder. 'Honestly, Dad. I meant you to call me when you had the time.' She put her finger in her ear. Wherever they were, it sounded busy. 'Where are you?'

'Venice!' he bellowed, more for his benefit than hers, she suspected. 'Your mum is dragging me towards a gondola – but, Tilly, what is it you need to talk to us about? Do you want me to put your mother on? She's just—'

'Actually, Dad, it's you I need to talk to.'

'Is it the house?'

'No, it's not your house.' Her heart was thumping hard against her chest. But she had to get this over with, just tell him. It wasn't right – two brothers never talking, not even acknowledging each other's existence. 'I've had a visitor to the shop.'

'What kind of visitor?'

She closed her eyes, pursed her lips together and then blurted out, 'Scott.'

'Scott?' he repeated.

Oh goodness, had it been so long since he'd thought about his brother that the name didn't even ring a bell? 'Yes, Scott.' She waited for more... but nothing came. 'Dad, are you there? You do realise the Scott I'm referring to, don't you?'

He cleared his throat, a sign he was figuring out what to say. 'What does he want?'

Was that honestly what he really wanted to ask? After all this time. 'He doesn't want anything, Dad. But I do.' Since they'd had their falling out she'd been determined to always say what was on her mind, to take a stance and not be swayed by others' opinions. 'I want to know why you never told me about him.'

She heard muffled sounds and the tail end of what was probably her dad excusing himself from her mum and whoever was nearby. His voice became much clearer after he'd moved away from the mêlée. 'It's complicated.'

When Tilly saw Lois milling outside the shop she rushed over to the door. She hadn't thought this through, that her dad might call straight away. She had her dad wait a moment, ushered Lois inside, and Lois was only too happy to man the till and the shop while Tilly ran upstairs with the phone.

Huddled in the front room above the shop, which wasn't all that warm – she never turned the heating up in these rooms like she did downstairs – she leaned against the wall and watched the icy rain pitter-patter against the window pane as she explained Scott's first appearance at the shop, how he'd been back many times since.

'It sounds as though he's been there a while. And he turned up just like that? The bloody nerve.'

'Dad—'

'No, Tilly. Lord knows you're your own woman, you're independent, but with this... you don't get a say.'

'What do you mean I don't get a say? He's my family! And he's your brother!' Her voice went up a decibel.

'Don't you yell at me, Matilda.'

'I haven't been Matilda since I was at primary school.'

'No, I don't suppose you have been.' He sounded exasperated – with her, with his brother's appearance, with everything.

'I've got to get back to the shop, Dad. I can't talk to you when you're angry.' Or when she was angry. She wasn't sure what she'd expected but she hadn't foreseen him warning her off before offering any other explanation. And it reminded her of how he was the day she announced she wouldn't be taking up her offer of a university place. She'd been standing at the bottom of the stairs, he'd just come in the front door, and she'd blurted it out just like that. He'd stood there as though she'd slapped him across the face and then he'd followed her around the house telling her what a mistake she was making.

Was this how Scott had felt? Had he taken a wrong turn and her dad and Shirley had been so angry they couldn't forgive him and move forwards?

What was wrong with her family?

* * *

A soft knock announced Lois's arrival at the upstairs of the shop. 'I locked the door and turned the sign to closed.' She found Tilly slumped on the floor and sobbing in the front room, her gaze fixed out of the window at the miserable weather unfolding.

Tilly leapt to her feet. 'I'm so sorry, what was I thinking? I have a business to run. And if I shut every five minutes it'll prove my dad right.' For Lois's benefit she added, 'He always thought that me running a shop selling bits and pieces wasn't the right career move when I could've had so much more.'

Lois tilted her head. 'That's very dramatic.'

Tilly gratefully took the tissue from Lois's outstretched hand and blew her nose. And as they went back down the stairs and lingered at the bottom, she recounted the whole story – her schooling, her career path and university plans and then the sudden change of heart. She stayed behind the curtain at Lois's insistence while Lois popped out to the shop front whenever she was needed.

'Barney told me you didn't have the easiest of relationships with your parents,' said Lois, hovering at the curtain, 'but he never told me the details. It's a shame they weren't on board with your choices.' Lois's soft Irish lilt was a balm for the soul and made Tilly want to confide in her.

'You know, I never really thought of them as unsupportive as such. It's not as if they're always telling me I chose wrong or they talk about what might have been. Those comments were only made once, at the start, but ever since then it's been more an air of disapproval I feel whenever I'm around them, particularly my dad. Mum isn't too bad – I think she got used to the idea of me changing direction – but Dad doesn't seem to have done so. I don't get it – it was good enough for his own mother; why isn't it good enough for his daughter to want to run a shop, surrounded by beautiful things, in a small seaside village?'

'I haven't known you all that long,' Lois smiled, 'but I can tell you're a determined young lady. Tell me, are you more like your mother or your father?'

Tilly smiled. 'I'm like my dad.'

'There you are, then. You're two strong-willed people and maybe it's led to things being expressed wrongly, or perhaps leaving things unsaid. He might've changed his mind, you know. He might not even think the same way as he once did. Have you asked him about it?'

She shook her head. Come right out and ask him whether he's over the shock, whether he's recovered from spending all that money on a private education for her to do something she could've done without those qualifications? No way. She'd never wanted to bring the matter up again. It was bad enough the first time. Occasionally she felt like asking him whether he was impressed with the shop and how she'd moved it forwards since she took over, but she'd lost her nerve more than once and they'd bumbled along with pleasantries whenever they saw each other.

Lois had gone back through the curtain into the shop to help a lady who was debating between a cushion with glittery reindeer on the front and one with a jolly snowman. Tilly went and splashed some cold water on her cheeks at the sink upstairs and, with a deep breath in and a big exhale, she pulled herself together. Time to get back to work and put the conversation with her dad out of her mind for now.

Downstairs again, she smiled at Harvey, who had just come into the shop with a bag slung over his shoulder. 'Are you shopping or just saying hello?'

'Barney said you might like a second quote for the work here.'

She wanted the ground to swallow her up whole. 'I would've always come to you, you know that, but I was trying to do right by family.'

Harvey smiled gently. 'I get it, please don't apologise. Now, show me the way and I'll give you that all-important second quote.' He leaned closer so Lois didn't think they were talking badly of her husband. 'It'll keep Barney happy, too.'

Lois offered to keep an eye on the shop a little longer while they went upstairs so Tilly could take Harvey through the details of what she planned to do. Harvey's full-time job as a loft fitter meant he knew plenty about projects like this since he'd done an apprenticeship with the company he still worked for so had several years' experience, plus he had the work he was doing to get his own renovations business off the ground, giving him a breadth of knowledge. He'd even brought a folder with him so she could see his previous work – something she hadn't been able to see with Selena.

They began in the front room, then moved to the bathroom, Harvey taking way more measurements than Selena had and asking a lot more questions. Tilly wondered whether this was how he usually worked or whether Barney had told him to be extra thorough. In the bathroom she ran through the changes she wanted, they talked shelving in one of the storage rooms, which walls up here would be painted, which papered, the new light fittings and electrical socket changes she had in mind. He took copious notes, asked a lot of questions, and they finished at the staircase and talked over the repairs needed there too.

Downstairs at the front counter Harvey took out a calculator as well as a big logbook and his iPad. 'I'll price it all up for you. And it's no trouble,' he added quickly, predicting she was going to say he didn't have to take time out of his busy schedule for this. 'You should really have three or four quotes, but I reckon Barney will stop worrying at two.'

She felt a little naive having not done so, blinkered by having family in her life again and swept along in all the excitement. But Harvey and Barney were both right. This would put her mind at rest and anyone else's.

The shop had got busy and Lois insisted on staying. She seemed to be enjoying herself, chatting with customers, helping them select Christmas gifts. Tilly had overheard Barney the other day when he was having a pint with Benjamin telling him that Lois could do shopping as an Olympic sport if there was such an event and Tilly could see why. She was in her element in here.

'Would you be interested in part-time work once I get the expansion finished?' Tilly asked the minute Lois's customer left satisfied and with two bags filled with gifts. Harvey was still tapping away on his calculator, intermittently scribbling down figures. 'Dessie isn't always available and if I have two floors, I'm going to need two people here at least so the shop isn't unattended but customers upstairs aren't neglected either.' And then there was the rest of it – the tea and lunch breaks, the cleaning surfaces and sweeping the floor, the times she went out back and looked on her laptop for new stock ideas.

'I actually would be,' Lois smiled at the same time as Barney came in to collect her for lunch and she repeated what Tilly had just asked her.

'Thank goodness for that, she's getting under my feet these days,' he winked, planting a kiss on Lois's cheek. 'Now, come on, those waffles are waiting.' He waved over to Harvey.

'Enjoy yourselves.' Tilly straightened up the cushions on display in the centre of the shop. Once the new year was upon them she'd have a short sale of any remaining Christmas items and those that didn't go she'd store for the following Christmas. Cushions, instead of having festive designs, would have woodland creatures or spring flowers, keeping up with the seasons.

'How's it going?' Tilly asked Harvey when he looked as though he'd finished his quote.

He was frowning. 'Just making sure my figures are correct.' He made another face she wasn't sure she could read and handed the completed quote to Tilly.

Tilly's eyes whizzed down the scribbled figures and settled on an amount at the bottom. She turned the piece of paper over but there was nothing on the back. 'Is this figure for the whole job?'

He nodded. 'I included everything you said.' He reeled off the work, pointing to each part of the calculation for her. 'Have I forgotten something?'

'No, everything is there.' Her lips twisted in thought. 'I suppose you went with the cheapest paint, wallpaper...' And then she began to smile. 'And I'll bet you've given me a massive discount on labour, too. Harvey, you shouldn't have done that.' But she felt better now because it explained why this quote was so cheap compared to

Selena's. By the way Selena was when she was here, it didn't take a genius to see she wasn't going to be giving any reductions simply because Tilly was related to Scott even though he kept going on about family discounts.

Harvey met her gaze. 'I didn't add in any discount.'

'Harvey, I know you and I know people who've used you to renovate their homes. You always give a friends-and-family discount.'

'I do, but I only knock off a percentage after the initial quote. That way the quote is comparable to others.' He seemed to be choosing his words carefully. 'This quote is full price and it's not the cheapest of anything. I've priced up on the basis of high quality, things that will last. I prefer to do it that way so my clients don't get a shock if they choose something top-of-the-range rather than bottom-of-the-range.'

'Right.' She was still staring at the figure he'd reached, a figure considerably lower than the one Selena had given her.

'Tilly, what was the other quote? How much?' Harvey persisted. And when she said nothing, he put a hand on her shoulder. 'You know what, you don't need to tell me. Judging by your reaction it's a lot more. Just tell me, does this other designer know you're getting more quotes? I mean, it's what most people would do – surely they realise?'

Tilly shook her head. 'I intended to even if it was without their knowledge, but I decided I wanted to trust my uncle. He looked upset when I mentioned anything about another estimate.' A thought occurred to her and she aired her concerns out loud. 'Selena might be tricking him too, using him to get to me.'

'It's certainly a possibility,' Harvey replied diplomatically. 'Look, I know what it's like to have family rifts, to not know the whole truth. So, I'm going to tell you what I know.'

He knew something? About Scott?

Luckily the shop was quiet once again, the only sound from passers-by going about their business unaware of how she was feeling right now, as though she didn't know who or what to believe, which way to turn.

'Barney did a bit of investigating.' He pulled a face. 'You know what he's like, he's looking out for you. You gave him the name of this interior designer and he looked online for her.'

Tilly had done the same. 'She says she's old school, doesn't want to be online because she likes to keep it personal with the clients. But Uncle Scott said the website would come eventually, it just takes time.' And Tilly wasn't online herself so she understood where Selena was coming from. Tilly's shop had a presence in the Cove, she got business when tourists came this way and she had visitors who'd found her by word of mouth.

'And while that's admirable, it's unlikely most businesses would survive that way. I know I wouldn't. This shop is different, most of the shops in the Cove are. They've been established for years and if they haven't, they're surrounded by businesses that have been and pull people here to the village. We get a lot of tourists in the high season, those people tell their friends, the friends come and tell others, and so on and so on. Local loyalty goes a long way as well.' He paused. 'Take it from someone who is establishing their own renovations business – there's only so much work you can get from friends and family. In fact, ninety per cent of what I've worked on already has been here in the village, but that'll end. People don't need renovations every year. Melissa has been working hard on establishing an online presence for us, not going too hard at it until I've built up more of a portfolio, so it's a delicate balance. But we have a website, albeit a basic one – just like the bakery, the pub, the waffle shack, Lucy's blacksmithing – and we're on several social media sites, too. Melissa is also looking for opportunities for press coverage as we need to grow.'

She slumped down onto the stool by the till. 'Perhaps I should just ask her. Maybe she's not tech-savvy.' It sounded desperate even to her own ears.

Everyone was always saying how positive Tilly was, how she saw the good in people, and she was proud of being that way. But, perhaps for the first time, today she saw her admirable qualities as something to be wary of. Had Scott come to the Cove to find a piece of his family jigsaw and put right the wrongs of the past or was it true that he didn't have the capacity to change? Had Tilly's positivity and her ability to give people the benefit of the doubt been her worst enemy this time?

'I'll leave you to it.' Harvey collected up his things with a quiet goodbye.

Tilly thought of the couple of thousand pounds she'd already transferred to Scott. And as she looked at a photograph of Grandma Shirley, the one that was in a frame on the wall behind the till, Shirley keeping an eye on Tilly and the shop, sadness flooded her body. She wished Grandma Shirley was here now. Although if she was, Tilly wouldn't be in the same predicament because she wouldn't be running the shop. But at least her grandma could've told her everything about the man who'd been a stranger until recently, she would let Tilly know what she was supposed to do.

Tilly stared at the piece of paper with all of Selena's scribblings, the calculations for the renovations to take her shop to the next stage, the development she'd been so excited about up until now. Was Scott lying to her? Or was he being deceived by Selena? She guessed there was only one way to find out what was going on but she knew she should tread lightly. She didn't want to offend, to ruin the friendship she was forming with her uncle, if it turned out there was nothing to worry about. Quotes came in vastly different from one another all the time, didn't they?

She picked up her phone and called Scott, who seemed pleased to hear from her, and the bond of family warmed her. But he sounded stressed – he was sorry but the breakdown service hadn't been able to fix his truck. He kept apologising over and over. And Tilly didn't mention Harvey doing the quote because she wanted to talk to him about it face to face. Only then would she know if Scott was trying to be a part of the family, whether he knew Selena as well as he thought he did, whether she really had anything to worry about.

By the time Tilly locked up the shop for the day she was exhausted. Even Melissa's text to say they were all congregating for waffles up at the shack couldn't tempt her and she walked home to her cottage, her head all over the place. She barely tasted the shepherd's pie leftovers she warmed up for dinner, she pulled on thick brushed-cotton pyjamas in a trance and lasted only an hour in front of the television before she climbed the stairs to bed.

She'd almost drifted off when her phone rang and, bleary-eyed, she picked it up. 'Dad? Is that you?'

The line broke up a couple of times until finally she could hear her dad a lot more clearly and he assured her that he and her mum were fine. That had been her first worry – that he was calling to say they'd been in an accident – because when the phone rang after the sociable hours the worst always went through your mind and sent that sinking feeling from the top of your head to the tips of your toes.

Tilly was relieved when it appeared her parents were both totally fine.

But that relief didn't last long at all. Not when her dad told her the real reason for his call this late at night.

18

Benjamin wasn't sure which was worse when it came to his parents – bickering and snide remarks or silence and the total avoidance of one another. Either way, it wasn't a great environment to be in and he did his best to ignore the way his dad was being secretive and disappearing off to places, saying nothing of where he was going. It wasn't unusual for some people, but Danny was a sharer and there was a time he'd tell them if he was heading out to grab coffees, a snack from the bakery, or a newspaper. Now, it was radio silence.

Benjamin had even begun to wonder whether his dad was having an affair and, with that thought, he hadn't wanted to go back to the house after work today. He finished the lunchtime shift at the pub and rather than heading straight back to the farm to help out or be there if needed, he took a long walk down The Street, hands pushed into his pockets to keep them from the icy chill. He'd intended to walk all the way to the end, around the bend past the Heritage Inn and out of the village, before looping round and down past the riding stables until he arrived back at the Cove and headed for Mistletoe Gate Farm. But he stopped his walk short when he saw the *Closed* sign on Tilly's Bits 'n' Pieces.

He went into the tea rooms to grab a takeaway coffee and once Etna had finished slicing a generous serving of carrot cake and popped it onto a plate for her customer, he asked whether she knew where Tilly was. 'The shop's closed,' he explained.

'Nice to see you, too, Benjamin,' she frowned.

'I'm sorry, hello, Etna.' His smile won her over. 'She doesn't usually close at such busy times of the day – it's odd, that's all.' And whenever she did close, she always put a sign up on the door to say she'd be back soon so she didn't miss valuable customers.

Patricia came out from the kitchen carrying two full English breakfasts, a popular choice at the tea rooms even well into the afternoon. 'I saw her head off after talking with Lucy. Lucy said Tilly wasn't feeling too well and had gone home.'

That settled it. He ordered his takeaway coffee and asked for a cup of the chicken-and-vegetable soup to go. He barely heard Etna telling him how her friend Kenneth – who some might say was more than a friend – had grown the carrots, the peas and the onions on his allotment.

Benjamin headed to Tilly's cottage and it took him a few attempts at knocking to get her to come to the door. Either she was in bed or ignoring him, and if it was the former, he still wanted to see whether she was all right, whether she needed any help at all.

'You've been crying,' he said the minute she opened the door. Not only were her eyes red and her cheeks flushed, she looked as though she'd used up all her fight and had nothing left.

She opened her mouth presumably to deny it but instead stood back to let him in. She looked cute, bundled up in a chunky, coffee-coloured cardigan that reached almost down to her knees, her hair twisted up into a clip at the back of her head, bangles on her wrist jangling as she closed the door again.

'For you.' He handed her the soup. 'It's chicken-and-vegetable and I'm pretty sure the vegetables are home-grown on Kenneth's allotment but I can't be sure, I wasn't paying attention when Etna gave me the low-down.'

She managed a small smile. 'She does like to go into detail. Sometimes the brain isn't up for it.'

He followed her into the kitchen, where she set down the container. 'It's still warm – eat it now, don't let it go to waste.'

She was facing away from him, towards the cupboards, but opened up the container and leaned in to smell the hearty soup, thanking him again. She took out a spoon and as she sat down at the little table to one side of the kitchen he gingerly sat down opposite and she didn't protest. She didn't seem to mind him being here and so he didn't ask questions, he waited.

'Thank you,' she said when she was halfway through. 'And please thank Etna, this is wonderful.'

'It's all in Kenneth's meat and two veg, I think.'

She almost spat the soup out trying not to laugh. 'Benjamin...' She shook her head but with good humour. 'I almost choked.'

'Apologies for that, but not for making you smile. When did you last eat?'

'Not for hours.'

'You closed the shop.'

She finished the soup and put the empty container in the sink ready to rinse and put out with the recycling. She wrapped her cardigan tighter around her body and came back to the table. With twinkly lights looped around the beams on the ceiling in here it was a cosy part of the cottage in its proportions and its ambience.

'I spoke to my dad late last night.' She looked at him, tugging at the loose strand of wool on her cardigan sleeve at the same time. 'He called me. We hadn't spoken since I told him Uncle Scott was here.'

She told him?

'Dad contacted one of the neighbours and had them go into the house to check something for him. You know, since the burglary.'

He wasn't sure where she was going with this. What did that have to do with Scott? 'I thought you said they'd already documented everything that was missing.'

'Dad had something specific in mind.' She didn't immediately tell him what. Instead, she launched into an explanation about her dad, his brother, his family, gaining momentum and confidence to share everything she now knew.

'Dad told me Scott began his teenage years in a mess, angry as though the world owed him a favour. Nobody ever really knew why – not Dad, not Grandma Shirley. He was disinterested in anyone but himself, he became controlling with my grandma, something I never knew and I don't think Dad knew the extent of until Grandma told him many years later. Scott took money from Shirley, lied all the time. Even when she was sick, he tried to tell her what medicines she should be taking, tried to overrule the medical experts and get her to try some hokey-pokey herbal remedies that would've done more harm than good. It sounds as though Grandma gave him plenty of second chances, opportunities to prove himself, but he wasn't particularly interested because he didn't think that he needed to change. He was a classic narcissist and as far as Scott could see, everyone else was in the wrong, never him.'

Benjamin wasn't sure how much to say. It hadn't exactly gone down well every other time he'd tried to share an opinion about Tilly's uncle. And so, he decided silence was the better option, at least for now.

'According to everything Scott has told me since he came to the Cove, he's wanted to make up for past mistakes, he says he's changed, he wants another chance. But now Dad has told me that he's never admitted to being wrong in any way, and now that he knows Scott is here and has questioned why, it's made me start to think a bit harder about things. I'm starting to wonder whether Scott is trying to deceive me the way he did the rest of his family.'

Benjamin put his hand over both of Tilly's, stretched out in front of her on the table, palms clasped so tightly together it would've taken quite some prising to get them apart. 'The question is, do *you* think he's changed? Do you think he deserves a chance to prove himself?' Because if she did, he'd go with it and be there for her.

'You know I always give people the benefit of the doubt.'

'But...' he said for her.

'Dad also told me that Grandma Shirley left Scott some money in her will, while she left Dad the shop. I already knew that, of course – Scott told me, and he said he'd felt touched so I assumed he was humbled his mum had thought of him even though they were estranged. Dad told me Grandma hadn't wanted to cut Scott off entirely but she also didn't want him to have the business or any portion of it because it meant a lot to her and already she could tell it was something I had a passion for, even though Dad didn't see it yet.

'Another thing Dad said was that Grandma Shirley had asked him to seriously think about how things were with me, how his disapproval for my career choices might be the thing that broke us. And now I know she was talking from experience, that she never wanted Dad and me to stop being father and daughter. So, it was my grandma who saw me having the shop as a way to bridge the gap between me and Dad again. It's just he never told me, and I suppose – how could he? He would've had to explain about Scott but he'd closed off that part of his life. He told me on the phone that Scott had made him angry, upset, he'd taken something from their mother right up until she died and that he couldn't ever forgive him for that.'

'Do you think he should?'

Tilly shrugged. 'I really don't know what to think.'

'What was it your dad wanted his neighbour to check at the house?' he asked, getting back to what had started the conversation thread, the topic before Tilly was side tracked by Scott's back story.

'Dad had begun to wonder why so much in the house was left untouched. At first he'd thought perhaps the burglar was interrupted but then he began to think along other lines once he found out Scott had been in touch with me.'

Benjamin had a sinking feeling about this already so he just listened.

'Scott would've known that the shop went to his brother because he likely remembered my grandma saying she wanted it to stay in the family. She was always saying it, even though she never elaborated on who she saw running it. What Scott wouldn't have known was whether Dad had sold the shop or taken it on himself. The neighbour Dad spoke to confirmed that when the burglary first happened, the study seemed to have been the prime target. More so than the bedroom, where there were several valuables still lurking apart from a couple of pieces of jewellery Mum identified as missing after I couldn't find them anywhere when I searched the house for her – her charm bracelet, for one, which she was devastated about. Dad said he'd bought it for her when they first got married and had added charms ever since – a dog for Curly, our family pet we got when I was five, a book because she loves to read, a daisy as it's her favourite flower, and a house charm he gave her when they bought their first home together. The neighbour also told Dad that some of the files had been taken out of the cabinet and were strewn around.'

She briefly floated into a cloud of nostalgia before she continued. 'I do remember the study being the messiest room of all when I was at the house – drawers open, papers not quite pushed into folders properly – but the shelves had clearly been ransacked because half of the stuff was on the floor. I assumed whoever had gone in there was looking for cash, bank account details, so I simply tidied everything up and didn't think much more about it. There were no bank cards, no password details – I assumed it wasn't anything to worry about. I never told my parents how bad the room had been because I didn't want them to be any more upset than they already were. Hearing how a stranger had gone through their home with such disrespect for their privacy and rights was something I thought could wait until they came home.

'Dad told me that in his study he kept all the paperwork for the shop before it was signed over to me as well as the agreement when I took over the business. He thinks now that it might've been Scott breaking in that night to find out who the shop has been transferred to. The neighbour told him where the papers were and they were apparently in a different folder to where they should be. They were likely part of the mess I randomly pushed into files because I didn't have time to pore over every document.'

'I don't believe it.'

'Me neither. I mean, Dad admits it's far-fetched as a theory but he's planted that little seed of doubt now for me and I don't seem to be able to do much other than dwell on it and worry. I closed the shop because I kept bursting into tears. Pathetic, I know.'

'It isn't pathetic. And I happen to think the theory has merit, it would explain Scott's sudden appearance. Otherwise, it's one hell of a coincidence.'

'How could I have been so trusting?' She balled her fists and thumped them onto the table. 'How could I let him reel me in like that?'

'Tilly, this is *not* your fault. One of your best qualities is that you give people a fair go, you don't make rash judgements.'

'Yeah, well, maybe I should. And what am I supposed to do now? Now that I've let him into my life.'

'I'm not sure what to advise. He's not dangerous, is he?'

Tilly managed a smile. 'Dad says he isn't. What he damages people with are words and actions but not violence.'

'Those can be equally damaging, in my view.'

'Dad partly blames himself about Scott. He thinks if he'd been a better brother or son, he might've been able to sort Scott out.'

'I only have one sister, who is pretty much on the right track, so I can't really say whether he's right, but look at Harvey and Daniel. Both of them soon realised they couldn't run the other one's life, Daniel took responsibility for the mistakes he made. And sometimes people just don't want help, Tilly, no matter how hard you try,' he added softly.

Her eyes pleaded for this not to be true, for her to have a part of her family nearby and still be as excited as she'd been a couple of weeks ago. 'Dad wanted to know whether I'd given Scott any money.' A sheepish look and he knew she had.

'How much?'

When she told him he took the information in and puffed out his cheeks. 'We can't let him get away with it.'

'If it's true.'

'If it's true,' he repeated, but the glance they shared told them both they knew her dad's out-there theory was probably spot on.

He stood up. 'Come on, let's get you back to the shop. We'll talk on the way and work out where to go from here.' And just like that, just as Charlotte had said, he was there to catch her as she fell, as Scott showed his true colours. Because there might be some doubt in her mind but there was absolutely none in his. Scott had come here under the pretence of caring and had taken advantage of Tilly's good nature, and now he had to be stopped.

Tilly tugged at his arm as they left the kitchen. 'Thank you.'

'For the soup?'

'The soup... and for being here for me.' She was looking at the flagstone floor beneath her sock-covered feet. He noticed that even her socks were colourful – bright turquoise with white and yellow daisies. 'You tried to tell me not to trust him and I thought you were interfering.'

He plucked his jacket from the hook in the hallway with his free hand. He didn't want her to let go of his arm. 'No apology necessary.' He wanted to kiss away the sadness, make it all disappear. And when her phone buzzed, he asked, 'Is that Scott?'

She dropped his arm, checked and nodded, holding the phone, unsure what to do.

'Answer it,' he said, thinking quickly, 'but don't say anything else yet. Just keep him talking.'

She answered it and put it on speakerphone. Scott was telling her that his truck was at last fixed but rather than bring over the furniture he wanted her to go with him to another vintage furniture fair tomorrow.

Benjamin had tapped out a note on his phone and showed her.

Tilly read out what he'd written, brow furrowed in confusion at where this was leading. 'I can't,' she said, 'I've got a terrible cold at the moment and wouldn't want to pass it on.'

'Another one? Jeez, that's unlucky.'

'Tell me about it.' She didn't need that written down, she adlibbed just enough.

'I'd offer to come over but I have another job – starting in the afternoon,' he backtracked, 'the fair is in the morning.'

'I'm fine, it'll pass, I'm sure,' she said, repeating Benjamin's typed-out speech. She pulled a face that showed she had no idea where all this was headed but Benjamin was keeping the conversation going by typing more notes and Tilly dutifully repeated them. 'I'm really excited about all our plans. But I've been thinking...

when I renovate, maybe I could push out the back of the shop too.' She was half-smiling at the conspiracy.

Scott seemed surprised but, true to form, fell into the trap Benjamin had wanted to plant with those words. 'Yeah, great idea. Don't get anyone in just yet, though, I've got a mate who can help, he's done similar here near my flat in Lowestoft.'

Benjamin rolled his eyes. Of course he had a mate, these sorts of men always did.

'Can you get me a quote?' Tilly asked, reciting Benjamin's next note. 'Only trouble is...' Her pause was partly to show hesitation but also because Benjamin's fingers didn't work that fast on the screen. 'I'm embarrassed to tell you this...' – another pause, more typing from Benjamin – 'but I'm in trouble. The roof at the shop needs emergency repairs and I have to do them or close... for health-and-safety reasons.'

Benjamin was typing as quickly as he could.

'I'm cashing in an ISA I forgot I had,' she said next. 'The amount will cover the repairs but I can't get it for another week or two. Is there any way you could lend me the money? I'll put it back into your account by Christmas and carry on as we were.'

Benjamin was glad Scott wasn't quite so quick-thinking that he came back with anything other than a few grunts that eventually gave way to, 'Selena has bought things already.'

Benjamin had a reply all worked out.

'I know, but it's literally a couple of weeks tops,' said Tilly, 'and then the roof will be done and I can return the money, with another few thousand or whatever your friend needs for the deposit for an expansion.'

The talk of thousands more got Scott excited.

'It's okay,' Tilly stammered, taking the reins, not needing Benjamin's dictation. 'I know it's too big a thing to ask so don't worry. I'll close the shop for a while and wait until I have more money. Only thing is, we'll have to put our plans on hold. Can't do anything until that roof is fixed.'

'No, don't do that,' Scott leapt in quickly. 'I'll transfer the money you gave me back your way, then you can do the transfer to me again. Do you think your money will be through by Christmas?'

'The bank assures me it will. Oh, thank you, Uncle Scott. I really think these plans are going to transform the shop.'

'They will, and what else is family for? We help one another, right?' He was almost high on the fact she'd announced she wanted the expansion to be bigger and better, giving him the opportunity to trick her into handing over more money.

'That's right,' Tilly managed and she only grimaced after ending the call. 'That was horrible,' she said to Benjamin.

'Could've fooled me, for a moment I thought you were enjoying it.'

She pulled a face. 'I kind of started to. It was nice to feel a bit in control. I seem to sway between being upset and being angry. But what if we're wrong? What if he finds out how much I've doubted him and, actually, it wasn't him who broke into my parents place?' One look at Benjamin and she added, 'We're not wrong, are we?'

He didn't answer, just helped her on with her coat and they set off for the shop.

'It's funny,' she said as they made their way down the front path and turned to walk along the lane. 'I don't feel so awkward admitting being wrong to you or to Barney or anyone else here, but telling my dad, confirming that he was right all along – I don't want to have to do that.'

'You think he'll say, I told you so?'

'In a way, although he'd never say it. I just don't want to disappoint him.'

He nudged her. 'I'm pretty sure you could never do that.'

And when she linked his arm with a smile, he knew he at least had his friend back. He wanted more, so much more, but for now it was enough for him to help her and see her happier.

He also knew now what he had to do and so once they'd reached the shop he told her he was heading back to the farm to help out, but he had absolutely no intention of doing so. Because he had somewhere else to go.

And if his hunch was right, this might just get Tilly the answers she needed.

19

Tilly was grateful that the shop had been incredibly busy in the days since she'd closed up and run home to her cottage, unable to fathom what to do next. It had kept her focused, and she'd drawn strength from Benjamin's encouragement not only that day but in the days following, when they'd come up with a way to deal with her uncle Scott. And now, three days after wanting to hide behind closed doors and make it all go away, she was ready for action.

Tilly waved to Scott when he arrived at the shop, smiling as though nothing was out of the ordinary at all. As far as he would know, it was business as usual.

'It's going to snow soon,' he said the moment he stepped inside.

She wished he wouldn't mention snowfall because she didn't ever want to associate anything so beautiful with his dishonesty and lack of integrity. Still, she could always make herself envisage the ugly, dirty slush that formed when the snow began to melt.

Benjamin had left her to it that day he'd walked her back to the shop but he'd returned at closing time. He'd confessed he hadn't really been to the farm like he'd said, but that he'd been somewhere else.

'Can we talk properly?' he'd asked her as she began to switch off the lights.

'Sure, how about a drink in the pub?' She felt she needed to make it up to him, to let him know how grateful she was to have a friend like him looking out for her.

He hesitated. 'I think this is a conversation you'd prefer to have in private.'

She led him out the back behind the curtain and they sat on the stools she had out there while he told her where he'd been.

'When I bumped into your uncle the first time, at the farm, I had a vague feeling I'd seen him somewhere before but I couldn't think where. It baffled me for ages. It was only earlier on when he called you and he said he had a mate who'd done work near his flat in Lowestoft that I twigged where it was I'd seen him.'

Tilly braced herself. 'Go on.'

'I went out in Lowestoft for a pre-Christmas get-together with some friends I've known since college and as we were leaving the pub, we heard shouting from a shop a few doors down and saw some man being thrown out on his ear.'

She'd closed her eyes briefly. 'Don't tell me... Uncle Scott.'

He nodded. 'I went into the shop today even though it was a long shot but when I talked about the night in question the owner remembered it – he said it wasn't often he got yelled at. He told me everyone assumes the owner of a pawn shop would get into lots of trouble but contrary to popular opinion, it's a relatively sedate clientele he has and this was his first whiff of bother in a long while.'

'What happened?'

'Scott had been in once before to pawn something and he clearly thought it was a good place to get rid of whatever he needed to, but this time he went back with a sports watch and a fancy clock. The owner told him he had reason to believe the watch was a fake and he didn't want to take either item on that basis. Scott got angry, then.'

Tilly closed her eyes. 'What did he sell the first time he went in there?' But she already knew the answer before Benjamin took something out of his pocket.

He handed her the charm bracelet her mum had treasured, with its house charm, the miniature dog, all the beautiful charms she'd collected along the way, and Tilly closed her fingers around it, all doubts about whether her dad was right about Scott gone.

Tilly had burst into tears that night in the shop after Benjamin told her and gave her the bracelet. He'd held her close for a long while until she felt ready to walk home and then they'd made the walk together to her cottage, where they'd drunk mulled wine beside the Christmas tree and talked until both of them could barely keep their eyes open. But that night, as well as Benjamin consoling Tilly, they'd come up with a plan.

Now, with the money back in her account from Scott thanks to quick thinking on Benjamin's part that day when Scott was on the other end of the phone, the ball was well and truly in Tilly's court. And today, she wasn't upset, or at least not *as* upset. She was, however, furious.

Tilly offered Scott a cup of tea – something she always did. She let him talk about a vintage fair he'd been to, her hands shaking as she picked up her own cup of tea, and suddenly she regretted not accepting Benjamin's offer to be here with her for this. But she'd got herself into this mess; she was going to get herself out of it.

'Look at this table, Tilly.' Scott turned his phone around so she could see a photo. 'You could sand it down, varnish it and sell it for eight times as much as you'll pay for it.'

'You think I should buy it?'

'Definitely.' And because she'd been quiet rather than her usual chatty and enthusiastic self, he finally asked, 'Something up?'

'I'm fine.' This was what she'd wanted – him here on her turf, sitting comfortably before she threw everything at him. 'I spoke to Dad.'

'Oh? How is he?' The penny took a while to drop. 'You told him I was here.' He scraped his hand through his blond hair that was greasier than she'd seen it before. 'And I suppose, judging by the way you're acting, he had plenty to say about that. Jeez, the man doesn't do second chances. And just like Mum, he never let me prove myself.'

'So you really *have* changed?'

He seemed put out she might be doubting it. 'I told you I have.'

Her heart thumping, she delivered her next line. 'Is that why you broke into my parents' house?'

The moment of gobsmacked silence didn't last long. He harrumphed. 'Now you're talking crazy, or your dad is, I'm not sure which of you came up with that little gem. It's a bit of a hike for me to do a burglary, isn't it? If I was going to rob someone, I couldn't be arsed going all that way. I'd be doing it a bit closer to home, save on the petrol.' He snorted when he laughed, a horrible sound, a sound so far from the man he'd let her believe he was.

'You're saying it wasn't you?' She'd have laughed if she wasn't so riled up with the lies he continued to spin and the disregard he showed for her feelings, for the hospitality she'd shown him ever since he came here to the Cove.

'Of course it wasn't, Tilly. What's got into you? I told you Nigel would do this if he knew I was here. This is exactly why I didn't want you to tell him yet – not until I'd had a chance to be on your side for a while, show I'd changed.'

He certainly was going all out to keep this little pretence going. Furthermore, he knew full well that her parents were on the cruise until well into the new year, so it wasn't too much of a risk for him that they'd get wind of his visit until long after he got his money back from Tilly and likely a whole lot more.

He ploughed on, pleading. 'Tilly, come on, we're working well together. I'm putting in all this effort to go to fairs to find things for you, Selena has done a lot of the chasing around for suitable materials, we'll be raring to go for you really soon. And I've found someone to come and do a quote for the extension. He can come tomorrow morning.'

She pushed her cup further away, having not even taken a sip. 'Why do you keep lying?'

It was like watching a child as his eyes widened and he insisted that he wasn't. 'I'm not. We're family, come on, Tilly.'

She reached beneath the counter and pulled out a small velvet pouch, which she upended until the charm bracelet tumbled out. But when she looked at him, he seemed oblivious. He was seeing a piece of jewellery with no meaning attached, something he didn't care about in the slightest. This bracelet, so special to her mum, to her dad, meant nothing to him. Family didn't mean much either and it had taken Tilly far too long to see the ugly truth.

'It's nice,' he shrugged. 'Someone will buy it,' he assured her, adding in a big noisy slurp of his tea on top.

'It's too special to sell. It means a lot to Mum, and to Dad.' He looked as though he was tired of listening. 'I picked it up in a shop in Lowestoft, actually – well, I didn't, a friend did.'

His cheeks took on a different colour and he had the grace to put his cup down. He stood and hoisted up his jeans that seemed way too big around the waist.

Tilly waited for him to say something, anything, but when he did, she liked it even less than she would've thought.

'This shop should've been mine.' He narrowed his eyes, his words coming out with spittle, his true character bubbling up to the surface. 'I was robbed when our own mother left it to Nigel and not me. You know, when I first met you, Tilly, I thought you were fair and reasonable. Try seeing this from my point of view.'

'Why don't you try seeing it from mine?' She folded her arms across her body. 'I trusted you, I let you into my life, and this is the way you repay me.'

'As I've said, I was robbed – half of this shop should've been mine.'

'Why would you think you were entitled to it?'

'Well, I'm more entitled than you are!' he snarled.

'Grandma Shirley loved this place.' Her voice shook and she hated that it did. 'She was proud of it. She threw all her energies into it and she passed it to Dad knowing he'd do the right thing. It turned out the right thing was for me to run it. You would've sold it!' Her voice rose but she gulped at the way she'd hurled the accusation – no taking it back now. 'You never cared about this family.' When he didn't try to convince her otherwise, she looked right at him as she said, 'Dad was right, you won't ever change.'

The expletives that came out of her uncle's mouth had Tilly frozen to the spot, unable to say much more at all. She let him run with it, the foul language assaulting her from all angles as his anger echoed around the shop about how life had dealt him crap, and it just kept coming – that his own family hadn't even helped him, it was as though the whole world owed him everything and he wasn't about to lift a finger to make changes himself.

When he marched around to her side of the till it was the first time in his presence she'd been scared. 'What are you doing?' she shrieked, stepping out of the way before he could push her.

He opened the cash register and positioned his body in such a way that she couldn't reach past him to close it again. He reeked of cigarettes, of clothes that needed a good wash. 'I'm taking what's rightfully mine,' he said casually as he snatched the notes out of the till and shoved coins into his pocket.

Tilly knew she didn't have the strength to fight him. She told herself that at least she had all that money back in her account. 'You don't have to do this.'

'What, you're going to give me a chance, are you?' he snapped. 'Nah, didn't think so.' And he looked around for what else he could take.

When he picked up the bracelet, she opened her mouth but nothing came out.

'From what I remember, this is worth a bit. Why do you think I took it? Plenty of pawn shops around, you know.' He held it high above his head, enjoying the game of Tilly trying to leap up and get it as he held it out of her reach.

By now she was crying and wondered what else he was going to take of hers. But a thunderous voice came from the door before he could ransack the entire shop.

'Stop right there!' the voice boomed.

'Dad!' Tilly ran towards him, straight into his arms, a place she hadn't been in years. It had been tentative hugs hello and goodbye, but right now she'd never felt safer.

'Oh, the cavalry's arrived.' Scott's voice dripped with disdain but her dad's gaze pinned him to the spot.

Her dad might be retired but he was like a big bear protecting its cubs as he left Tilly by the bay window and advanced towards Scott. Scott, for all his bravado, stood wide-eyed as though he was waiting for Nigel to tear him apart.

Nigel took the bracelet from him. 'The police are a phone call away, Tilly, if this goes sideways.' He didn't look at her, only at his brother. 'I don't want to call them, I don't dislike you that much, Scott. I feel sorry for you.'

Scott didn't say anything. It was odd seeing the two of them face to face, men who were strangers in everything except the biology that gave the same straightness to their noses, the same naturally blond hair that for one had evolved over time but for the other had been covered up with something fake.

'Why did you come back?' Nigel demanded. 'Why now, after all this time?' He shook his head when Scott said nothing. 'You know what, I don't need to know. When Tilly said you were here, at first I panicked and then I thought about my daughter doing her best to give you a chance. I thought of her kind nature, I thought perhaps I should try to be a bit more like her and do the same. It took me less than a couple of hours to realise that that's Tilly, she's trusting – oh, she's savvy, too, but she'll let you prove yourself first – and I decided I wanted her to know all the facts rather than just what you've shared with her.'

Nigel didn't let his brother get a word in and, for once, it seemed Scott had become the silent type. 'I wasn't a hundred per cent sure it was you who had broken into our home but I followed my gut feeling.' He looked at the bracelet in his palm. 'And now I know for sure.' The anger had faded and now there was a sadness Tilly would never understand as an only child. She could only imagine how it must feel to be betrayed by someone you thought would never do such a thing.

'This shop should've been mine,' Scott spat, repeating what he'd already said to Tilly.

'You never would've kept it in the family.' It was as though all of the anger inside him had almost deflated Nigel but still he stood tall. 'You would've sold it the first chance you got. That's why Mum didn't want to leave it to you.'

'This is worth a lot more than the cash I got.' Resentment laced his every word as he nodded here and there around the shop, at its four walls and everything in it.

'That's all this is to you, isn't it?' said Nigel. 'It's all about money.'

'Hey, money makes the world go round.'

'And so does family, loyalty, kindness.'

Tilly could tell Scott wasn't taking in a word of this at all. Some people deserved a second chance, some people made the most of it when they got one, but Benjamin was right, there was only so much you could do and not everyone even wanted to be helped.

Scott pushed past Nigel and Tilly backed away as he stormed out of the shop into the pouring rain and didn't glance back once.

It was then that Tilly's legs buckled. Her dad caught her in time and rocked her as though she was still his little girl. She was vaguely aware of Benjamin coming in and her dad telling him he had everything in hand, she saw her dad's arm turn the sign on the shop to *Closed*, and later she could remember being led through tears out the back behind the curtain and up the stairs, away from it all.

* * *

In one of the rooms above Tilly's shop, Nigel handed Tilly a second mug of coffee topped with a shot of rum from the hip flask in his pocket.

'Dad, it's ten in the morning,' she giggled as she took the coffee. 'I don't want to be drunk on the job.'

'Just don't tell your mother.'

The rum had quite a hit but it was welcome. After the shock, her dad had settled her up here, called her mum at the tea rooms to quickly update her, and he'd made them both a steaming mug of coffee laced with alcohol.

'You know, I might not get up from this position at my age.' Tilly had put down two huge cushions for them to take a seat and her dad patted the cushion beneath him after he screwed the top back on his hip flask, the gift Tilly had sent him for Christmas last year, made specially by Lucy at Lucy's Blacksmithing.

Her parents had left their cruise soon after Nigel called his daughter. Nigel hadn't been able to get out of his head the worry that Scott was here in the Cove, that Tilly had given him money, that he was pretending to be on her side. If Scott really was being honest then so be it, and Nigel had come with a semi-open mind, but when he'd arrived at the shop it had been apparent that, much as he hadn't wanted to be, he was right. The man had been taking his kind-hearted, trusting daughter for a ride.

'I'm so naive, Dad.' Tilly looked at the floorboards, the hole down which she knew a lot of dirt was lurking.

'Don't beat yourself up. He's clever, he reels people in.'

Tilly nodded and suddenly a thought occurred. 'Are you staying with me at the cottage?'

'Gracious, no,' Nigel chuckled. 'We wouldn't do that to you. We're staying with Barney.'

'Barney?'

'We tried to book in at the Heritage Inn but it's fully booked with Christmas coming and with Melissa's wedding. Your mother called Barney and asked if he could suggest anywhere close by and he insisted we stay with him. The bags are still in the car but Barney intercepted us outside the tea rooms. He looks out for you, you know. I get the feeling if he'd known Scott was coming into the shop today, he would've been one of the first to be here for you.'

'I wanted to confront him on my own.' She looked at her dad. 'Probably not the best idea. I don't know him, after all.'

Her dad put his hand over hers. 'He'll never admit to being wrong. And your grandma used to wonder how he could possibly be a part of this family. She'd say it jokingly but she meant it, and it made her sad.'

'It must have made you sad, too.'

He sipped his coffee, pulling a face for a moment at the hit of rum. 'It did when I let it. Not talking about him, ever, was my way to manage it over the years. Perhaps I shouldn't have kept it all so quiet, we could've avoided this whole fiasco.'

'He might still have found a way,' Tilly said to make him feel better. None of this was his fault, none of this was anyone's fault apart from Scott's. 'I'm glad you got here when you did, Dad.'

He cleared his throat. 'I know I haven't always been forthcoming with praise when it came to this shop and your insistence on following a career that you think I never approved of.'

'You don't,' she said, not unkindly, just as a fact.

'I didn't, not at first. I said some terrible things to you about what you chose to study, how textiles was nothing more than a hobby, how retail was dead-end. I'm embarrassed at the things I said, Tilly.'

She gulped at his recollection. Had those words plagued him the way they had her for a long time, yet he'd said nothing? 'You wanted what was best for me, I get that.'

'Oh no, do not let me off the hook. This is an apology as well as an explanation, from the bottom of my heart. I didn't approve then because I was all too aware of what might happen if you didn't follow the right path. I've told you that when I used to let myself think about things, I'd get sad about Scott – so I pushed those thoughts away where I believed his estrangement from our family and everything that led to it wouldn't affect me. But I see now that it did. I let Scott's behaviour influence my way of thinking. Without me realising it, he was always at the back of my mind. He had as many opportunities as I did but chose not to stay in school – which might be the right choice for plenty of people but he took it as his licence to bum around and do whatever he liked. He wasn't bad at school, which is why it never made sense that he left. He could've had a very different future if only he'd tried. I don't think I'll ever understand why he didn't go and look for a job or find an apprenticeship. Instead, he spent his time on the seafront in the amusements, wasting his money, occasionally winning big, declaring he was going to game his way to the future. He wanted to enter quizzes and win prizes, he wanted to gamble, and for a while all of that kept him going.

'As soon as his luck ran out, he looked elsewhere to make what I can only assume he regarded as a living – petty theft, mostly. He stole a bike once, got caught by the owner, who took pity on him when he apologised and gave him another chance. But he never took it as a warning he needed to sort himself out. He'd steal money from Mum, come here to the Cove when she first got the shop and put his hand in the till, all the while pretending he was here to spend time with her. And he was her son; it took her a long time and a lot of courage to refuse to give in to his demands any longer and tell him to stay away. I was at university during the worst times, when she found out just how much he'd stolen from her. He tried to make her think she was getting forgetful, that she might have dementia.'

'That's cruel.' Her heart broke a little bit to think of her grandma being manipulated like that.

'The cruellest thing was that she actually began to wonder whether she really was losing her mind. She lost her confidence. I came home one summer and found him stealing, heard him telling her to put her accounts in his name so she didn't fall prey to a scam. I confronted him, he gave me a few choice words, and that was the last time I spoke to him.'

He smiled. 'You get your determination from your grandma, and your capability. Mum was the one who finally sent Scott on his way, you know. She told him she didn't want him in her life after she caught him stealing her jewellery – the eternity ring your grandad had given her, a bracelet from her own christening, the carriage clock from your grandad's retirement. She realised then that Scott wasn't ever going to change. It can't have been easy to admit that about her own son.'

Tilly shook her head. 'Poor Grandma. It must've been horrible for her.'

He smiled kindly. 'Having you around so much mended her heart a little. She adored you right from when she first cuddled you as a newborn. But she took the pain of losing a son to her grave. And I'm afraid that I took his failures and worst characteristics and turned them into my own fears.' He looked around the room, bare now but right above a shop filled with beautiful things in a community filled with so much friendship and love. 'Coming here, I see you've done everything right and I shouldn't have worried. I'm really very proud of you, Tilly.'

Her voice caught. 'We've never spoken like this before.'

'And that was wrong.' He smiled. 'Maybe we're both a bit stubborn.'

She let his comments settle before she told him she'd got carried away with the idea of expanding the shop. 'I saw it as a way to really prove to you that I was more than just a shop girl; I wanted to show you I was a business owner, a forward-thinking one who excelled.'

'Tilly, I saw that in you way before I gave you the shop. It's *why* I gave you the shop. I wanted it to stay in the family, of course, but more than that, I knew you had a creative side I hadn't respected, a colourful side just like Mum had, and when I signed those papers giving you ownership, I was excited.'

'You were?'

'Of course. My little girl was going to run a business that had significant sentimental meaning for me – that meant the world. And whether you kept it as a candle shop or turned it into the equivalent of the famous Liberty store in London made no difference to me. Do you see that now?'

She nodded, tears in her eyes. 'I do.'

When he leaned across and put his arm around her shoulders, she had a sudden pang of guilt. 'What about your cruise? Can you join it again somewhere? I feel terrible you left to come and help me.'

'We probably could if we really wanted to, but I don't think we will. Your mother looked happy as anything as we drove into the Cove and she saw all the decorations, the nativity scene outside the chapel, the shop fronts all festive. I'd have no chance of getting her back on a boat this side of New Year.'

'Heritage Cove does do Christmas well,' Tilly agreed. 'You wait till you go into the pub. Benjamin's Christmas menu is delicious – try the sticky date pudding and you'll never look back.'

'Benjamin? He's the young lad who came by the shop earlier.'

'That's right... what's that look for?'

'He was worried about you.'

'We're good friends.'

Her dad nodded, presumably knowing he was unlikely to get any more details. 'Tilly, do you need to reopen the shop straight away?'

'I don't have to. Why?'

'How about lunch and a piece of that sticky date pudding?' He pushed himself up to standing.

And with a smile she told her dad, 'That sounds like the best idea I've heard in a long while.'

20

Today was the last day of trading for trees at Mistletoe Gate Farm for the next forty-eight hours or so because at four o'clock they'd be closing the business to make way for the final preparations for tomorrow's wedding and the day after that would be dedicated to clearing up. Danny was out somewhere again – Benjamin had no idea where, only that he'd been gone ages – and Benjamin had volunteered to chop more logs, which were selling fast. The temperatures weren't much above zero in the day and with the holidays fast approaching, it seemed everyone wanted to stock up for their log burners and open fires.

As Benjamin chopped, he thought about Tilly. He'd been relieved to see her walk into the pub yesterday with her dad and even more relieved at the look she cast his way that told him she was doing fine, that the drama was over for now and hopefully for good. Her dad commanded a presence and not only could Benjamin see why he and Tilly had butted heads often enough, he could also see how Nigel's appearance in the Cove would've left Scott in no doubt that if he messed with Tilly, he'd have him to answer to. Watching them as they waved Tilly's mum over and settled together at the table at the rear corner of the pub, Benjamin could already see Tilly basking in the attention from her family that she'd craved for so long. He hoped it was the start of them breaking down some barriers and beginning to repair any of the damage. She was warm-hearted, a beautiful person through and through, and he got the impression her dad might be the same.

Nigel had come to the bar to order drinks as his wife and daughter looked over the menu for their main course, although they'd already decided on sticky date pudding for dessert.

'You look like you could use this,' said Benjamin when the pint of Guinness was ready.

'I think I've aged ten years since Tilly told me my brother was in Heritage Cove.'

'How's Tilly doing?'

'She's fine. A bit numb, I think; beating herself up for being so trusting.'

'Tilly wouldn't be Tilly if she didn't give people the benefit of the doubt,' he shrugged, sharing a smile with her dad.

Nigel looked over his shoulder to make sure they wouldn't be overheard. 'She told me you tried to warn her about Scott from the start.'

'Tilly has a strong family ethic, which I think she learnt from you, and she did what she thought was best. Scott played his hand very well, by the sounds of it. I'm just glad she realised the truth before he did a lot more damage.'

Nigel shook his head. 'Doesn't bear thinking about, does it?'

'You think he's gone for good?'

'Let's hope so, but Tilly will be on her guard. Thank you for looking out for her.'

'What are friends for?' Benjamin had set all of the drinks onto a tray for Nigel.

Benjamin hadn't had a chance to talk with Tilly on her own but he'd caught her eye a few times as the family ate their lunch and she'd smiled back at him, and it was that smile he thought of now as he finished stacking a pile of logs and Danny reappeared.

'Thanks for the hard work, son.' Danny patted him on the shoulder.

'No worries, keeps me fit.' They shared a knowing laugh. 'What took you so long?'

'I took a load of trees to the florist.' With the farm closed to visitors on days when they would ordinarily get a lot of custom, Danny had spoken with Valerie at the florist and they'd agreed she would stack a whole load of trees out the front. Heather would put a sign up tomorrow morning directing customers to the florist rather than buy from here at the farm.

'You were gone a while.' The more his dad had sloped off elsewhere, the more he'd wondered whether Danny was having an affair, especially when he was so evasive about where he'd been or why he'd taken so long. Might that be the real reason for the divorce? He'd noticed yesterday that Danny had even had a haircut, when usually it took a lot of nagging for him to get it done. Benjamin had toyed with the idea of getting it over and done with and asking one or both of his parents outright about the divorce but he knew deep down that it wasn't a good idea right before the wedding. The last thing he wanted was tension in the air, and he also wanted his sister by his side for this.

'We have a lot of trees,' Danny shrugged. 'That's why it took a while. And besides, I got to enjoy a cuddle with baby Thomas while Valerie was serving a customer.' His breath came out cold against the air as he smiled. 'Took me back to when you and Charlotte were babies. She'll be here in a few hours.'

Nice change of subject, Dad. The conversation was over and as Danny was distracted by something on his phone, Benjamin took off his work gloves. He watched customers milling around, he breathed in the scent of pine and the feeling of home. But the warmth he felt soon turned to a chill when he realised their days were likely numbered. The Doyles and Mistletoe Gate Farm could be coming to an end and it was the saddest thing he'd ever known.

* * *

The sun hadn't had a chance to rise before Benjamin's alarm woke him the next morning in time to get organised for the wedding of the year. He smiled. Today he got to see two very good friends get married and start the next phase of their life together. And he also got to see Tilly.

Some of the wedding preparations had been done last night – his dad had jet-washed the veranda the day before and so they'd been able to sweep and wipe down parts that had inevitably got dirty with it being so close to the working tree farm. It meant that this morning it would only need a once-over to be clean. Even though the trees were all well-shaped, those closest to the wedding set-up had been given a bit of extra attention to ensure they were perfect. By the back doors they'd lined up boxes of decorations, the sets of fairy lights they were going to thread into the row of trees closest to the house for a sparkling backdrop to the wedding, vases, candles, all the paraphernalia Melissa and Harvey had selected, ready to put the whole lot up this morning – they hadn't wanted to risk doing it last night in case there was a freak storm or a gusty wind that ruined everything.

Benjamin put on a pot of coffee in the kitchen. It was so early the heating hadn't really been on long enough to feel warm and he let his coffee toast him up as he stood at the kitchen window looking out over the veranda into the darkness but to where he knew the grass was ready with the dancefloor area that had been delivered so late last night they'd panicked it wasn't coming.

'Brewed enough for two?' Charlotte's voice broke into his thoughts as he stood there. She'd been held up in traffic last night and hadn't arrived till much later than planned, practically wanting to fall into bed when she got here. Only a look between them both had told Benjamin that she was just as apprehensive about what was going on with their parents as he was but that it could wait for the time being.

Benjamin took out another mug from the cupboard and did the honours by making his sister a coffee and, both cradling a brew, talk at last turned to their parents.

'Mum seems quieter than usual but she hasn't told me anything,' said Charlotte. Both of them had wondered whether she would perhaps open up to her daughter even if she hadn't tried with her son. Charlotte had always been able to talk to Heather, but maybe it was their mother's way of protecting her children to keep it bottled up. And Benjamin supposed both of his parents were tactful enough not to let anything blow up until after the wedding.

'I think Dad might be having an affair.' His words were like bullets, but he'd held the thought in for so long that it flew out before he could think of how it might make Charlotte feel.

'Are you serious?'

'He's nipping out more than usual, he's evasive when I ask where he's gone, and he had a delivery the other day – his favourite aftershave, which I know he stopped wearing a long time ago because the bottle has been gathering dust in his bathroom for years now. I saw it when I went to borrow toothpaste one night and asked him why he didn't throw it out. He just shrugged. But now, all of a sudden he's got more in.'

'That doesn't mean he's having an affair, Benjamin.'

'He got a haircut the other day, too – without being prompted.'

She smiled because she likely remembered their mum nagging their dad about how his hair was well over his ears and looked terrible. Danny's response usually was to pull on a hat to cover it and his actions had even made his wife laugh.

'There's no other explanation that I can see,' said Benjamin, 'unless it's a financial problem that has really come between them. That's another good reason to hold a wedding here – if finances are the problem, it might be another arm to add to the business and switch things around.' He looked at Charlotte. 'I know, it's wishful thinking.'

'Finances would be enough to break the strongest of couples,' she frowned. 'But Mum and Dad? I never thought it would break them. I never thought anything would. Do you really think it's too late? Did those papers get filed? I mean, you said they were here, you found them – maybe that means things never reached the point of no return.'

At first he said nothing but after another swig of coffee he told his sister, 'This is Harvey and Melissa's day, but once the wedding is over we'll talk to them. I know it's their relationship, but they need to be honest if the business is struggling. I take it you're still interested in taking over one day.'

'Of course,' she sighed. 'I've always wanted it, ever since I was a little girl. But I assumed I had at least five or ten more years before Mum and Dad wanted to slow down or retire.'

'Are you in a position to take the business on now?' If she was, at least it would stay in the family. If the farm got sold then she'd never get it back again.

'I'd have to do some figures and talk with my bank manager.' Her gaze drifted outside rather than on him. 'They were both so quiet last night. Usually, no matter how late I arrive, they're up for talking into the early hours. I tried to tell myself it was because of all the wedding preparations, but maybe not.' Her voice wobbled when she said, 'This is where we grew up. Mistletoe Gate Farm is the stuff of dreams – it's as beautiful as it sounds. Remember how we used to run up and down the track as kids, getting told off if we went beyond the gate?'

He began to laugh. 'I remember you kissing Lee Maynard by the gate and Dad catching you there.'

'Dad couldn't stand him,' she winced. 'He was a total bad boy. He couldn't kiss, either.'

'Whoa sis, way too much information.'

'Talking of love lives—'

'I wasn't aware that we were.'

'We are now... what's the deal with you and Tilly?'

'We're good friends, I'd like it to be more,' he confided before he told her everything that had gone on with Scott, the way her parents came to the Cove, how she'd had a narrow escape but got all her money back.

'Talk about drama,' she said with a shake of her head. 'But now her uncle is out of the picture, what's stopping you from telling her how you feel?'

He hesitated before he admitted, 'I think Zoe took away some of my confidence when it comes to women.'

Her fingers poked through the handle of her mug as she held it securely to take another sip. 'You never said that before.'

He looked outside at the sun beginning to brave rising, golden, highlighting the frost that had been there all along but was almost invisible before in the dark beyond the glass. 'I thought Zoe and I were in a good place, but once she ended things I realised we hadn't been right for a long while. Despite that, I was trying hard to keep the romance alive, I did what I could to keep her happy, but perhaps that was my mistake. Maybe if I'd been more myself and accepted that things weren't working then it wouldn't have been such a bad breakup. I mean, people change, it's life.'

'So why has that dented your confidence?'

'Zoe and I were horrible to each other in the end. I think she got nasty in the hope of driving me away, I see that now. But we aren't in touch any more and for a while I missed the laughs, the friendship.'

'And you think the same could happen with you and Tilly.'

'I'd hate to lose her as a friend. I'd rather have that than nothing at all.' He turned his back to the window and leaned against the sink. He looked across at their indoor tree, the branches laden with ornaments they'd collected over the years, memories from childhood and family times brought forward from past to present. He'd switched the lights on the second he came in the room – the first person up always did – and already he knew he'd hate it when they took it down once the season was over, perhaps for the very last time.

Charlotte set down her mug. 'It sounds to me as though Tilly is always willing to see the best in people, to believe in the good rather than the bad. So if you got together and it didn't work out, she seems the sort who would stay friends. I mean, you both live here in the village and that's kind of how it works in the Cove. And, Benjamin... stop talking about you and Tilly breaking up when you haven't even got together yet.' She smiled and nudged his ribs. 'And Tilly is great, I can imagine having her as a sister-in-law.'

'Steady on – you tell me off for talking about breaking up when we're not even together. I think it's a bit presumptuous to be talking marital bliss.'

'I never liked Zoe, you know.'

'Oh, I know,' he grinned, amused that she thought she needed to tell him.

'Actually, that's not right. It wasn't that I didn't like her, it was more that she never fitted in. She always hated going out into the fields – she was constantly worrying about her hair or her make-up or her footwear. There's nothing wrong with that, but the farm is a very big part of who you are. Even with your own career as a chef you still help out here and I know you enjoy it. I mean, can you imagine having kids and them wanting to run around here and have fun? She'd have been right on top of that and they'd have had to sit on the veranda sensibly, stay clean.'

'All right, you've made your point,' he laughed, because it was all true. 'And now you've gone from marriage to kids.'

'I should stop, shouldn't I?' she teased with another nudge. 'You know, Mum suggested a few years back that you and I might take on this place together one day.'

'She mentioned that to me, too. But you're the business woman, sis.'

'With my business sense and your culinary skills we could do so much.' She ploughed on. 'I visited a Christmas tree farm near where I live – you know me, no way was I having the lead-up to Christmas without a tree to look at – anyway, they had a small restaurant on site.'

'You want to open up a restaurant here?'

'It's just an idea and it's always nice to dream, isn't it?'

He nodded but their conversation stalled when they heard footsteps. It was Heather.

'Both of my children in the kitchen together,' she announced as if they didn't know it already. A smile had quickly taken the place of the weary look she'd had as she came into the room. Benjamin wasn't sure whether the look now was genuine or put on for their benefit. 'It's just like old times.' She put an arm around Benjamin's shoulders even though it was a stretch for her, her other arm around her daughter. 'I've missed this.'

'Mum, it isn't that long since I came to stay,' Charlotte insisted as Heather got on with pouring herself a mug of coffee. 'And you know how much I love it here.'

'Do I smell coffee?' It was Danny come to join them and he patted Benjamin on the shoulder, gave Charlotte a hug and grabbed a mug for himself. 'It's going to be a glorious day.'

Benjamin and Charlotte looked at each other. Their dad so full of the joys was puzzling when they both knew the truth.

'Snow is forecast for later,' Danny grinned, mopping up the spill of coffee from the bench before he headed off with his mug and a call over his shoulder of, 'It's the most enchanting time of the year to be tying the knot.'

Heather's expression gave away nothing despite Danny's air of joviality that suggested he was high on the occasion rather than merely running a venue to put on someone else's wedding.

Benjamin was tempted to call after his father that it was indeed a very enchanting time of the year and no time for thinking about divorce.

But for now, he had to shut his feelings down.

This was Melissa and Harvey's day. The rest could wait.

21

Tilly arrived at Mistletoe Gate Farm with her parents. Melissa had seen them both at Barney's and insisted that they come along to the wedding today and they'd been delighted to accept.

As they went through the mistletoe gate, Barney and Lois joined them. Barney and Nigel were soon talking about the barn repairs but Barney seemed happy with the outcome and declared it was lovely to be a guest rather than having the responsibility of ensuring it all went smoothly. 'I'm just grateful Tilly came up with the farm as the alternative and that the Doyles were in agreement.'

Tilly had pulled on flared jeans for the walk up to the farm, her bridesmaid dress being already there waiting for her. 'As soon as I saw the picture of Heather and Danny's wedding it just made sense.' What she didn't mention was that it felt odd now that the place her friends would share their vows would soon be the place where Benjamin's parents brought their own marriage to its conclusion.

'Dig the wellies, Tilly!' Gracie, who walked Harvey's dog Winnie regularly, caught them up on their walk towards the farm. 'Like mine?'

'Yes!' Gracie's were purple with yellow flowers on them. 'Where on earth did you find them?' Harvey and Melissa had had fun writing the invitations, specifying that outfits should be practical and footwear suitable given the location. *Wellies are welcome!* they'd added at the foot of the card.

'They're a charity-shop find – I know they're not one of a kind, but it makes me feel as if they are.'

'Well, I think they're classic,' she complimented.

Looking around when they reached the end of the path and found others milling, Tilly saw that there were plenty of wellington boots worn by the women and the men. Most were the usual khaki or black, but some guests had gone for the bright colours – yellow, one person in a pair of purple psychedelic wellies that would be better placed at Glastonbury than here in an unassuming village on the east coast of England, another pair in bright orange.

Tilly left her parents talking outside with Barney, Lois, and Gracie while she went in to the join the girls and finish getting ready. She took the steps up onto the veranda, passing free-standing heaters that emitted a warmth for the guests at grass level. On the veranda itself were another couple of heaters to keep the bride and groom toasty as they said their vows but Tilly had a feeling that with this many people hoarded together, nobody was going to feel the cold anyway.

On the veranda, tied around every post was mistletoe in sprigs beautifully tied off with either white, red or green bows. Several glass vases with big, white candles inside were positioned at intervals on any suitable wooden surface around the place, and holly and ivy adorned vessels and accompanied the mistletoe arrangements so generously that it almost felt as though the veranda was part of the outside landscape. Melissa had also taken on her suggestion of floating candles in glass bowls, one at the table for the register's signing, another at the side table behind that. It was one of the most romantic sights Tilly had ever seen.

Tilly smiled over at Harvey, who stood with his brother Daniel in his tux with navy cravat and a white boutonnière and looked a bundle of nerves even though Melissa was his childhood sweetheart and this marriage had been written in the stars for years. When the wedding got underway, Tracy and Tilly would be the first to emerge from the double doors to the sitting room at the opposite end of the veranda – doors that usually opened only in the summer months – and they'd walk the short way along the veranda before Melissa followed on to meet Harvey.

'Good morning.' Benjamin was hanging around in the kitchen when she went inside. Dressed in a suit with tie and a pale-blue, checked shirt, he almost took her breath away before she managed a hello.

'Good morning,' she beamed before taking in the mistletoe in here too. It made the room even more welcoming than it was already.

Heather was downstairs before they could say anything more. 'How do I look?' She did a twirl to show off her navy, silk dress that clung to her svelte figure. She had on the beautiful dragonfly brooch she'd bought at Tilly's shop a month ago and a pair of diamond drop earrings that sparkled as she moved.

'Fabulous,' Tilly declared, with Benjamin agreeing.

Troy and Brianna, who usually worked at the waffle shack, were today working the wedding and had just finished filling champagne glasses at the other end of the kitchen. Heather lifted up a tray of them and told everyone she was heading out to greet the masses.

'I'd better get upstairs to meet the girls and get changed,' Tilly told Benjamin. The spare room had been allocated for Melissa to finish getting ready and the bridesmaids to do the same. 'How are you?'

He knew exactly what she meant and smiled softly, unable to look away. 'I'm fine, not thinking about it today. More to the point, how are you? We haven't had a chance to talk.'

'I'm sorry, I've been busy with Mum and Dad.'

'In a good way?'

'In a very good way,' she assured him.

Charlotte interrupted them and bustled the missing bridesmaid upstairs, where Tilly became swept along with Melissa's excitement.

Tilly was zipped into the midnight-blue bridesmaid dress, Tracy positioned tiny white flowers in her hair that was pinned up with only a few loose tendrils hanging down, and with bouquets in hand, at last they were ready. Melissa wasn't even nervous a bit, she was organising them all, and Tilly hoped that one day if she ever got married she could be as calm as that. The only dent in Melissa's outwardly confident exterior was when Barney came upstairs to meet her and emotions got the better of him as he prepared to be the one to give her away. Tilly knew she was thinking about her parents when her hand moved to the locket that had their photographs inside and it made Tilly realise how lucky she was to have her mum and dad in her life. It was something she would never take for granted. And no matter what Scott had done, he'd not managed to dent her belief in family, her trust and bond with those who mattered. In fact, him turning up in the village had even helped to strengthen her relationship with her dad by bringing her parents here sooner than anticipated.

* * *

Tilly couldn't imagine how nervous Melissa felt doing this walk because going from the doors over to where Harvey and Daniel were standing and taking her position off to the side had taken a lot of concentration. How much of her own nervousness was down to the walk and how much could be attributed to Benjamin's eyes following her, she wasn't sure.

Melissa captivated everyone in a champagne, A-line gown with Chantilly lace beneath a beaded bodice, her auburn hair curled in loose waves that tumbled around her shoulders. Barney looked proud as anything by her side and knowing how much both the bride and groom meant to him had everyone's emotions on the rise.

The vows became a blur as they talked about their days at the barn as kids, how time apart had made them stronger, how lucky they each were to have the other now and forever. And Tilly kept her gaze on them, because if she looked at Benjamin again she thought her legs might buckle.

When Melissa and Harvey finally shared a kiss, everyone roared their applause. Chatter erupted as they signed the register, and they had their photograph taken so many times that Tilly wondered whether their faces would begin to hurt from smiling.

Before long there was music, there was dancing, congratulations passed to the happy couple – who held hands the entire time, not wanting to be separated even for a moment. Barney was talking avidly with Etna and Patricia at one side of the veranda, Jade and Celeste were laughing about something along with Nola and Terry from the pub, and Harvey's mum Carol was standing with Jade's boyfriend Linc's dad – rumour had it they were keen on each other and Tilly knew that if any romance was on the cards then surely this place would encourage it more than any other.

'Wonder if Melissa will take him to the bathroom with her,' Heather whispered when she paused at Tilly's side having conferred with Brianna and Troy about which canapés to circulate with first.

Tilly looked over at Harvey and Melissa and giggled. She wasn't sure they had let go of each other's hands since they'd finished the photographs. 'I wouldn't mind betting on it.'

'They seem to have loved every minute of their day,' Heather gulped, a hint of nostalgia in her voice that some might not pick up on but Tilly did, knowing about that form she and Benjamin had found. It was in this very place that Heather herself had married and now here she was at someone else's nuptials facing the end of her own happy ever after.

'You've done them proud with this place,' Tilly assured her as they looked at the sprigs of mistletoe, the flickering candles, the lights in the pine trees lining the border of the crowds.

'You certainly have.' It was Barney, come to thank Heather. He took her hands. 'Thank you from the bottom of my heart. You know that I was devastated not to put on their wedding, they both mean the world to me. But here...' He took in the farm, the open air, the atmosphere on the veranda and beyond. '...here is very close to perfect.'

The talk between Heather and Barney turned to work needed for the barn and Tilly went over to Jade, who was looking worried. 'You look more nervous than Melissa and Harvey were.'

'Hey, I'm *always* nervous when it comes to unveiling my masterpieces. Each time I have the same panic that people won't like the cake, that they'll think it could've been better.'

Danny took over from Tilly and reassured Jade she had nothing to worry about. He took her inside to make sure they had everything ready for the cake-cutting.

'Surely all it needs is a knife,' Benjamin joked, appearing beside Tilly.

'You'd think,' she replied.

'You look stunning, by the way.'

'You don't look so bad yourself.' For once she didn't find herself looking away. Maybe it was the glass of champagne that had given her a bit of extra confidence.

'Your parents are having a wonderful time. I just left them talking with Kenneth about his allotment.'

Tilly giggled. 'That should take a good few hours.'

'I hear they'll be around for Christmas.'

Tilly nodded. 'We need to put in the order for lunch at the pub.'

'Christmas lunch? You're not having a quiet family event at your cottage?'

'They want to be in amongst it all, they told me. And that means being at the pub with everyone else. I think even though they've visited enough times, they want to really get to know people.'

'That's a very good sign.' He seemed to be waiting for more but told her, 'And two more at the pub is no problem.'

'Will you get to enjoy the food as well as cooking it?' she asked.

He smiled that smile she'd been falling in love with ever since the summer. 'Always. But it's seeing the pleasure of others when they eat my food that really makes my day.'

'Dad's still going on about the sticky date pudding.'

Benjamin laughed. 'I'm pleased it was a winner. Just you wait until he tries my turkey with cranberry sauce.' He turned more serious. 'Are you really all right after everything that happened?'

She felt blessed that he worried. 'I really am. I don't think Scott would dare to come back – he'll know Dad wasn't bluffing when he said he'll call the police if he does. And I've already contacted a security firm to put in some CCTV at the shop. It was about time, anyway, as most shops install them these days.' She had stopped referring to Scott as Uncle Scott, too. Somehow it no longer felt right and he didn't deserve the description.

'I'm glad you're so positive. I'm glad he didn't change you.'

She was glad as well. She'd still give people the benefit of the doubt, she'd still trust, she wasn't going to let Scott take anything else from her. She'd given him her time and her thoughts and kindness and very nearly her money, and that was enough.

'I have some time off between Christmas and the new year,' she told Benjamin. 'Mum and Dad are manning the shop and I'm under instruction to take a decent rest. Dad seems quite excited about it.' And although he'd told her how proud he was of her, this went one step further and showed her. 'They're going to help me plan the expansion, too. Properly this time, no cutting corners, and by the time I get around to it, Harvey should be able to fit me into his schedule.'

'I'm really pleased for you, Tilly.'

She locked eyes with him as his arm brushed against hers, his fingers lifting slightly as though he was about to take her hand and tell her or ask her something.

But when Danny came close to them Benjamin looked worried. 'What's up with him?'

Tilly glanced over and Danny definitely didn't seem himself. He was running his fingers around the inside of his collar as though it was choking him, he was taking deep breaths in and out.

'Oh God, you don't think he's going to confess all to Mum now, do you?' Benjamin followed the direction of Danny's gaze and, sure enough, he was looking directly at his wife, his movements suggesting he was plucking up enough courage to go over to her.

'Surely not, this is a wedding.'

But there was no more time to debate what was or wasn't happening because Danny had climbed up onto a small stool beside the registry table and he was clapping his hands together, requesting everyone's attention.

Tilly looked around and saw confusion on the guests' faces as they'd been told there wouldn't be any speeches today.

Danny's voice shook as he began. 'Thank you, everyone.' He

cleared his throat. 'And thank you to Melissa and Harvey for agreeing to let me do what I'm about to do.'

Tilly put a hand on Benjamin's arm as he started forwards as though he wanted to halt this train wreck before it happened. He stopped, his other hand reaching up to his throat, running across the stubble on his chin.

'As most of you know,' Danny went on, 'Mistletoe Gate Farm has been in our family for a very long time. This farm is where Heather and I married. It's where we raised our children, Benjamin and Charlotte.' He covered his eyes. 'But you all know their names, I don't need to tell you.' He looked out at the crowds, his eyes casting about. 'Forgive me, I'm nervous.'

He gave up searching among the throng for Heather, who Tilly knew had ducked inside for another tray of champagne. Danny probably had no idea she hadn't come out yet as he moved on with his speech.

'At the farm we've seen dry summers that threatened growth, harsh winters that uprooted trees and the latest storm even tried to do its worst except that we wouldn't let it.' It was then that Heather came out, tentatively, onto the veranda and walked slowly around so that Danny could see her. He looked directly at his wife, a sense of calm now in his voice. 'We've seen plenty of people come and go every Christmas, my favourite time of the year, and it means the world to me that we've had the privilege to bring you folks such pleasure and delight with our trees, and of course our mistletoe.'

Tilly didn't dare let go of Benjamin's arm and as she murmured the question, asking whether he was all right; he took her hand instead of answering, squeezing it just a little bit more than was necessary as he braced himself for what looked to be an announcement that this would be the last season of selling trees for the Doyles.

'Mistletoe Gate Farm is special to me,' Danny continued, chin held high. 'But nothing... and I mean *nothing* means as much to me as my family, especially my wife, Heather.'

Heather and Danny were looking at each other as though they were the only two people here on the veranda with its magical lighting, enchanting mistletoe decorations, and the frost-tipped trees beyond.

Danny stepped down from the stool and walked over to his wife. 'Heather, I proposed to you right here at the farm – at the gate, I do believe, surrounded by mistletoe. I seem to remember getting down on one knee and falling into the bush as I lost my balance.' Heather smiled and guests chuckled. 'But ever since then you've been the thing that held me steady. We got married right here at Mistletoe Gate Farm and over the last few weeks as we've pulled out all the stops to make this day memorable for Harvey and Melissa, it's reminded me of the promises we both made, promises that I never want to break.

'You sometimes get frustrated with me when I don't take action, when it takes me forever to make a decision – whether it's choosing a paint colour for the living-room walls or what time to eat dinner. But now, Heather, it's time I seized the day.'

The crowd gasped as he sunk down onto one knee in front of her. 'I am sorry I treated any of your dreams outside of this farm as frivolous, a hobby, when they're an important part of who you are.' He reached for her hand when she looked about to protest that it didn't matter. 'You've always supported me and I want to do the same for you, always. I never want to lose you. I want to grow old with you, spend the rest of our days together, but I know I need to make changes, let you follow paths that I never envisaged. And those paths can be your adventure or they can be ours.' He shook his head, annoyed he might not be getting this right.

Tilly watched on, mesmerised. Nobody but the two of them had any idea what he was on about but it didn't take away a single ounce of the romance.

'Please say it's not too late for us.' Danny's face searched hers.

'I hope it isn't.' Heather's voice wobbled as she told Danny, 'I should've shared how I felt earlier. I've let my frustrations bubble up until it all got too much.' She hadn't had a chance to rehearse this as her husband probably had and she took her time to find the right words. 'I'm sorry I assumed it would be easy for you to let go of the business and just leave at a moment's notice to indulge my whims.'

Tilly wondered whether they'd heard any murmurings or gasps from the crowd at the mention of the business, the farm, that seemed to be a point of contention. Tilly heard someone query somebody else about whether they were selling up. Another person asked where they would all get their trees from if this farm disappeared.

'They're not whims, I know that.' Danny's voice was so soft you could hear the love he had for his wife in every syllable.

'I don't want to sell the farm,' said Heather and Tilly wasn't sure whether she'd imagined it or whether she really heard a wave of relief wash over the guests. 'I'm not ready to leave this place yet.'

Danny smiled. 'I was kind of hoping you'd say that.' Still on one knee, in a lower voice he added, 'Otherwise, I'd be feeling pretty stupid right about now.'

Danny cleared his throat and projected his voice once again so everyone could hear, even those farthest away near the border of trees. 'Heather, you are the woman by my side and the only one I want. I hope to share your dreams and go places with you. As long as we're together, that's all that matters.'

Tilly noticed the celebrant hadn't left yet and when she took her position at the front, things began to fall into place. She held on tight to Benjamin's hand, smiling up at him, warmth intensifying between them as he realised, too, that whatever he'd discovered before had been a sign that things weren't right in his parents' marriage but not a sign that things couldn't, and wouldn't, be fixed.

'Heather,' said Danny, grasping his wife's hands in his, 'would you do me the great honour of renewing our vows – here, right now, with our closest friends and family present?'

Heather could only manage a nod as he reached out and wiped a stray tear that trickled across her cheek bone, and without words he led her to take her place alongside him in front of the celebrant.

* * *

The ceremony was just as special as the one preceding it. Valerie brought out a stunning bouquet of red and white roses with rich green foliage, pine cones, and delicate, white gypsophila flowers. Danny had been planning this for weeks, along with the eternity ring he presented to Heather after they stumbled over the vows they both recalled from years ago, knowing they hadn't got the wording exactly right but happy with the sentiments.

It turned out there were two cakes – a triple-layered, lemon-and-elderflower buttercream cake for Melissa and Harvey that had gingerbread reindeer on top and a base that resembled a tree trunk, with forest flowers and greenery in icing around the edges, and a red velvet cake for Heather and Danny, the same flavour they'd had at their wedding all those years ago.

'Your dad is a romantic,' said Tilly when she finally managed to get a moment with Benjamin again. He and his sister had been talking for a long while with their parents.

'He actually is.' He told her that his mum had divulged to both him and Charlotte her passion for languages and travelling, something she'd never made very much of. 'Dad always thought it was just talk, he feels bad for how he didn't take her seriously. He knew his whole life was and still is this farm but he's beginning to see that Mum might need a little bit of herself in the equation.'

'But she still loves the farm.'

'Of course.' Benjamin took a deep breath. 'I'm so relieved, Tilly.' He leaned in so close it sent her heart fluttering. 'At least now I know why Dad kept ducking out and not telling me where he was going.'

It made sense now they knew – the ring, the cake, the celebrant, his haircut, the aftershave and his newly fitted suit that was a step up from what you usually wore as a guest at a wedding. 'Did you ever mention you'd seen the divorce papers?' she asked him.

'I didn't see the point.'

She nodded in agreement and as guests began to mill on the makeshift and compact dancefloor, he asked whether she'd like to dance.

'Let me get my wellies,' she grinned.

But by the time she came back, red wellies on in place of the heels she'd worn as a bridesmaid, it was time for Harvey and Melissa to wave their goodbyes. They thanked their hosts before Harvey turned to Melissa and said, 'Come on, Mrs Luddington, it's time we left these folks to carry on partying without us, we've got a plane to catch!' And with that he grabbed her hand and they took the stairs down the veranda as guests used the pouches of fresh rose petals allocated at the start of the night to send them on their way.

'Christmas and New Year in New York will be amazing.' Tilly shivered as they waved until the car was out of sight, the bride and groom heading to America for a few weeks.

Benjamin stood behind her and rubbed her arms, warming her right the way through. The partying had resumed, Heather and Danny held each other as close as they could, swaying in time to the music, Barney and Lois, Tracy and her husband Giles – happy couples everywhere, and friends, danced with the farm as their backdrop.

'I don't really want to dance with everyone else,' Benjamin whispered into her hair. 'How about we grab our coats and get away from the crowds?' His eyes twinkled in the moonlight.

'Sounds good to me.'

Once they had their coats on, Tilly slipped her hand into Benjamin's as they crept away from the crowds so nobody would notice them leaving.

His skin was warm to the touch, unexpected when the temperature outside was plummeting. They walked from the farm, the noise fading into the background as they made their way down the track that brought customers and visitors here like clockwork every Christmas, all the way towards the mistletoe gate.

They stopped when they reached the gate and Benjamin leaned on the wood and she rested her body next to his. It felt good to be just the two of them, nobody watching.

'I'm sorry again for the way I reacted when you tried to warn me about Scott,' said Tilly. It felt the right time to make her apology again.

'Like I said before, friends look out for one another.' But this time, rather than leave it at that, with one arm still on the gate he moved to stand in front of her so that her body was pressed against the wood and he was almost holding her. 'Is that what we are, Tilly? Just friends?'

She gulped and then giggled when a sprig of mistletoe on the bush beside him blew in the breeze tickling his neck and made him lash out thinking it was something else.

When the laughter subsided after he'd sorted out the shrub he was still waiting for his answer. He was so patient, always had been, and here he was knowing what answer he wanted yet still waiting to get it.

'I think we're maybe a little bit more than that,' she confessed, aware of the rise and fall of her chest, the longing between them.

And Benjamin wasted no time in reaching out his hand and pulling her closer to him until their lips met.

Surrounded by mistletoe, Benjamin and Tilly had a long-lasting friendship, they had each other, and more than that, they had the promise of a new beginning.

EPILOGUE

The snow hadn't come on the day of the wedding, just a light frost that had added to the romance of the occasion but not interfered with the practicalities. It was a completely different story today, however. Following the wedding, icy temperatures had at last given way to a snowfall that blanketed the whole of Heritage Cove, buildings along The Street sparkling in all their glory beneath the winter sun.

Luckily the weather hadn't stopped anyone from showing up at the barn on Barney's land and it was all systems go again, the same way it had been since the day after Boxing Day, two days after the Christmas lunch at the pub when the residents of the village had had their stomachs filled with festive fayre and enough alcohol to put plans in place.

Lois was complicit in the plans – she'd booked a very-last-minute, post-Christmas escape for four nights in Southwold, where she and Barney would enjoy bracing walks with Harvey's dog Winnie who they were looking after, they'd visit nearby beaches, enjoy pub lunches, and have some down time after the wedding and following festivities. Those four nights had given the people of the Cove enough time to give back to Barney, the man who cared so much about this community, the man who was always there with a shoulder to lean on no matter what for – whether it was your car breaking down, or trouble with a parent, or help needed to get through a difficult day. Barney had always been there for others and now they were here for him.

With Harvey away on honeymoon, Terry had got three of Harvey's work colleagues who were regular customers at the Copper Plough on board – he'd given them each a voucher for a meal at the pub, plus another for bottomless drinks on a night of their choosing. Daniel had thrown in vouchers for free waffles at the Little Waffle Shack right up until New Year and Etna had told them tea and coffee was on the house while they were in the village doing this important work; she even hand-delivered it to the workers every few hours, enforcing a break for their well-being. Volunteers from the village had been on hand to take away the tarpaulin that had been used to temporarily protect the inside of the barn after the roof was damaged, Jade and Celeste regularly delivered even more food for the workers to keep them going, Tilly and Benjamin helped to revarnish some of the woodwork once it was ready for coating.

Now, Tilly checked the varnish was dry on the barrels Barney used as tables for events.

'Ready for me to move them?' Benjamin asked her. Barney was due back today so Tilly, like everyone else, had been constantly checking the time. And despite the snow, Barney and Lois had been lucky that the roads were relatively clear beyond the village and the gritting lorries had been out early enough this morning that their journey home should be reasonably smooth.

'They're ready,' she smiled.

Since the day of the wedding and then Christmas, life had been a bit of a blur for both Tilly and Benjamin. They'd spent the whole of Christmas afternoon and night with each other – her parents had been happy to remain at the pub and then head over to Barney's for the evening – and they'd really talked. They'd got to know each other on a deeper level, they'd shared their fears, why they were both scared of losing the wonderful friendship they already had. They'd also exchanged gifts – Tilly had wrapped up the bistro-style chalkboard from her shop that Benjamin had admired and he'd bought her an amethyst pendant he found in an antiques shop. They'd shared plenty of kisses beneath mistletoe that day, too, because Benjamin seemed to have put sprigs of it up all over Tilly's cottage without her even noticing and he insisted that whenever they passed beneath it they had to kiss.

The barrels had only just been moved when Patricia called over that Barney and Lois had pulled up outside. She'd been on door duty and on the lookout.

Barney would've seen the repaired barn door by now – that had been first on the list of repairs when Lois took a call from the suppliers to say they could get the timber to them earlier than expected – but he had no idea of the efforts that had been put in by everyone in the village since he and Lois had left the Cove for Southwold.

Everyone inside hushed and huddled together, giggling at this covert affair. Tilly had set up a table at the side of the room already with glasses from the pub on top, a space for the big pan of mulled wine that was warming in Barney's kitchen to Benjamin's recipe, a tray of orange slices ready to drop into the vessels. She leaned back against Benjamin's chest as they waited and turned to kiss him on the lips. She felt so at home with him, like they had always been destined for a relationship but it had just taken them a while to get there. Tilly had said as much to Jade, who totally gave in to the soppiness of the sentiment – especially after she let Tilly into a secret: she and her boyfriend Linc were expecting a baby. It hadn't been planned – family was a long way off for them, or so they'd thought – and for now she was keeping it quiet. Tilly looked across at Jade, who had delivered pastries moments ago, and grinned. If she and Benjamin could be half as happy as Jade and Linc then she'd consider herself very lucky.

'What's all this?' It was Barney, inside at last, misty-eyed, his cap in his hands, coat still on and complete shock showing in his expression. He looked around – at the stage, no wet patches anywhere, the barrels shiny and varnished, up at the roof that looked as though it had never been damaged at all. 'I don't know what to say.'

'That's a first!' Etna called out, much to everyone's amusement.

'I wish Harvey and Melissa could see all of this,' he said, still in disbelief. Winnie was already doing the rounds for a fuss now she'd been let out of the car.

Tilly retrieved the iPad from the table, clicked a few times and had what she needed, because they'd had this planned all along. 'They can, Barney.' And she turned the screen to face him.

'We're here!' Harvey and Melissa called out in unison, huddled together with a spectacular backdrop of Central Park carpeted in snow. They were both wrapped up with chunky scarves and hats but their smiles beamed across the miles.

Winnie's tail wagged at the sight of her owners and Barney took over the iPad to show how wonderful the barn looked. Benjamin ducked out briefly and was soon back with an enormous pot of mulled wine, the smell wafting into the barn with him. As Barney continued to chat to Harvey and Melissa, Tilly took over service and ladled out wine for anyone who wanted it and it became another party inside the barn, the place of so many memories, the place that meant so much. Everyone talked about their next community project, which, once the snow stopped and the ground softened a little, was to be a working bee at the chapel. The cemetery was a mess and would take some clearing but, with so many willing volunteers, they should have it shipshape in no time.

'I'm warmed right through.' Tilly linked arms with Benjamin. They'd both finished their wine and sloped off without anyone noticing. They were getting good at doing that.

They watched their footing outside the barn where at the edges of the courtyard it was slippery since the snow had hardened and refused to budge and they made their way around to the front of Barney's house, setting off up the road towards The Street as they talked about everything that had happened to the folks of Heritage Cove this winter. They didn't dwell much on Scott but they did talk about Tilly's parents and their love of her shop, the shop they'd been looking after for her so she could take a break herself.

They reached the pub and turned down the street towards Mistletoe Gate Farm. 'I wonder what your parents are up to right now,' she said.

'I don't really need to know,' he grimaced.

She put her gloved hand against his chest, laughing. 'I didn't mean that. I just meant I wonder what they're seeing, experiencing. I wonder how much Italian your mum is getting to use, whether your dad will learn it, too.'

Heather and Danny had gone to Sicily until the new year. Danny had had it booked for weeks, sneaking off to a travel agent in one of those moments when Benjamin had wondered where he was. And when he'd told his wife where they were going, she'd cried. Right now, they'd be soaking up the sightseeing with fewer tourists than in the warmer months, their love enough to keep them as warm as they needed – at least that's what Danny had told everyone, embarrassing Benjamin and Charlotte in the process.

Benjamin and Charlotte had spoken with their parents after they renewed their vows. They'd agreed that they wouldn't let on to them about the divorce proceedings they'd been aware of, but they still needed to know what was what when it came to the farm. And they were told that along the way the farm had done better than well – business was, in fact, booming. So, for now, Charlotte would spend time really learning what it would take to manage the family business while she carried on with her day job.

Benjamin stopped Tilly beside the mistletoe gate. 'I should whisk you off somewhere romantic, too. You deserve it, you know. We could go anywhere.'

'The world is our oyster?'

'Exactly.'

'But where would we go?'

'You choose.' He kissed her lightly on the lips.

But she merely shook her head. 'You know what, I don't need to go anywhere else but here, Benjamin. You've made me the happiest girl in the Cove this Christmas. I'm surrounded by mistletoe and Christmas trees – what more could a girl ask for?'

And when he kissed her, she had her answer.

She couldn't ask for anything more. She had exactly what she'd been looking for.

ACKNOWLEDGMENTS

Firstly I'd like to say a huge thank you to the entire team at Boldwood for offering me a book deal to write new books and bring some of my backlist to even more readers in even more formats. In particular I would like to thank Nia Beynon for the initial chat regarding Boldwood as a publisher and Tara Loder for many lengthy conversations about my series books and next steps. It took a while to work out a way forwards and I'm so pleased to be working with you all.

A very big thank you to Jessica Redland, an amazing author and friend who has found a home with Boldwood and introduced me to the team. Jessica is always generous with her time and her advice and I'm so glad to be a part of the writing tribe known as The Write Romantics who are there for each other along the way. Social media keeps us close and the constant support and encouragement is something I could never imagine being without.

My thanks goes to Katharine Walkden for being a whizz with editing, grammar and punctuation, as well as spotting potential plot holes. Her care and precision are second to none and she is a pleasure to work with every time. I'd also like to thank Emily Reader for giving the story a final polish to make it sparkle.

Thank you to my husband for encouraging me when I have doubts, for cooking delicious meals during the week, for managing my website and being there as my sounding board when I need to work out plot problems or issues with my characters. I love my job as an author and I know how incredibly lucky I am to have his unwavering support.

And finally, to my readers... an enormous thank you for buying this book. I hope it was a pleasure to read and that you continue to enjoy the series!

MORE FROM HELEN ROLFE

We hope you enjoyed reading *Winter at Mistletoe Gate Farm*. If you did, please leave a review.

If you'd like to gift a copy, this book is also available as an ebook, digital audio download and audiobook CD.

Sign up to Helen Rolfe's mailing list for news, competitions and updates on future books.

https://bit.ly/HelenRolfeNews

Christmas at the Little Knitting Box, the first book in the New York Ever After series, is available now.

ABOUT THE AUTHOR

Helen Rolfe is the author of many bestselling contemporary women's fiction titles, set in different locations from the Cotswolds to New York. Most recently published by Orion, she is bringing sixteen titles to Boldwood - a mixture of new series and well- established backlist. She lives in Hertfordshire with her husband and children.

Follow Helen on social media:

twitter.com/hjrolfe
facebook.com/helenjrolfewriter
instagram.com/helen_j_rolfe

Printed in Great Britain
by Amazon

86934971R00149